I0645392

If We

Get There

A Novel

Also by Jon Gosch

Deep Fire Rise

If We Get There

Jon Gosch

If We Get There
Copyright © 2020 Jon Gosch

All rights reserved. No portion of this book may be reproduced in any form without permission from the publisher, except as permitted by U.S. copyright law.
For permissions contact: editor@latahbooks.com

This book is a work of fiction. Any references to historical events, real people, or real places are used fictitiously. Other names, characters, places, and events are products of the author's imagination, and any resemblance to actual events or places or persons, living or dead, is entirely coincidental.

Book design by Kevin Breen and Gray Dog Press

Cover image derived from Adobe Stock Images

ISBN: 978-0-9997075-9-3
Cataloging-in-Publication Data is available upon request

Originally published in June 2013

Manufactured in the United States of America

Production by Gray Dog Press
www.graydogpress.com

Published by
Latah Books
Spokane, Washington
www.latahbooks.com

Author may be contacted at jongosch@hotmail.com

Dedicated to my parents,
Shawn and Vern

Thanks for the life

The sun had not yet risen, and the river they puttered out into was well-water black and gently roiling from the steady downriver breeze. Nearly two miles across, the northern bank of the Columbia was incandescent with the sprawling lights of the paper mill, and the play of the lights against the motion of the water was like a masterwork of impressionism that could repaint itself at every instant.

His father attached green glowsticks to the fore and aft of the boat and then told Cash to give it some throttle. Soon they were clipping upriver, the boat bouncing with thuds against the turbulence while his father sat rigging the poles and baiting the hooks. Cash was heading out toward the middle of the river. He heard his father holler at him and looked back over his shoulder.

"The shelf," his father hollered again, pointing toward the Oregon bank.

By the time they were finally anchored and had both hooks in fifty feet of water, the sun was halfway over the foothills and crowned with several orange hues. Cash and his father drank coffee and ate doughnuts out of a box, watching their poles bob hypnotically. Cash took the last bite of a maple bar and wiped his hand on the side of his jeans.

"What's the biggest sturgeon you ever caught?" he asked.

"The biggest I caught or the biggest I hooked into?"

"Both."

"The biggest sturgeon I ever caught was fishing off the jetty at County Line. It was just under six foot. I was actually fishing alone. As soon as I hooked into it, I thought, whoa, and then the line just went out zzzzzeeoooo. These Orientals down on the rocks saw it jump, and I heard 'em going, big fish. Big big big beeeeeg fish. They actually drug it up on the rocks for me. Weighed a hundred and forty pounds."

"And the biggest you hooked into?"

"It was longer than the boat we were in. I'm not kiddin' you. When we finally got it up alongside the boat, everyone was marveling at it, and I said, how long is this boat anyway, and they said twenty-four feet, so I said, well this fish must be twenty-six feet long then cause it's two feet longer than the damn boat. You remember that fire at the furniture store? Yeah, well, all my pictures of that fish were boxed up in the attic."

"How do you catch one like that?"

"You don't."

His father removed a cigarette from his pack of Marlboros, lit up, and put the smokes back in his jacket.

"I'll tell you a story," he said with a smoky exhale. "Bunch of years back there was this dam inspector, this Italian guy, who went to have a look at the Bonneville Dam. He goes underwater for about two minutes and then he pops back up and leaps out of the water. Telling everybody there's a sea monster down there. Everybody just laughed at him and told him it was a sturgeon of course, but he kept saying, it's gonna eat me. It's gonna eat me. They never could get the guy to go back down there."

Cash chuckled. "Sea monster."

"Damn good eating, these Columbia River sea monsters."

Cash brought his own pack of cigarettes out of his jacket, and his father shook his head sadly but refrained from saying anything. Cash lit his cigarette, and the two of them smoked and listened to the riverwater gurgling against the boat.

"So, how's your mother?" his father finally asked.

"Jeez, Dad. Isn't it awful early in the morning to be talking about her? Think we could at least wait 'til lunch."

"Come on. I'm only asking how she's been doing."

"Why don't you ask her?"

"Cause she won't speak with me is why."

"She's fine," Cash said. "But don't think I'm gonna be your arbitrator or anything. It's shitty enough as it is."

"That isn't what this is about, son. I'm just asking how she's doing."

"Well, she's fine. Now can we please just fish."

As if in answer to his demand, Cash's rod began jiggling and he leapt up and set the hook. His father reeled his line in quickly and put the pole aside while Cash fought the fish. He cranked a handful of turns while letting the tip of the pole into the water and then heaved back and reeled in a dozen more. His father came around with the net, and when the fish finally appeared at the surface, he scooped it and brought it aboard.

The sturgeon was a pale olive-gray, scaleless with a spiked back, and just short the length of a man's arm. It knew it had no use for the net and it thrashed its tail violently and bent itself nearly double and attempted to roll and then thrashed its tail more until it finally appeared calm and resigned and looking up at them.

"It's too small," his father said.

"It might measure out."

His father put on a pair of thick rubber gloves and he held the fish down with one hand while with the other he worked the hook out of its mouth with a pair of needle nose pliers. Once the hook was out, he set to untangle the net from where it had wrapped around the spikes. His father was having difficulty removing the fish, and Cash bent down to help him.

"I've got it," his father said.

"Let me help."

"Those spikes are sharp."

Cash had nearly unworked the net when the sturgeon flailed again. Cash withdrew his hand with a hissing inhale.

"Cut you, didn't he?"

"You little bastard."

Blood trickled down his middle finger, but he merely looked at it and finished undoing the net. Once it was free, his father held the sturgeon flat on the deck while Cash put the tape measure beside it.

"What's the minimum again?"

"Thirty-eight inches."

"Can you stretch it some?"

"I'm already stretching it."

"Then it's an inch too short. Half an inch maybe."

"Back you go then."

His father took the sturgeon in his hands and lifted it over the edge of the boat and lowered it into the river. For a moment the sturgeon just lay there in his palms like it had grown accustomed to being handled and then it casually flapped its tail and disappeared into the gloomy, green depths of the river.

They brought three more sturgeon aboard the boat that morning. One which was half the size of the others and was tossed back without measuring, and then two more that were less than an inch too short to be kept legally. The last fish was so identical in length and appearance to the first that neither Cash nor his father could say for certain that they hadn't caught the same fish twice that morning. Cash told his father it meant they were supposed to keep it, and his father told him it only meant they should have fished somewhere else.

After the last sturgeon was released, Cash's father pulled the anchor up by its chain and they cruised back to the marina. Cash rode in the stern tossing bait to a dozen seagulls that had picked up the scent and glided behind the boat, diving and squawking at each fresh piece he threw. When the bait was gone, Cash rinsed the bucket in the river and went up and sat next to his father.

"So what kind of roofs we got on the slate after this church job?" Cash asked.

His father dodged the boat around a piece of driftwood and kept his eyes downriver.

"Dad? I said what kind of roofs we got—"

"I heard what you said."

His father turned and looked at him.

"Tomorrow, you and Charley are gonna be working the last job. I've sold the business to an outfit in Vancouver."

"You can't be serious."

"I wish to God I was fibbing."

Cash sat back in his chair, dazed and blinking.

"They've been trying to buy me out for six months now, and I just kept telling myself that we could hold on and make it work. Every month I held on their offer went down. Guess I finally realized I needed to quit kidding myself. If this business was gonna turn a profit, it sure as hell would have turned one by now."

"What about the bank? Couldn't you ask for another loan?"

"They told me I'm tapped out. Can't even say I blame 'em."

"And you thought this was a good time to tell me? After the fact."

"When would have been a good time? Besides, the deal just went through yesterday. The owner of this Vancouver outfit, Fred Norris, he walked into the shop about four in the afternoon and handed me a check. Said it was the last offer I was ever gonna get from him. I saw that he meant what he said and that he'd come back up on the price some, and that was that."

"So how much are we gonna walk away with?"

"Shit. After I pay off the loans? Nine hundred and nine dollars."

Cash spit overboard with disgust and sat shaking his head.

"What the hell am I supposed to do, Dad? Things are already tight for me."

"I already talked with Robbie over at Fibre. He says he can probably find something for you."

"Working the mills? Man, it's just a bunch of deadbeats over there."

"Cash, half your friends work in the mills."

"Half my friends are deadbeats."

"It pays the bills, son. We don't always get to be discriminating in how we bring home the bacon. Shit, it ain't like roof cleaning is the most glamorous profession anyhow."

"At least I got to do my own thing. Only had to take crap from you."

"Son. If you think you've got it rough, you should try marching in my shoes these days."

Cash ran his hand through his hair a few times and then just stared into the river with a bleak expression. Downstream a freight ship bellowed long and baritone as two cormorants flew past with their wings beating furiously. His father took a drink of his coffee and watched Cash watching the water, while underneath them a thousand and more fish were swimming easy and smooth.

Cash and his girlfriend sat on the tailgate of her truck, drinking beer and gazing down at the lights of the city. It was a familiar scene, a dead-end lovers' lane high on the hill where they had spent many evenings making love and arguing, often in the same night. Though it was now autumn, and after dark, the air was balmy and pleasant. Cash wore only shorts and a t-shirt. He swallowed the last of his beer and then pitched it over his shoulder into the bed of the truck, where it clanked loudly.

"Shuusshhh," she scolded.

"Whoops."

Gracie was a petite young blonde, twenty-one years old but appearing younger. She was dressed up and pretty in the way she saw was fashionable in her magazines and smoked a cigarette because he always did.

"How was fishing?" she asked.

"We caught four."

"That's great, baby."

"But we had to put 'em all back."

"Aww. Crummy."

"How was work today?"

"Oh, gosh. You wouldn't believe it. Marcy was in for a trim today. You know Marcy. From the casino. She said that Doug Klein came on to her at the blackjack table. Said he could get them a nice hotel room in Portland whenever she wanted. Can you believe that?"

"Yeah. I can believe that."

"What? How can you believe that?"

"Cause he's a horny old dude."

"But Marcy said he was wearing a wedding ring."

"So what?"

"He's married. It's just, I don't know, just despicable."

"He probably doesn't get any at home."

She made a face of disgust at him.

"Why you gotta look at me like that? It's not like I'm the one trying to cheat on my wife. I'm just saying that's the way things are. You know, this salon business is turning you into a queen gossip."

"No, it's not."

Cash raised an eyebrow.

"It's not."

He raised the other, and it gave him a look of alarm.

She laughed at his goofy visage and pushed him down and sat on top of him. He lay back with his hands linked behind his head.

"Is this where you mount me?" he said.

"You're awful."

Cash looked up and saw the night faintly littered with stars. In the distance below, a train hooted its passing through town, and after it had gone everything was very quiet, only the occasional yap of a small dog in the neighborhood. The two of them simply lay there for a while until she spoke again.

"What are you thinking about?"

"Nothin.'"

"Yeah, ya are."

"How do you know?"

"Cause, you can't not think about something."

"Why can't you?"

"Cause, you can't."

"Well, I wasn't thinking about anything until you brought it to my attention. Now I'm just wondering what the heck I was supposed to be thinking about."

"Ah, you were. You were thinking something. You just don't wanna say what it was."

"Gracie—"

"It's okay. You can have it to yourself."

"Alright then. If thinking is so important, what were you thinking about?"

"Kids."

"Why are you thinking about kids?"

"I can't help it. Just like thinking about 'em."

"Oh, man."

"What?"

"Nothing."

She bent down toward him some and sought out his eyes which were slow to match hers.

"You know I'm not trying to rush you, baby. I wanna be young for a while still."

"How long?"

"I don't know, baby. Until it's time. Until we know we're ready. I can't put a date on it. We'll just know, you know?"

He was silent for a while and then said, "You really wanna know what I was thinking about?"

"Of course."

"It's the worst kind of news."

Her eyes widened with morbid worry.

"Relax, Gracie. Nobody died."

"Thank goodness."

"My dad sold the business. It's all over."

She gasped and threw a hand over her mouth.

"He suggested that I might work in the mills."

"Oh, baby. Oh, I'm so sorry. I know how much you've been hoping this business with your dad would start taking off."

"Feels like I've just wasted the last two years."

"But what about working the mills? That wouldn't be so bad, would it? At least you'd be making a steady paycheck."

He watched the sway of the trees, a slight breeze fanning through the leaves like the sound of a distant waterfall.

"Maybe this is a sign," she said.

"A sign for what?"

"That you should go back to school like I've been saying. Another quarter or two, and you could have your associate's degree."

"And then what?"

"Well, I don't know. I guess you could keep going for your bachelor's. My mom was saying they're looking for a new pharmacist at Safeway. You could study to do something like that. She said they make like fifty dollars an hour."

"You want me to be a drug dealer?"

"I'm talking about a pharmacist."

"Is there a difference?"

"Why do you always have to be so disagreeable? All I'm saying is that you're smart enough to go to school and be whatever you want to be."

"School."

"You say it like it's the penitentiary."

He looked off past her.

"Everything's going wrong," he said. "Just wrong."

She waited for him to go on talking, to say something reassuring, something raunchy even. But he didn't.

A hot noon heat, inexplicable for the second week of autumn. He and his brother, Charley, sat in the shaded flat of a church roof and ate their lunches out of bright red coolers. Both of them were slim and fit, and their disheveled hair made them appear rakish and untroubled by vanity. Cash had two days' worth of stubble, which his brother could not yet grow. Around them the trees were boisterous with the sounds of myriad birds all seemingly crazed for the world to hear their song above any other, and a squirrel fat from acorns dropped from an oak branch onto the crest of the roof and regarded the brothers with a bewildered sense of invasion.

All about the spacious roof, lengths of hose lay snaked on the pitch. Two of the hoses were connected to pressure washing machines inside a trailer marked with the words Dawkins Family Roof Cleaning, and a third hose was slung over the front of the church and attached to a water spigot. Next to the brothers on the flat rested various pressure washing guns, as well as a wrench, a broom, a shovel. Steam was lifting steadily from the portions of roof they had just worked.

When the two of them finished their lunches, they packed the garbage into their coolers and then leaned their backs against an eave while Cash smoked a cigarette.

"It's your turn," said Charley.

"I can't think of anything."

"Just come up with something. It doesn't have to be good."

"You do another one."

Charley thought for a moment. "Okay. Would you rather eat a skunk or a sack of toenails?"

"How big of a sack?"

"Like one you'd put our sandwiches in."

"How much of the skunk would I have to eat?"

"The whole thing. Eyeballs, nose. Everything."

"Could I grind it up?"

"How you gonna grind up a skunk?"

"You let me worry about that. Would it be allowed?"

Charley huffed. "Yeah, I guess so."

Cash smoked and thought it all over.

"I'd eat the toenails."

From the nearby thoroughfare they heard a rush of traffic swoosh past, ten or twelve cars in a row just released from a red light and punctuated by the final thundering of a muscle car. Afterwards, they listened to the birds again.

"I got another one," Charley said.

"Shoot."

"Would you rather be killed by a shark or an alligator?"

"An alligator."

"How'd you know so fast?"

"Cause a shark would rip you apart, but an alligator would probably drown you first."

"Really?"

"Sure."

"How do you know?"

"Cause I'm brimming with knowledge."

"Interesting. I'll have to remember that."

"Alright," Cash said. "I've got one."

"Finally."

"Would you rather live with just Mom or just Dad?"

Charley looked at him with an expression of profound distress.

"That's not a good one. I don't want to play that way."

"It's just a fantasy thing, bud. Don't get all upset."

"But that's not how we play this. It's supposed to be funny stuff. Like sniffing butts or whatever."

"There's lots of ways to play, Charley."

"Yeah, but I don't want to play that way. Ask me another one."

"Ok, I'll make you a deal. You answer that one first, and then I'll ask you one you'll like afterwards."

"But. But you can't tell them okay. You have to be discreet."

"Discreet?"

"Yeah. Like you can't tell anybody."

"I know what the word means."

"I'd rather live with just Mom."

"See, that wasn't so hard."

"But I'd rather live with them both together."

"Yeah, well, that ain't ever gonna happen again."

Charley shot a glance at Cash and looked off sullenly. Cash took a last drag of his cigarette and then stubbed it out and tossed it over the edge of the roof. They sat.

"They might get back together," Charley said finally. "You don't know."

"I know enough."

"No, you don't know because you don't live with them anymore like I do."

Cash rubbed the back of his hand against the stubble of his jaw and watched Charley closely.

"You're right, bud. Let's just forget about it. I'm sorry I asked the question."

"I'm sorry you're an asshole."

Cash just nodded, and Charley turned around and set his eyes upon him full on and brazenly.

"Did you hear me? I called you an asshole, asshole."

"I hear you."

"A fucking prick."

"Yep."

"Uh . . . uh . . . sexer of dogs and flabby old blind women."

Cash chuckled. "Flabby old blind women?"

"You owe me my question. One I'm gonna like."

"Ok, Charley. Here goes. Would you rather lick a vaginal wart for five minutes or wear a diaper filled with someone else's poop for an hour?"

Charley's face brightened with exuberance. "I'll need a minute to consider this one."

When they were finished with the job, they blew the debris into the bushes and then loaded the hoses and the tools. Working in tandem, they hoisted the extension ladder on top of the trailer and fastened it down with bungee cords. Cash walked around the building and came back swinging a gas can and threw it in the bed of the truck and then got inside and started up the engine. They rolled out of the parking lot and turned onto Nichols Boulevard, each of them with their windows down, spitting sunflower seeds into the wind.

As they came along the high school, they looked over to where it stood across the soccer field in its old brick grandeur. The bell tower clock showed a quarter to five. Cash spit another seed out the window and turned back toward his brother.

"Looks like you're gonna have to come up with another senior project, bud."

"I was just thinking the same thing."

It was the first Friday of the month, and the tavern was clamorous with men and women eager to drink their way into a new paycheck. Cash and Gracie sat out on the patio and were halfway through their second pitcher of the cheapest beer available. Across the street were businesses that specialized in the sale of logging supplies, bolt supplies, and propane, and if Cash or any other bar patron had wanted they could have stood up and chucked a beer bottle into the Longview Fibre log pond.

From across the parking lot there came the clopping of high heels, and soon a trio of girls in mini-skirts approached the entrance. Cash looked over at them and back at Gracie.

"You can check 'em out if you want," she said.

"Already did. Bit too gangly if you ask me."

"I'm not gangly, am I?"

"No. I'd say you're slender."

"I like slender."

A man in a greasy Carhartt jacket held the door for the girls as they entered the bar, nodding politely to each one, and then craning his neck at their backsides once they'd passed. Cash lit up a cigarette and Gracie picked at her nails as a deep industrial boom issued from within the neighboring pulp mill.

"Okay, let's try this," she said. "If you could be anything in the world, what would it be?"

"Is this really the best we can do for conversation?"

"Come on. It's a good exercise."

"Is it though?"

"So, what would you be?"

"You mean anything? Not just what I'm qualified for?"

"That's right. Anything."

"I'd be a sherpa."

"What the heck is a sherpa?"

"They're the guys who haul rich people's crap up Mount Everest."

"Come on, I'm serious."

"Oh, you're serious. In that case, I'd like to be a race car driver."

"Yeah, but it's not like you can just go to school for that."

"Gracie, I'm still goofing with you."

"Dangit, Cash. I wanna know."

"Then that makes two of us."

Cash gulped down the last of his beer and refilled the glass.

"Aren't you curious?" she asked.

"You mean, about what you most want to be more than anything in the whole great wide world?"

"Quit teasing."

"What is it?"

She said a veterinarian, but Cash was already up out of his chair and walking with his arms outstretched toward a slightly older, slightly more handsome, and far better-dressed version of Cash himself. As the stranger drew near he reached out his arms, and the two of them made a manly, back-pounding embrace. They returned with their arms linked over each other's shoulders.

Gracie was beaming a huge fascinated smile. "Who is this?" she exclaimed.

"This is my flesh and blood," Cash told her. "Came all the way from Florida to surprise the hell out of me tonight."

"I'm Spencer," he said, holding out his hand.

"Oh, I love it," she said. "Sit with us."

"Have a beer, cousin. I'll grab a glass."

Spencer waved him off. "I'm buying shots. You like tequila, Gracie?"

"I love tequila."

"Beautiful. Cash, if this isn't already your girl, then she oughta be. I like her already."

Spencer squeezed Cash's shoulders and tousled his hair and went inside the bar. When he returned, he was gracefully balancing a tray that held ten shots of Patron, along with a salt shaker and a bowl of sliced lime. Gracie said, oh my, and Cash just grinned and shook his head.

"I hope you know I'm too broke to return the favor," Cash said.

"Don't even sweat it, cousin. I'm rich."

"How did you get rich?" Gracie asked. "I mean, if you don't mind me asking."

"First, let's all take one of these."

Spencer offered the tray with a sweeping mockery of elegance. Gracie and Cash each salted their hand and grabbed a shot and a lime wedge. Spencer set down the tray and held a glass aloft.

"What are we cheersing to?" he asked.

"You bought 'em. You call it," Cash said.

"Alright. Here's to family."

They touched glasses, tapped them on the table, and tossed back the tequila. Spencer set his empty glass on the tray, grabbed another, and tossed it back as well. He kissed the empty glass and set it aside the other.

"Thirsty?" Gracie asked.

"Just like to start it off right, you know what I mean? Now, what am I telling you? Oh, yeah. I'm a bartender. Best one in Fort Myers Beach. And I'm not really rich. Not like a lot of those fat bastards you see down there anyways."

"What are you doing in town?" Cash asked. "Why didn't you call me?"

"Just a last-minute thing. Had some time off, so I figured, what the heck. Might as well spend some time with the folks. All that jazz. Called up your mom this morning, told her I wanted to surprise you, and she said you'd probably be out here. God, this place brings back some memories. Remember that bee that Donny ate? No, you weren't old enough yet, were you?"

"I was there. That was when I was still sneaking in."

"That's right. You were a clever kid."

"Until they got wise to me."

"Yeah, what, after twenty times."

"Probably."

They sat for a moment, each of them reminiscing wild days gone by.

"You know, Cash. You look just like I remember you."

"Pretty much like looking in a mirror isn't it?"

"What? Don't sell me short. I'm dapper. I've got jawbone."

"Fuck off, you vain ass."

They both smiled and then took another shot of tequila. Afterwards, Spencer pulled his chair near Gracie and asked questions about her life in an earnest, charming way that was his bread and butter as a bartender. Cash smoked, quietly listening. When all the shots had been taken, Gracie announced that it was her turn to buy a round and staggered inside.

"So, what are you doing with yourself these days?" Spencer asked.

"Not much. Is languishing the right word? I think I'm languishing here."

"I have no idea what that word means, but it doesn't sound good. What's the problem?"

"My dad sold his business, which means I lost my job. My

parents are separated, and I might have to start working the mills to make ends meet."

"That is bad."

"Depresses me to even say it out loud. I'm living in this pitiful little studio apartment on Louisiana. And Gracie? Don't get me wrong. She's a nice girl, but—"

"But she's a little dull, and one of these days you're gonna knock her up by accident and . . ." He made the sound of a wooden bat hitting a baseball. ". . . there goes the life of Cash."

"That's about right."

They both sat there thinking it all over until Spencer finally said, "You need an exit strategy, bro."

"Like what?"

"Come out to Florida. I've got a spare room you can crash in until you get your feet on the ground. Pretty sweet pad. Got a pool in the backyard, nice big kitchen. And the house is right on this canal that leads into Estero Bay. Full of dolphins and manatees and jumping fish. All kinds of cool shit. Got a kayak. I mean, I'm set up."

"What would I do for work?"

"Who cares? Even if you were a custodian, at least you'd be outta this place."

"You're probably right."

"You know I'm right. Look, I've got a buddy out there who's the GM of a pretty fancy restaurant. This guy owes me a favor. I'll bet I could talk him into having a job waiting for you when you arrive."

Cash rubbed his neck, looking seriously affected. "You know this all sounds too good to be true, right?"

"What the hell. We're kin."

"Only one hitch."

"What's that?"

"How do I get there?"

"You fly, dummy."

"I need to have my motorcycle."

"That little two-fifty?"

"Nah, I got a new one last year. I'm making payments and I can't just split out on it."

"So, sell it."

"I could try, but you know how long that can take. Especially going into winter."

"What about your truck?"

"It's in the scrap yard."

Spencer leaned back in his chair and gazed at Cash levelly. He nodded to himself and leaned forward again.

"I can see what you're about to say," Cash said.

"Saddle up, cuz. You're fixin' to have yourself the journey of a lifetime."

"I already feel sore thinking about it."

"Don't be a pansy."

"You realize it's already October, right?"

"Ya, ya. And this is Washington, not Florida. It's gonna be so wet and cold and dreary. Ya, ya. What else you got?"

"Hold on. I'll think of something."

"You're a goddamn champ, Cash. Now get your ass to Florida!"

"Florida."

"Fort Myers Beach, baby!"

"How many girls will you have waiting for me?"

"More than you can handle."

"I imagine I could handle a lot."

"More."

"Will I get rich like you?"

"Damn right."

"Can I get back to you on this Florida deal?"

"Sure. But while you're thinking about it in your sad little studio, imagine me on the beach with the sand in my feet, beer in my hand, and surrounded by scandalous little party babes. I don't need you out there. I'm extending an invitation."

"Gracie. That's gonna be tough."

"Speaking of her, where is she? Thought she was getting us a round."

"Just keep it mum around her, ok?"

"I feel you. Zip lip around the girl. But where is she?"

A moment later, Gracie trudged up to the table and slumped into her seat. Her mascara had run down her face, and her eyes lacked any focus. She groaned once and looked somewhere between Cash and Spencer.

"I threw up," she said.

His father pointed the pool cue at the two ball, then the four, and said combo. He hitched his jeans up and leaned down over the table. There was the clack of balls, and the four dropped into the corner pocket.

"That was a heck of a shot," Cash said.

"I've always blown all my luck on the things that don't matter. Except you boys. They called out all the right numbers with you two."

It was a Tuesday afternoon, and the pub was nearly empty. One withered crone was slumped over the video poker console, and a bored mill worker was playing a basket of pull tabs. The barmaid had her back to the bar and was watching SportsCenter highlights.

His father looked the table over. "Six ball. Side pocket."

He hunkered down and hit his shot. The ball grazed the corner of the pocket and then fell. He picked up the chalk and worked it around his cue and gave it a blow.

"So, what's your plan now?" Cash asked him.

"Don't know. Guess I'll think of something. Maybe Walmart's hiring." He pointed to the table. "Seven ball. Same pocket as last time."

The ball dropped.

"And how about this deal with Spencer?" Cash continued. "You think I should go for it?"

"I think you're twenty-two years old, which means I think you oughta be making your own decisions."

"I'm not asking you to make up my mind for me. I'm just asking what you think."

His father had been stalking around the table and he stopped and planted the stick into the floor, his hands fisted around it chest high.

"I'll say this. I was nineteen years old when you were born. Life got awful serious in a hurry for me, and it never did seem to let up after that. I'm not saying I regret it. But you don't get that time back. Two ball. Corner."

"Do you think the bike will make it?"

"The bike? Sure. Those Suzukis are pretty reliable as long as they've got oil in 'em."

His father sank the ball.

"And how about me? You think I'll make it?"

"It's a long, long ways across, son. Lotta things can happen."

"You're saying you're not sure?"

"How could I be sure?"

He watched Cash's look.

"That's not the same thing as saying I don't think you're man enough. I'd just say I believe labeling anything a certainty is inviting along a whole lot of potential for grief."

He surveyed the table. Five stripes and the eight ball remained. His only chance at it was a long difficult bank shot, and he picked up the chalk and walked along the table reading the angles.

"What does Gracie think about this?" his father asked.

"I haven't told her yet."

He looked across the table at Cash. "You leave without telling her anything, I'll hunt you down like a rat."

Cash snorted.

"I'm serious."

"I know it."

His father walked back to the cue ball and tapped the corner pocket twice with his left hand.

"In here," he said.

He leaned over, steadied himself for a long time, and then struck the ball with a dull and barely audible precision. The eight ball caromed off the wall, and Cash shook his head and set his stick down on the table as it dropped in the pocket.

"You oughta poolshark for a living."

"Can't win with scared money, son."

He leaned his stick against the table and took a drink of his whiskey.

"You and I both know you're leaving," he said. "You're just trying to gauge how much of a rebel it makes you when you do it. Truth is, it probably runs in your blood. Always was west though. Now I suppose you'll all start running the other direction. I just want you to understand that this isn't such a bad place to settle down as you might think. You'll see."

He unzipped his flannel jacket down to his navel, removed something from his inside pocket, and zipped it back up.

"This is yours," he said.

Cash took the credit union check made out in his name and signed for nine hundred and nine dollars.

"I'm sorry things didn't work out like we'd planned. You woulda made a fine crew boss."

"I don't blame you, Dad. You did the best you could."

"Well. You just be careful out there. Make sure to wrap it up when you're with any of them strange birds."

Cash tried not to grin.

"I know your motives," his father said.

"You wanna look over my route with me?"

"We'll study some maps tonight."

"Another game?"

"Rack 'em, loser."

She lived six blocks from his father's house, and Cash walked the streets without hurry, the last of the day's sun casting the neighborhood in a bronze, cinematic glow. He turned the phrases over and over again in his mind, and then he tried them out loud, and then he just walked.

When he arrived at her ground-floor apartment, he went to knock at the door but instead stepped back and lit a cigarette. He was still pacing along the sidewalk as Gracie came outside carrying a trash bag.

"Hi, baby," she said. "Why didn't you call?"

He shrugged.

"You look bothered about something. You alright?"

"I need to talk with you."

"Let me toss this bag first before it spills all over my shoes."

He watched her walk over to the alley, swing the bag into the dumpster and return. She looked so pretty he doubted whether he was in his right mind.

"Come inside, baby," she said.

"Is Darlene in there?"

"Yeah."

"Can we talk out here then?"

"What's the matter with you? You look like you've got your tail between your legs."

He stood there gazing at the sidewalk.

"I'm not even gonna guess what the problem is, so you better just tell me."

Finally, he looked up at her. "Gracie, I'm moving to Florida."

"What? Florida? But you haven't even discussed it with me yet. How do you think my family is gonna like that idea? Besides that, my lease isn't even up until February."

"I'm saying, I'm going there alone."

She mouthed some words, but nothing came out. Then her chin went down to her chest, and her whole body seemed to go limp as she stood there convulsing with quiet whimpers. The sound of her crying was agonizing to him and he fought the instinct to take it all back. He stepped forward and put his hand on her shoulder, and in this state her roommate appeared at the door.

"Gracie, you're letting all the dang bugs inside again," she said. Then she saw what was happening and shut the door behind her.

When Gracie had finally stopped crying, he sat her down on a bench in the garden and took her hand.

"It's what I have to do," he said.

"Why can't I come with you?"

"For a whole lot of reasons."

"Your cousin convinced you there's a bunch of sluts out there, didn't he?"

"This doesn't have to be unpleasant."

"For you maybe. How do you think I feel?"

"Gracie, there's plenty of boys in town who will treat you a lot better than I have."

"They're just a bunch of hicks."

"I'm a hick."

"No, you're not."

As Gracie continued to snuffle, Cash watched children in the park across the street run a shrieking game of tag. Twilight was coming. A father called out time for dinner, and a child waved goodbye to the others and scampered home.

"Do you hate me?" he asked.

"No. I love you."

He took a deep breath in through his nose and let it out slow.

"Tell me why I can't come," she persisted.

"Because it won't work out for us. We're different people."

"You're giving up too easy. On everything."

"I just need a new deck of cards, Gracie. That's all."

"Then I guess that makes me something you're folding, huh?"

"Don't put this on yourself. It's better if you think of me as an asshole."

Gracie shook her head and wiped the tears out of her eyes. Then she composed her face into one of bravery and put her hand on his thigh.

"I'm not letting this happen to us. I'll fly out there if I have to."

"Gracie—"

"I will. I'll just fly out there then."

"I've already decided."

"I love you, Cash."

"I know."

"Why won't you just let me love you?"

He couldn't look at her anymore, so he turned and watched the children now playing keep away with a small boy's hat.

"I'm going to show you something," she said suddenly standing. "I'll be right back."

He watched her walk into her apartment. When she was out of sight, he stood up and went away down the alley.

The garage smelled of firewood and gasoline and a decade's accumulation of dust. Patches of oil greased the cement, and a heap of childhood toys brightly clogged one whole corner. Up in the rafters the remnants of a long-abandoned plywood fort abounded with cobwebs. Some tools and rusty sawblades filled a wonky bookshelf, and behind that was a clutter of carpentry projects their father had left unfinished. Cash and Charley stood among these artifacts, only concerned with the pair of Suzuki motorcycles that stood side by side on their kickstands. A black and squat GZ-250 mini-cruiser rested next to a taller, leaner, faster VS-800 Suzuki Intruder which was painted a bright turquoise and draped with leather saddlebags.

Earlier that afternoon Cash had loaded the saddlebags with clothes and shoes and camping gear and they were bulging full. Atop one saddlebag he'd secured his tent to the frame of the bike with a handful of zipties and atop the other his sub-zero sleeping bag had been fastened in the same manner. Cash went around the bike demonstrating for Charley how he'd rigged everything, elucidating in great detail what he had selected to pack and what in the end he'd be forced to do without. Cash made another lap of the bike and then stopped to quietly admire the economy of it all. When he looked up across the two bikes, Charley was staring at him wistfully.

"I've got a surprise for you," Cash said.

"What is it?"

Cash removed a folded paper from his back pocket and walked around and handed it to Charley, who unfolded the document and regarded it with confusion.

"I don't get it."

"Don't you know what a title looks like? I'm giving you my old bike, Charley. I've already signed it over to you. That two-fifty's yours now."

Charley looked at the title again, this time with amazement. "It's really mine?"

"Sure. I'm not gonna need it in Florida."

"Wow."

"I do have one stipulation though, Charley. You need to take a class for your motorcycle endorsement before you start riding it all over. I know you've been riding dirt bikes since you were a little kid, but it's a lot more dangerous out on the street. You gotta get that endorsement, ok? Mom and Dad are gonna hold you to it."

Charley had been nodding his head in agreement when their mother opened the door from the house and shouted that their pizza was ready. She was tall and still pretty, especially for her age, but she wore an anxious and wearied look.

"Mom, guess what?" Charley called.

She muttered something neither of them could hear.

"Cash is giving me his old motorcycle."

"I told him that you and Dad are gonna hold him to that class," Cash said.

"You two get in here and eat some dinner."

The kitchen smelled deliciously of cheese and dough and fresh vegetables, and although it was only a pre-made pizza she'd bought from Papa Murphy's, the boys complimented their mother's fine cooking. She watched her boys pile slices onto their plates and then she served herself and joined them in the living room. They sat in deeply cushioned couches with paper towels in their laps and watched news on the television. A group of Muslims had firebombed a U.S. embassy in North Africa, and four Americans were dead. Their mother made a disconsolate clucking.

"It's so awful," she said.

"What's this one about?" Cash asked.

"They killed all those people just because of some video a few wingnuts made about Mohammed. It's absolutely senseless."

"What'd they say about him in the movie?"

"Oh, I don't know. Does it matter? Should anything anybody says end in this? I mean, how barbaric! Killing innocent people over a video they had nothing to do with. It gets me worked up. It really gets me . . ."

Cash had hit the power button on the remote, and the television expired.

"Take it easy, mom," he said.

"You can't just turn off my feelings. I'm upset about this."

Cash looked at his brother for assistance, but Charley only mouthed, I don't know.

"It's all a long way from here," Cash said.

"That doesn't make it any less important. Think of these people's families. Can you imagine?"

"It is awful, Mom. We agree. I've just never known you to be so concerned with this kind of stuff."

Their mother sighed, and she took a long time doing it.

"I'm just nervous," she said.

"About the Muslims?" he asked tentatively.

She looked at him sidelong and said, "About you leaving."

Cash put his plate on the coffee table and went over and sat next to her.

"Lots of people ride their motorcycles across the country, Mom."

"Yeah. And not all of them make it back."

"But I'm top notch."

"It's the other drivers that scare me. And the weather. And what if your chain breaks while you're on the freeway? Have you thought about that?"

"It doesn't even have a chain, Mom. It's a shaft drive."

"Whatever. You know what I mean."

"I'm vigilant, Mom. I'm always watching out for—"

"And now Charley's gonna be riding around on your old bike. Great."

"What the heck, Mom. Dad was a motorcycle mechanic when you married him. You used to ride with him all the time."

"That's how I know how dangerous it is. How many screws does he have in his elbow?"

Cash buried his mouth into his bicep, groaned, and then faced her with exasperation.

"Why are you doing this now? For Christ's sake, it's too late to go back on it even if I wanted to. We should be enjoying our last night together, not dwelling on fears and what-ifs."

"It's easier for you. You don't think of the consequences like me."

"Yes, I do. But I don't worry. That's the difference. I don't worry when it won't do me any good. Now buck up, or I'll go spend my last night at Dad's."

Her eyes bulged as if she'd been slapped. It took a few exhales, but she finally breathed it all out and suddenly her whole demeanor softened and she almost looked like a different person.

"I'm sorry, honey. You're right. You are. I'm almost like a child when I'm like that, aren't I?"

They hugged, and Cash rubbed her back while telling her to take it easy, take it easy.

When she released him, she smiled and said, "Okay. You're leaving in the morning. Are you all packed?"

"Yep."

"Did you pack socks and underwear?"

"Yes, Mother."

"How many pairs?"

"I've got a backup of each."

"A backup?"

"I'm kidding, Mom. I packed four or five pair."

"How about a first aid kit?"

He shook his head.

"You need band aids, at least."

She went into the bathroom, and he heard the sound of her shuffling through cupboards. When she returned, she gave him a bag containing at least twenty band aids of various sizes.

"How often are you expecting me to hurt myself?"

"Just take them."

As she continued to pepper Cash with questions and advice, he took notice of Charley gazing into the carpet.

"You're awfully quiet over there, bud," Cash said. "What's going on?"

"He's just sad like me that you're moving to the other side of the country," their mom answered for him.

"That what it is?" Cash asked.

"Pretty much," he said.

"Well, I'm not gonna be gone forever. Just need to try something new for a while. I'll be back."

"How long do you think you'll be away?" their mother asked.

"I really don't know."

His mother woke him from the couch with a gentle hand on his shoulder, and when Cash had finally blinked her into focus he saw she was holding out a hundred-dollar bill.

"I don't need that," he said.

"It'll pay for a couple hotel rooms," she said. "It's bound to rain somewhere."

He looked at the money doubtfully, as if it were bad luck.

"Please take it."

"Mom," he said and took the bill.

"Now give me a hug. I have to go."

Cash sat up, and she clutched him fiercely.

"My brave son," she said.

When she released him, he saw her eyes were wet.

"You come home for Christmas, ok? That's all I ask."

"I'll try."

"You come home for Christmas."

After she was gone, Cash stood up and stretched and then stuffed a few last things into his backpack. Quickly, he ate a bowl of cereal and drank a cup of lukewarm coffee and then gathered his gear. He pulled on his jeans and over them his padded rainpants. Then his sweatshirt and his leather jacket and his boots. He pondered what he may have forgotten and then leaned over the side of the couch and pulled his phone charger from the wall.

Finally, he walked down the hall and pushed open the door to his brother's room. The creak of the hinges woke Charley, who rolled over to face him in the half dark.

"I'm leaving, bud."

"Yeah, I know."

"Just came in to say goodbye."

"Bye."

"That's all you're gonna say?"

"Be safe. I'll miss you. Wear condoms."

"That's more like it. Alright, bud. Adios."

Charley rolled back to sleep as Cash closed the door. He went through the house and into the garage and pushed a button on the wall that made the door clank open. Cash walked up to the Suzuki Intruder and pounded himself in the leg. "I'm really doing this," he said.

He rolled the motorcycle out of the garage and then shut the door and went around the side of the house. When he came back to the bike, he put his key in the ignition, pulled on his helmet and gloves, threw a leg over the seat, and let out the choke. With his left hand he squeezed the clutch, and with his right he disabled the kill switch. Then he rocked the bike to an upright and knocked back the kickstand with his heel. Finally, he thumbed the starter, which made a quick electric whine, and the engine exploded into a deep, hammering tempo. Once the bike quieted, Cash pushed in the choke and stepped into gear and rolled down the alley.

It had rained in the night, and the streets were all glistening in the mild, morning sun. He rode past the church where his parents had been married, crossed over Lake Sacajawea, and then passed the empty skatepark and his father's storage unit. On Industrial Way he shifted gears, smelling the sulfuric tang of the pulp mills. He went around Mount Solo and then stopped for a red light at the last intersection. When the light blinked green, he made a left onto Highway 4 and soon Longview receded and was gone.

The highway followed the Columbia River as it coursed and swung its last leg out to the Pacific Ocean. Cash rode easy at first, letting himself and the bike warm into the rhythm of a long day. Around the sharpest corners, Cash would give his rear brake a touch, downshift, and then bend along with the banked curve, not turning but leaning bodily until the highway straightened for him to rise and flick up a gear and rock back the accelerator. As Cash navigated this twisting asphalt, he was amazed by the newness of everything, a road he'd traveled countless times made foreign by the spirit of his enterprise. He felt intoxicated by the uncertainty of the day and all the days after, as if his destiny had suddenly been unleashed. He rode those first miles with a massive grin tucked behind his visor.

Down the road, Cash noticed his left rearview mirror was angled too far to the ground, so he knocked it with his palm until the single headlight of another motorcycle was visible a quarter mile in the distance. He passed County Line Park where a few fishermen sat on the bank in lawn chairs and then a little cove where on the beach the rusted hull of a wrecked ship had long resided. A logging truck approached from the other direction, and it went past with a raucous whoosh and a gust of turbulent air. Later, he came to a series of tight corners that doubled and tripled back above the bank of the Columbia, and as he leaned with them Cash felt as though he were somehow dancing with the land itself.

He soon passed Cathlamet and Skamokawa and the highway left the river and became engulfed by forest. As the road elevated into low hills, he came to a passing lane and got right and saw if anyone would come up from behind. A black Camaro shot up the incline, and Cash watched the car pass and then decided to keep pace. His body lurched back as he accelerated and flew through the new misty and moss-green farmland. Cows fed in overgrown pastures, and scattered throughout the valley old, forsaken houses and barns slumped an interminable rot. The trees were falling away much faster now, and his corners required more of a lean. Coming around a sharp turn, Cash looked slightly over his shoulder and saw the motorcycle still riding the same distance back.

He was low on fuel, and when he came to a rural gas station he pulled up to the pump. A faded, handwritten notice instructed customers to prepay, so Cash went in and gave the old woman a twenty. As he was filling his tank, he looked back from where he'd come and saw the same motorcycle pulled off on the side of the highway. The rider appeared to be staring at him. He tried to make out the bike or the rider, but it was too far away. He finished pumping and went inside for his change. When he returned, the rider was there as before.

Cash fired up the bike and took off riding through a gloomy, shadowed forest. He checked his mirror and saw the rider had commenced to follow again. Cash rode the speed limit for a while and then picked it up, and the rider stayed. He slowed back to the limit and then well below, and the rider stayed. Finally, he pulled over on the side of the highway, and the rider did the same. Cash turned around on the seat, and all he could tell was that the rider appeared to be wearing some sort of a pack that humped up behind his helmet.

He sped west, and when the rider immediately followed, he knew he'd had enough. He braked hard and swung around sharply and rode directly at the rider, who had pulled over again. Cash stopped so close their two front tires were nearly touching. He pulled off his helmet and walked straight up to the rider.

"Gig is up, dufus."

Charley sat on the little 250 in full gear. He wore a tremendous hiking pack that looked as though it were concealing a twin brother, and which rested on the backseat like it was his passenger.

"What are you doing?" Cash asked. "Running away from home?"

"You are too," Charley said, his voice muffled by the helmet.

"I'm twenty-two. I'm entitled to do what I want."

"So am I."

"Charley, you're a senior in high school. You're not even entitled to buy a six-pack."

"So, what?"

"So, what do you think Mom and Dad are gonna do if I let you come along?"

Charley shrugged.

"They're gonna disown me and then beat you sillier than you already are."

"I have everything I need."

"Charley, you don't need anything, cause you're going home."

"I have it all in this bag."

"Oh, yeah. You got any gas money?"

"Almost a thousand dollars."

"From roof cleaning?"

"Yeah."

"Well, I'm sorry bud, but you can't come along this time. Couple of years, you finish school, we'll do something like this together. Okay? I'll see ya, bud."

Cash started up his bike and waved farewell as he took off west again. Several miles along he thought Charley had turned back, only to see him rise a crest nearly a half mile in the distance. One after the other they left Highway 4 and turned onto a road that ran them south through Naselle and back again to the river, the Columbia gargantuan there before the mouth, and the Astoria Bridge spanning it for miles. Cash rode over the dizzying last expanse of the bridge and then circled around the off-ramp and came into Astoria. He pulled into the parking lot of a hotel under the colossal green girders of the bridge and waited for Charley to come alongside.

"Let me put it to you another way," Cash said from his seat. "My bike has eight hundred cc's and that's about as small of a bike as you'd ever want to take across the country. The one you're on is a two-fifty. You see what I'm saying? You'd never make it. I mean, do you even know how far away Florida is from here?"

"All the way."

"That's right. All the way across the damn continent. There is no way you can make it there on a two-fifty. And look at that humungous pack. That thing must weigh as much as you do."

"I feel fine."

"Charley, you've rode fifty miles. Florida is another three thousand, minimum."

Charley gave no sign that the distance impressed him.

"This is like convincing a kamikaze pilot out of his mission. Go home, Charley! I will slash your tires if you keep following me!"

Cash fired up the bike and zoomed out into the road, cutting off a truck that blared its horn at him. Traffic moved languidly through Warrenton and Seaside, and Charley stayed a dozen vehicles back. Past Cannon Beach, Highway 101 finally opened up, and Cash resolved to simply out-ride his brother. He made a couple illegal passes to reach the vanguard and then rode with the throttle pinned back. Charley went out of sight.

Once Cash lost his brother for good, he finally began to enjoy the scenery. At the Neahkahnie Overlook, the highway bent high above the ocean, and Cash took the corner slow. The sky, the beach, the ocean—everything—was tinted a metallic silver as if the world had recently been polished with chrome. The silver haze had washed away the natural contours of the Coast Range hills so thoroughly that they appeared only silhouettes of themselves, looking like kindergarten renderings of mountains rising up from the sea. Descending from the overlook, Cash sped around Nehalem Bay, then through the towns of Rockaway Beach, Garibaldi, Bay

City. Soon after he caught the first heavy cow smell, he pulled into the Tillamook Cheese Factory.

He ordered a cheeseburger and fries and brought his tray of food to a table by the window. As he ate, he fantasized of Florida and imagined the feel of the sand and sun and all the new things that would be his. He pictured the girls on the beach, and a gale of excitement swirled inside and made him giddy. For the first time, his life had wheels. He was really gone and going.

When he finished his burger, Cash ordered a waffle cone with two scoops of huckleberry cheesecake ice cream and walked outside with it. He turned toward his bike and nearly ran into Charley standing on the sidewalk with his pack on his shoulders.

Charley smiled and said, "I knew I'd find you here licking a stupid ice cream cone."

They left Tillamook riding twenty yards apart through a flat, green farmland populated by dairy cows. To the east, a vast gray hangar was painted with the words Air Museum and beyond it the jumble of dark hills. They entered the Siuslaw Forest where the road ascended steeply and windingly, and Cash had to slow for Charley to keep pace. The low summit was announced with an elevation sign, and then the brothers twisted down again past the community of Beaver and into their first drops of rain, which plinked against their visors and slid away with the wind. The rain kept up, and soon their visors were full of it. Cars passed slishing water up under their tires and sending the brothers along with a cold draft. In Hebo they pulled under the carport of a gas station and dismounted. Charley was barely able to stifle shivering.

"Ain't so fun now is it?" Cash said.

"I'm okay."

"Look at you. You're freezing your ass off."

Charley had dropped his pack against the pump and was digging through the top pouch for his wallet.

"Put your damn sweatshirt on, will you."

"I don't have one."

Cash made his voice go up an octave. "I've got everything I need," he parroted. "Isn't that what you said?"

Charley swiped his card and unlocked his tank and began

gassing it with a trembling arm. Cash looked up at the roof of the carport and shook his head. He was cursing to himself as he unzipped his jacket and removed his sweatshirt. It hit the back of Charley's head and fell to the ground.

After Lincoln City it quit raining, but it didn't get any warmer. By the time they stopped at a Fred Meyer's, Cash was trembling worse than Charley had been before. They went inside and bought another sweatshirt and then walked across the street to a Starbucks. A chipper, young, redheaded girl awaited Cash at the register.

"Hello, sir. Would you like to try our pumpkin spice latte? It's our autumn special."

"I just want your biggest coffee."

Cash took his coffee to a booth and sat huddled up with both hands wrapped around the paper cup. A minute later, Charley joined him with a small hot chocolate, which he was blowing into. He took a scalding sip and then continued to blow. Finally, he looked up at Cash whose face was all harshness.

"That's the last time I sacrifice myself for your stupidity."

"I know."

"This was supposed to be my trip. You were never part of the bargain."

"I know."

"If you screw this up for me, I'll really leave you stranded. In the desert. You get what I'm saying?"

"I get it."

"We're gonna set some ground rules right now. First off, I lead, and you don't be lollygagging behind me. You buy your own food, your own gas. That bike is yours now, so you're responsible for checking the oil and tires. If you blow the engine, tough shit. I'm riding on. And I don't want to hear you whining when I go out to the bars at night."

"What are we gonna tell Mom and Dad?"

"You're the fugitive. You figure it out."

They sipped their drinks. A barista called out an order, and a thin man in a suit walked up and leaned against the counter in an awkward posture of forced relaxation. He was trying to chat with the barista, but she was pretending she couldn't hear him for the steam and hiss of her machine.

"What's the name of this town again?" Charley asked.

"Newport."

"Have we been here before?"

"I think Mom and Dad took us to the aquarium once."

"Is this the town with the sea lions?"

"I think so."

"Are we gonna go look at them?"

"No, we're not gonna go look at the goddamn sea lions!"

"Ok. Jeez. I thought since we came all this way, you might want to look at them for a minute."

"It's obvious you don't appreciate how long a ride we've got ahead of us. You say you know, but you don't have a clue."

Charley almost started a rebuttal and then thought better of it.

Cash swigged the rest of his coffee and stood up from the booth. "Finish that kiddie drink, and let's go."

Beyond Waldport, the ocean whipped up the fog and mist, and soon the sun was concealed for the day. Clouds of vapor whorled across the highway like the ocean's exhaust, and the brothers rode through the hanging wet as if they were motorized ghosts. Occasionally the fog was sucked back, and they watched mighty sea convulsions torment the rocks and cliffsides with a boom and a belch that jetted foam skyward, only to spatter back into itself and begin again. A relentless gray-green sea, savagely beautiful, it made the seaside cottages and saltwater taffy shops appear almost unbearably tawdry in comparison.

Soon after dark, they rode through Coos Bay and found a

cheap motel at the edge of town. They pulled into the parking lot, and Charley unshouldered his pack and dropped it heavily to the ground. Cash went inside the office, where an old snow-haired clerk glowered as Cash told him he wanted their most basic room.

"Do you smoke?" the man asked.

"Yeah."

"I asked if you're a smoker."

"Yes. I—"

"Cause there's no smoking in the rooms."

"Sure thing. I would never—"

"And there's no smoking outside the rooms either. You wanna smoke, you gotta do it at the far end of the parking lot there."

Cash said the smoking would be no problem and that he'd like a room. He held out the hundred-dollar bill his mother had given him. The clerk looked at Cash skeptically and finally grasped the bill wide apart at the edges and held it up to the light for inspection. He peered down, and Cash smiled.

"She look legal?"

"Better than the guy who come in here yesterday. Looked like he'd photocopied a hundred-dollar bill at the local library."

"What'd you tell him?"

"I told him to get the hell out, but he wanted the money back, so I ripped it up and threw it in the trash and told him to get the hell out."

After the brothers had each taken a hot shower, they walked downtown to find dinner. The first place they came to was a Chinese restaurant, and they went inside. A waitress came over with waters and wrote down their orders and walked back and handed it to the chef. Cash drummed his fingers on the table as he watched a beta fish swimming in a tank across the room.

"She's gonna be pissed," Charley said.

"Gee. Ya think?"

"Can't we just call tomorrow?"

"We? You are calling Mom tonight. She'll have the whole town searching for you if she doesn't get a call soon."

Charley deliberated and then pulled out his phone and hit Mom. She answered on the second ring, and he affected a confident breezy tone.

"Hi Mom. No, I won't be home for dinner. Well, that's why I'm calling. I'm uh . . . I'm in Coos Bay. With Cash. Wait, I can explain. You know how people study abroad, well—"

He held the phone out to Cash. "She told me to shut my mouth."

By the end of the call, both their meals had been served and eaten and no agreement had been reached with their mother except that from Coos Bay on they were to stick together at all times. Their father was gone hunting for a few days, but she told them they could be sure to hear from him soon and that he might just decide to drive down and wallop them both. On the walk back to the hotel, they discussed the likelihood of this, deciding that the safest bet was to get an early start in the morning.

Back in their hotel room, they each changed into shorts and a t-shirt. Cash brushed his teeth in the bathroom, while Charley lay in bed watching television.

"Are we always gonna have to sleep in the same bed like this?" Charley called. "It's kinda weird."

"We'll see," Cash said, his voice deep and gargled with toothpaste. "Don't wanna blow our whole wad before we get there."

"How long will it actually take us?"

"I was hoping a week, but I don't know. Ten days. Maybe more."

"It was really fun riding through that fog. It would have been a perfect day if only we'd gotten to see the sea lions."

Cash poked his head out the door.

Charley laughed and said, "I'm kidding."

Cash spit out his toothpaste and rinsed his mouth with water a few times. He checked his face in the mirror and then pissed and flipped off the bathroom light. He went and sat on the edge of the bed and began removing his contacts.

"How far are we going tomorrow?" Charley asked.

"Far as we can get. Somewhere in California."

"I've always wanted to go there."

"Charley, we went to Disneyland."

"Oh, yeah. I forgot about that. But that was back when I was a kid."

Cash almost said something but instead he just screwed the caps back on his contact container and then slid under the sheets next to Charley.

"Turn the boob tube off, Charley. Let's get some rest."

Charley flipped it off, but he stayed sitting up against the headboard. "I was wondering," he said. How come we're not taking the freeway?"

"Well, I was going to, cause I'm anxious as hell to get to Florida. But Dad convinced me out of it. He told me, there's some things you might only ever get to do once in your life, and you may as well do 'em right."

"Enjoy the ride," Charley said.

"That's right. Enjoy the ride. He said that once we get south of San Fran there's supposed to be a highway along the coast that blows this one out of the water. Highway One, I think."

Charley wormed down under the covers as Cash turned off the light. Both of them rolled onto their sides away from each other. Their hotel was right along the entrance to the highway, and now in the silence of the room they listened to drag races of souped-up trucks. Two of them went off in a roar, and then it drew quiet.

"You're gonna be glad I'm coming along," Charley said.

"I sure hope so."

Cash led them out of Coos Bay under a dull morning drizzle, the highway slick and windy and altogether uninviting. In the town of Bandon, they filled up on bagels and coffee and then gassed their bikes and rode on. For the next thirty miles the highway kept them within smell but not sight of the ocean. They were yearning to look on it again when they finally came to Port Orford and passed along a beach strewn with rock formations. Beyond those, an array of spires and sea stacks loomed above the breakers. Swiftly, they came around a bend where a tidepool was nestled in the serenity of a cliff-encircled cove. Monoliths and more rock formations continued to appear in the distance, and as much as they reveled in these sights, their attention was diverted by the wind which now howled and bullied them around their lane.

Sometimes it was a headwind screaming into their faceshields, but more often and more pernicious was when the wind swarmed from the side, forcing them to maintain their balance by leaning into the pavement at unsettling angles. As soon as they grew accustomed to this, the wind would suddenly vanish so that for a moment they were toppling over and had to quickly jerk back upright. There was no special method by which either of them could predict these vagaries of weather, but only a constant, clenching attention.

Eventually, the sun broke through and everything began to dry. The wind abated, and Cash and Charley both loosened their grips on the handlebars. They relaxed back into cruise postures and opened their visors to hear the ocean rolling in melodic. A seabird dove down and splashed into the water, and the brothers were craning their necks and squinting to see if the bird came up with a fish when—blam—a gust ripped through the lull, slamming them broadside, and sending their bikes into a shudder.

By midday they reached the bottom of Oregon and stopped at a checkpoint on the border. A woman in uniform came out of her booth and asked if they were transporting any produce. Cash said no, and she nodded them along. Immediately, they felt warmer, and to them the smell and the look of the land seemed greatly altered from a mile before, the thought of California powerful upon their minds.

In Crescent City they pulled into the parking lot of a gas station to stretch their legs. Cash was removing the wrapping of a new pack of cigarettes when a dirty, white Honda Acura pulled alongside them. An old, hippy dude with long, gray hair tied into a ponytail held out a Marlboro and said, "Here. Free."

Cash looked at the man and the cigarette judiciously and then took it and lit up. "Thanks," he said.

"Where you headed?" the hippy asked.

"Florida."

He showed no surprise at the distance, only nodding slightly as if to agree that it should be so. "Not many of you getting around these days."

"What do you mean?" Cash asked.

"Voyagers. Vagabonds. That type."

"How do you know that's what we are?"

He waved toward their bikes and Charley's pack and said, "It's pretty obvious to one who was one."

Cash waited for the man to say more, and when he didn't he thanked him again for the smoke and walked back to his bike. The man put his car in drive and as he passed them he called out, "You're doing it right, boys," and turned into traffic.

Once they'd gassed their bikes, they got back on the highway and arced around the crescent-shaped beach for which the town was named. Past this they labored up a long, steep incline and entered their first forest of redwoods where they were initially stricken not so much by the girth of the trees but by the darkness they created. The canopy had swallowed up all but a few ethereal piercings which threw angelic beams on the ground of ferns and against the gnarled bark of the trees. The road itself was unpredictable and preposterously zigzagged in its accommodation of the redwoods, some of which jutted out so far, they were like living guardrails. The brothers threaded the bulk of those mammoths and navigated a number of lethally blind corners until they were positively dizzy with trees. They bent their bikes around another unbelievable curve and then were suddenly splashed with light, the forest all gone behind them and the ocean again in sight.

They went on past Eureka and Fortuna in the last slanting bronze before sunset, both of them a little high from the last hour's ride. In the town of Rio Dell, they had hotdogs and chips for dinner and then inquired at the hotel across the street. The prices were extortionate, so they decided to ride on. Soon they entered the Humbolt Redwoods, and in this new forest, darkness was upon them almost immediately. When Cash spotted a sign for a campground, he hit his turn signal and Charley followed him down a dirt path. At the end of the drive they came to a small white house and a sign for the campground host.

The brothers walked up onto the porch where Cash buzzed for the attendant. Nobody came, and he buzzed again. Charley knocked on the screen door, and finally they turned and got back on their bikes and searched for a site on their own. The campground was largely deserted, but there were a few trailers scattered about.

When they came to a nice, flat site with a tree in the middle, they pulled in and Cash aimed his bike where he wanted to pitch their tents. He shifted the bike into neutral and set it on the kickstand, and by the glow of the headlight they began assembling their camp. Together they unfolded Cash's tarp and laid it out under the tree. Then Cash cut the zipties from his tent with a pocketknife, while Charley dug his tent out of the bottom of his pack.

"This is great," Charley said.

"When's the last time we went camping together?"

"It's been a long time."

"I can't even remember. You'd think Dad would try and take us more often."

"He's too busy."

"He's not too busy to hunt and fish."

"He'd probably starve if he didn't."

Cash laughed as he aligned the last link of a tent pole. "I never thought of it that way, but you're probably right."

They got their tents up quickly, and Charley began arranging his stuff inside, while Cash dug through his saddlebags with frustration.

"Crap," he said.

"What?"

"I can't find the rainfly. Guess I just thought it'd be in there."

"I don't know where mine's at either."

Cash looked up. "That tree looks like it's got some good cover, doesn't it?"

"Pretty good, I'd say."

"I told myself not to forget anything stupid, but I went and did it anyway."

"We'll be okay."

"What the hell. We're already pitched, right?"

"It'd be cool if we could have a fire."

"I don't wanna have to track down wood tonight."

"We should get set up earlier next time. Then we can make a fire and cook hotdogs instead of having to buy them at the store."

"Now you're thinking, bud. We'll do that."

Both of them were lying on top of their sleeping bags and looking up at the murky shapes of tree limbs rocking in the breeze.

"So where do we go tomorrow?" Charley asked.

"We keep going south. I was thinking that since we're being so economical tonight, we might splurge a little and stay in San Francisco. What do you think?"

"Shoot. We can stay with Aunt Susan, can't we?"

"That's San Diego."

"Oh."

"You need to learn a little geography, dude."

"I get 'em mixed up."

"I can see now that we're gonna have to do some road schooling. Make this trip an educational experience for you since you're skipping out on classes."

"I know some things."

"What's the capital of California?"

"Sacramento."

"You got it."

"I read it on a magazine in the gas station earlier."

"That's cheating then. How about Oklahoma?"

"Oklahoma City?"

"That was too easy. New York?"

"New York City?"

"It's Albany."

"I've never even heard of that town."

"How about South Carolina?"

"Beats me."

"It's Charleston. You gotta remember these now. Your future prosperity depends on the memorization of such factoids."

"That's what the teachers want you to think anyways."

"Knowledge is power, Charley."

"Shut up."

"Chant with me, brother. Knowledge is power. Knowledge is power."

"I'm serious. Do you hear that?"

Rain had begun pattering on the leaves of the tree.

"Christ," Cash said. "Is it getting through to the tents?"

"I don't think so."

They listened as the rain intensified and soon they could hear it popping against the roofs of their tents. Dark splotches began to form and grow until they were wet to the touch. The tents were all but raining themselves when they finally got out and broke them down in the sopping rain, while trying to keep the rest of their gear out of the muck. Cash hastily zip-tied his tent back onto the bike, while Charley simply folded his up and strapped it to the exterior of his pack. They started up their bikes and rode back to the highway like a pair of beleaguered tramps.

They headed south without a clue how far it was to the next town, only that it'd been a ways since the last. Already it was a fierce rain, and the sound of it falling in the trees was as loud to them as their engines. Rivulets of water ran across the highway like miniature floods, and as they forded these they tried gloving the rain off their visors, but it was entirely futile. As the condensation grew, the warmth of their breaths caused the inside of their visors to fog and obscure their vision so badly, they were forced to open their helmets to the rain as it pelted them in the face. The path of the highway was difficult to decipher, and they had slowed down to thirty miles an hour to be sure they didn't ride off the road by accident.

As dangerous as it had been, it worsened when they began to encounter billows of fog that hung across the highway like wind-teased curtains and hid the road from them for a moment, sometimes two moments, and then a curve originating too soon. Cash tried not to make these turns too drastic. He wondered about his traction, and then he wondered what he would do if one of them crashed, and he couldn't think of a thing. The rain had seeped through his leather jacket and through his rainpants and was saturating its way into his underlayers. His legs began to shiver and shiver, and he focused on them not shivering, and they shivered. An SUV finally passed going the same direction, and the wild-eyed expression he took from their faces terrified him more than anything.

Despite it all, Cash became transfixed by a mysterious luminescence that filtered through the fog above a ridge to the east. Brilliantly white and seeming to pulsate, it looked so strange and alien there in the forest. For a moment, Cash imagined it might actually be a UFO touchdown, and then a minute later he made out a sign and realized it was the town of Miranda.

The brothers got off the highway and backtracked to the source of the light and stopped at what appeared to be the only lodging around, a cluster of cabins along the main road. In the office, a pretty young girl was working the desk, and the brothers felt almost more embarrassment than relief as they stood there dripping on the tile floor. She said the nightly rate was a hundred and forty-five dollars, but since it was so late or else because they looked so pitiful, she said she could give them a cabin for eighty-five.

"We'll take it," they said.

Cash woke to the sound of the rain. He thought it was still night until he opened his eyes and saw the morning slitting through the blinds. He rolled over to find Charley's head half on each pillow, and his mouth wide agape. Cash sat up and looked at his phone and then twisted a few cracks out of his neck. Charley stirred.

"It's still raining?" he said.

"Mother nature ain't doing her best by us."

"Let's keep sleeping."

"It's already ten. We slept for eleven hours."

"I'm still tired."

"I'll make us some coffee. They don't have hot chocolate. Coffee's better for you anyways."

Cash got a pot started in the kitchenette and then went into the bathroom where their clothes were hanging everywhere. The heat had been up as hot as it would go, yet their jeans were still damp. He touched his riding pants, and they felt as wet as when he'd taken them off. In the kitchen, he found a small garbage bag, stuffed it with their wet shirts and socks and underwear, and then squeezed it into a tight wad. Neither of them had an extra pair of pants, so they kept their gym shorts on and pulled the jeans over the top. Cash lifted his leather jacket, and it was pounds heavier than usual. Charley was kneeling over their boots, which were open as wide as they'd go and lying sideways in front of the radiator.

"They're soaked," he said.

"You'd better drink some of that coffee."

Without cheer or much discussion, they packed up and squished into their gear. Cash returned the room key, while their bikes idled out front. Once the engines sounded warm, the brothers walked out into the light rain and threw a leg over their seats and knocked in their chokes. They rolled back out of their spots, faced themselves south, and then stepped into gear.

Past the town of Garberville, the rain petered out and quit, and they found themselves charmed by the luscious and tangled green of the country. Charley waved for them to stop, and they pulled over and pissed in the bushes. Cash was gazing into some distant thickets when he saw a cluster of horns, and then the sets of eyes motionless and scrutinizing. Cash pointed them out to his brother, and they counted four bull elk. Charley shouted, "Hey elk," and they silently dissolved into the forest.

Soon after this, they rode into another redwood grove where they were halted by standstill traffic. In a clearing to their left, a herd of elk grazed not more than twenty yards from the highway. Cash and Charley made different counts, but each agreed that it was the largest herd they'd ever seen in person, certainly never so close. After a couple minutes, the car in front of the brothers began honking, and a few of the elk perked their heads up with mild interest.

"Why isn't anybody moving?" Charley asked.

"I don't know."

"You'd think they'd take a couple pictures and move along."

"I was thinking the same thing."

Cash put his bike on the kickstand and stepped out into the oncoming lane. "You gotta take a look at this," he said.

Twenty cars ahead, an ungodly stout bull was straddling the painted centerline and singly obstructing both lanes of traffic.

"Look at the rack on him," Charley exclaimed. "How many antlers do you think?"

"He looks like a six-point. Seven. At least a seven."

"I'm gonna take a picture for Dad."

"You'll give him wet dreams with that."

The bull turned and modeled its other profile, and then gave a neck-flexed posture of defiance to anyone or anything that would dare trespass against him. Traffic continued to pile up on both sides before the bull finally sniffed the air and sauntered back into his harem. Cars resumed driving, and the brothers followed into a new flurry of rain.

Within ten miles, their boots had filled up with water, and their clothes had again become saturated. They exited the highway at a minor tourist village and pulled up to a diner that had been closed for the season. Huddled under the dripping eaves of the restaurant, each of them wrung out their gloves and put on a fresh, dry shirt. They tried shaking water out of their jackets, but it was useless.

Charley said, "listen to this," and as he shook a leg, they could hear water sloshing around inside.

"My toes are boot soup in there," he said. "I mean, I'm wet to my dang balls."

After Charley had dumped out his boots, they wandered over to the gas station and bought a bag of chips. A kid not much older than Charley was running the store, and Cash asked if he minded them hanging out until the storm subsided.

"Don't matter to me," he said. "Not many folks around here, so I never really get sick of people."

"Thanks," Cash said.

"But I don't think it's gonna quit raining for a while. You oughta go hang out with the guys next door. They got the football game on. You can get some real food."

Next door at the sub shop, seven or eight local guys stood outside under a leaky veranda watching a football game through the windows. The guys were mostly young and scruffy, and they welcomed the brothers and sympathized with their recent plight. Cash was about to ask them why they were all watching the game outside when one of them pulled a fat joint out of his pocket. He lit up, puffed on it, and passed it around to the others.

The joint made its way around the circle to a wiry, thin guy who wore a camouflaged poncho over nothing but shorts and a t-shirt. He took two long drags and offered it to Charley. "You want a hit of this?"

Charley looked at the joint and then at Cash uncertainly.

"None for us," Cash said. "Only thing crazier than riding this road in the rain would be doing it high."

"I feel you on that," one of the others put in. "I used to ride myself and I feel you for sure."

Almost without pause, the locals continued to pass around joints until they'd been smoked to the nub, and as soon as they were, someone would pull a baggy out of their pocket and roll another. Cash was surprised at how little guarded or suspicious they were about having a pair of strangers around, but he figured they just did things differently in Mendocino County. They were all eager to talk, and while dodging clouds of smoke he learned that most of them were laborers in the surrounding hills. A few admitted that they did nothing. At halftime, Cash went inside for a sandwich. One of the guys followed him in, took his order, and then went into the kitchen to prepare it.

Near the end of the football game, the rain appeared to be slackening, so Cash paid their tab and they rode back to the highway. Cash felt desperate to make some miles, but the weather only continued its assault, and within another fifteen minutes they had pulled off again at a rest stop. In the bathroom, they took turns warming their hands by the automatic dryers, and afterwards they stood outside under the roof of the bathroom and watched cars swooshing past in the hard, slant rain. Cash lit a cigarette, and he looked at Charley who was red-cheeked and wiping snot with the palm of his hand.

"You look miserable," Cash said.

"I am miserable. And my stomach keeps doing this weird thing, like I'm having spasms or something."

"It's your body trying to keep you warm."

"I don't like it."

"I know, bud."

"What's our plan?"

"I think we should give it one more try."

"I don't want to ride in this rain anymore."

"Give me twenty more miles, Charley. If it's still raining, we'll get us a hotel and watch movies all day."

"Ten miles."

"Alright. Ten."

With jaws clenched and their faces dogged against the discomfort, they rode on. By the time they came into the town of Willits, it had already been twelve miles and it was still raining. Cash wanted to give it one more town, and as he left Willits he expected Charley to stop, but he kept pace. They went on with the land broadening and the sky softening from cobalt to a dirty white. Their visors went silent, and they rolled onto the first dry slab of road in a hundred miles. Cash accelerated as fast as he thought Charley could manage, and they zoomed down the straight highway under a burgeoning bliss of sun. Vineyards went past in a blur, and they began to warm and dry. In Santa Rosa, they stopped to gas their bikes and then hurried on. After all the misery and delays, the city seemed possible again, and Cash sang out San-Fran-Cis-Cooooo like some merry, gay sailor.

Darkness fell south of Petaluma, and the Marin County landscape was all a fogged gloaming. The nearer the brothers approached the city, the more crowded the highway became, and when roadwork constricted traffic to two lanes, the cars swelled against the temporary concrete barriers. Vehicles were already traveling faster than the speed limit, but drivers still prodded at bumpers and darted about for insignificant advantages. Without a shoulder to escape to, the brothers felt trapped in a manic procession with too many potentialities for carnage. The fog thickened the closer they came to San Francisco, until their most reliable form of navigation was simply to follow the taillights ahead of them. Then suddenly the road unwound itself and laid down straight. Cash caught shredded glimpses of red railing amidst the fog and realized they were on the Golden Gate Bridge.

They paid the toll, and after a whimsy of random turns, they came into the periphery of downtown where they marveled at the compactness and neon complexity of the city. At a red light, Charley said he was starving, and two blocks later they spotted a late-night pizza joint and parked and went inside.

Behind the counter, a guy in a bright, flannel shirt with ears hooped by gauges greeted them. "Hey, bros. What's good?"

"I don't know what you mean," Cash answered.

The pizza guy laughed. "It's an expression. Like what's up. What's good. You see?"

"Oh, I got you. We just rode in from . . . Hell, I don't even remember the name of the town."

"Miranda," Charley said.

"We just rode in from Miranda."

"Cool, cool," he said nodding. "Like Easy Rider. Cool. Well, pick your poison, guys."

"I'll take two of those," Charley said, tapping the glass.

"Pepperoni. It's a classic, but I'm gonna let you in on a little secret. This one here," the guy said pointing his spatula at a pie heaped with meat, "This one is wicked tasty. Five kinds of meat."

"It does look good," Charley said.

"I designed it myself."

"We'll take four of the wicked one then," Cash said.

"Now you're talking my lingo."

The pizza guy scooped up four slices and put them on a baking sheet and stuck them in the oven.

"You know where we can find a hotel around here?" Cash asked.

"Depends on your budget."

"Probably sixty bucks."

"Oakland maybe. This town is expensive, bro."

He followed Cash's dismayed reaction. "You know, what you guys oughta do is check into a hostel."

"Like from that horror movie?" Charley said.

"No. Well, yeah. But it's not like that. I stayed at one in Canada once, and it was cool. Just a bunch of young people traveling around on the cheap."

"There any nearby?" Cash asked.

"I know there's some down on Post Street. That's just a few blocks."

"We'll check it out."

"Yeah. We'll check it out," Charley added.

"I might just be a pizza guy, but I've got my eye on things."

He opened the oven and put the slices on doubled paper plates and laid them on the counter.

"Say, we're a little wet still from our ride," Cash said. "Is it alright if we sit in your chairs this way?"

The pizza guy squinted one eye. "I'd be disappointed if you didn't."

They found a hostel on Post Street like they'd been told and walked up the steps. The lobby was crowded with a bustle of patrons all chattering in foreign tongues, and Charley knocked people with his bag, saying, "sorry, sorry," as he followed Cash through. A tour guide summoned the group to quiet down and listen to the itinerary of their pub crawl as the brothers approached a pale, young woman seated behind the check-in desk. Cash got them beds in a dorm room, and they went down the hall as two tiny Asian girls passed smiling at them and saying, "herro," in their accents. A map of San Francisco nearly filled an entire wall, and around its border were pictures of parks and buildings and activities with strings connecting them to pushpins throughout the city.

Their room was the size of an average bedroom with three bunkbeds set against a different wall each. Two of the bottom beds were made up, and on one of them was a makeup kit and a computer. Immediately, they took turns in the bathroom, peeling off their wet layers and taking hot showers that seemed lavish beyond anything. Afterwards, they bundled up their clothes and brought them to the basement in search of a dryer. Instead they found a spacious rec room full of young people drinking beer and shooting pool and having ardent conversations on the sofas.

"This is way better than a hotel," Charley said.

They went on into a little dining hall, and around the corner a kitchen equipped with pots and pans and an abundance of dinnerware.

"See, we can even cook," Charley said.

"Since when do you like to cook?"

"But we could if we wanted."

They walked back down the basement hall and passed a darkened room where a dozen people were watching a movie projected onto a screen. The next door was labeled laundry, and they went in and stuffed their clothes into a dryer and set the timer.

"I challenge you to a game of foosball," Charley said.

"I knew you'd say that."

"And I'm gonna whup you," he said as he imitated playing the game like a berserk monkey might.

"Let's go for a walk."

"A walk? You sound like Grandma."

"Don't be a punk. We've got our whole lives for foosball. Let's walk the streets a bit. Never know when we'll get to make it back here."

For an hour and half, Cash led them wandering without destination like some beatnik in search of gritty, street wonder. He didn't know what it was about San Francisco that inspired him, but he kept feeling compelled to walk one more block. One more, and then they'd turn around, he kept telling Charley. He watched an old man bent and hobbling with his bags over a smoldering sewer drain, and he found himself curious, about the man, about what was ailing him, about all he may have seen in those so many evident years. The more he watched people with this heightened curiosity, the more he found to wonder at. The finely tailored couple clinking glasses over a plate of roasted duck. A young, tattooed ruffian eyeing them for an angle, finding none, eyeing the next. A smutty, old, black lady asking, "what you need, sugars," and displaying a toothless bottom gum.

As they were heading back toward the hostel, Cash said, "Big day for us tomorrow."

Charley grunted a meager response.

"Highway One. You remember me telling you about it, don't you?"

"The one Dad recommended."

"That's right."

"What's so cool about it, anyways?"

"Supposed to be a biker's paradise. Just gorgeous."

As they crossed the next street, they looked up to the nearest parked car and saw two women kissing inside. The brothers stopped. Cash quickly shook himself from it and began to walk again, but Charley stood there like a gawking statue. The women were cupping and stroking the other's cheek, and they played their tongues in each other's mouths deliberately and with a moving tenderness. Cash grabbed his brother by the belt and began dragging him across the street.

"Hold on," Charley begged. "I need this. Please."

In the morning, they went out to where they'd left their bikes leaning against the steepness of the street. Above them, the surrounding high-rises framed a window of pure, blue sky. The brothers were rested and dry, and already the air was warm.

"This is gonna be a good day," Charley said.

They made their way back to the highway, patiently enduring the heavy Bay Area traffic through San Jose. Past the town of Gilroy, the road opened up, and the country air was ripe with the smell of eucalyptus. They left Highway 101 at Salinas and went on toward the ocean around Monterey and into the town of Carmel. Cash led them down to the beach through an opulent commerce district where the sidewalks brimmed with joyful women tasked with their next exquisite purchase. They came to a parking lot, and Cash pointed out the Pebble Beach Golf Course, and then they rode on. In a Safeway, they bought hot lunches from the deli, wrapped them up tight, and brought them along looking for a place to picnic.

With great anticipation they left the town behind, and as they made their first sweeping turn at Point Lobos, their stomachs went all aflutter. In a daze of awe, they crossed the Bixby Creek Bridge and wound along the two-lane track as it rimmed the utter edge of cliffs that towered above the surf. The ocean swelled to the rounded reaches of the horizon where one blue immensity met the other, and the sun was sprinkling a glitter on everything. Fuzzy white puffs of cottonwood pollen wafted on the lazy breeze before them. Among all this, the brothers leaned along with the jagged crust of the continent, doubling back on the hairpins, and rolling on the accelerator when it straightened south. Each time they crested a rise or came around a blind corner and were given a new vista, they said, wow, and wondered if the other were saying it too. Time seemed a petty thing in those miles, and they didn't realize until much later that they had discovered a new space. A territory upon which clocks had no influence. They were in such harmony with the scenery and the bending of their bikes that afternoon, it was as if they had been born on those machines, as if the world had just recently begun and soon after would be gone forever, and that all their lives were and all they would ever be was on those bikes, on that cliff road, with five thousand angles by which to view perfection, and ten thousand reasons to say wow.

On a lofty hill near Big Sur, they stopped and sat on the grass to eat their lunch. Both of them tried to express what the ride had done to them, but their words sounded like feeble instruments and they gave it up. As they were munching their food in silence, a balding man walked by and said they'd picked a nice spot, and the brothers agreed. They expected him to walk on, but he stood near them and gazed at the ocean with a serene look. After a moment, Charley turned to the man.

"What do you think about when you look out there?"

"Honestly?" the man asked.

"Sure."

The man paused and then said, "The hand of God." A moment later, he asked Charley what he thought.

"I guess I'm not thinking about much of anything. I'm just sure glad I'm here to see it."

The man nodded very sagely and then strolled along, humming to himself as he went.

After they'd finished their lunch, Charley asked if he could lead for a while, and they rode on like this, savoring each mile. Cash was happy he'd let Charley lead, for he enjoyed watching his brother ride, proud to see him handle his old bike so gracefully. They came to a bend where several fist-sized rocks had tumbled onto the highway, and Cash watched his brother split them deftly and then come out of the corner accelerating as fast as the two-fifty would take him. Cash was throttling hard to keep up when suddenly he saw Charley take both hands from the bars and raise his arms up into the air. Carefully he splayed them out until his arms were wide open, palms cupped to the sky. Charley was approaching a turn, but he held this speeding hallelujah so long it made Cash tingle with fear. At the last moment, Charley regripped the bars and made the corner.

Cash quickly overtook him and turned into the next pullout. "What the hell were you doing back there?" he shouted.

"Something I felt like."

"That was stupid. A stupid stunt."

"It wasn't a stunt."

"Then what was it?"

Charley shrugged.

"Goddamnit, Charley. I could just see you crashing. If you crash—"

"I knew I wouldn't crash."

"Charley—"

"I just knew I wouldn't."

Cash threw him a disgruntled wave and walked alone to the edge of the cliff, picking up a handful of rocks and hurtling them into the ocean. When he was spent, he stood motionless with his back to his brother. Timidly, Charley approached. He came up from the side giving plenty of berth.

"You can't do stuff like that," Cash said firmly but much subdued. "It would be my fault. It would all be on me."

"I'm sorry, Cash."

"You can't do that to me."

Behind them, an elderly woman had been taking photographs of the ocean. She called out to the brothers, "Boys, would you like me to take your picture?"

They turned to the woman.

"I'd be happy to do it," she continued.

"Thanks," Cash said.

He took his camera out of his bag and passed it to the woman. The brothers posed for her as she took several shots.

"Let's take one with the bikes," Charley said.

"Do you mind?" Cash asked the woman.

"Not at all."

They started their bikes and staged them at the edge of the cliff. The woman asked if they were ready, and the brothers nodded. Cash sat sideways on his seat and appeared very serious. Charley stood and grinned and held up a peace sign. The woman snapped the photo, and they thanked her and saddled up and rode on.

In the diminishing sun, the brothers passed Pismo Beach, watching surfers ride purple, mercurial waves, and then some miles past full dark they entered the town of Santa Barbara. They found another hostel across the train tracks from downtown, their dorm room vast and crowded and smelling of feet. After showering, they walked down State Street in search of dinner.

Charley pointed out the trendy sports bar their concierge had recommended, and they went inside where twenty-three separate televisions showed the same Monday Night Football game at incredible volume. They took a table as the announcer bombarded them with news of a first down. After a couple minutes, they looked for their waitress, but she passed them by without acknowledgement. One of the teams recovered a fumble, and patrons cursed and pounded their tables melodramatically.

"Let's go," Cash said.

"What?" Charley shouted.

Cash stood up and threw his head at the door, and they continued walking along the boulevard.

"You know that book Catcher in the Rye?" Charley asked.

"Not really."

"Didn't they assign it to you in school?"

"Probably. Doesn't mean I read it though."

"Anyways, I was reading it for class before we left, and what's funny is I just felt like the main character, Holden Cauffman, in there."

"In where?"

"In that restaurant. It was weird. I was looking around at all those people inside and I kept saying to myself, look at all these phonies. That's what Holden Cauffman says about people all the time in the book. That they're all a bunch of phonies. I never really knew what he meant when I was reading the book, but just now in that restaurant it clicked, and I knew exactly what he meant."

"I think you should write that teacher of yours a letter. Tell her what a valuable service she's doing."

"You should read that book."

"Naaah."

"It's not so boring as most of them they make you read."

"What do you think of this place?" Cash asked.

They were standing in front of a quiet diner. All the booths were empty, and one man sat at the counter.

"I'm starving. I'll eat anywhere."

A man behind the counter turned from his grill and greeted them with a deep, raspy voice.

"Hey, guys. Take a seat wherever you'd like. I'll be right over."

They sat a few seats down from the man at the counter who nodded and said hello as they opened their menus. The cook wiped his apron and picked up a plate of food and set it in front of the other patron. Then he came over with a pitcher of water and filled them two glasses.

"What looks good to you, fellas?" he asked.

"I'll take this mac and cheese," Cash said. "And a pint of that nut brown ale."

"And for you, my man?"

"What would you say is the most food?"

"This one's hungry. I'd go with the cheesesteak."

The cook took back their menus and began preparing their meals. He made conversation with the brothers as he cooked, and he seemed impressed they'd come all the way from Washington.

"I worked in Everett for a while," he said, "but I got tired of the rain and moved back down here."

"Same thing happened to me," said the patron. "I went away to college in Portland for a semester, and that was all it took. Too much rain."

"It can get to you," Charley sympathized.

"So, how'd you guys stumble upon this little place?" the patron asked.

The brothers explained their impressions of the sports bar, and both the cook and the patron agreed that it sucked.

"That's what most of Southern California is like," the patron said. "From Crescent City to Santa Barbara is God's country, but south of here? Ahh. Just keep driving 'til you get to Mexico."

Spry and unkempt, the brothers left Santa Barbara under a flamboyant, southern sun. They passed Ventura and Thousand Oaks and then rode due east into the bundled, highway mayhem of Los Angeles. They were slowly approaching a sign for Universal Studios when two motorcycles vroomed past, quadrupling the speed of traffic by splitting the lanes. Cash looked back at his brother, and Charley was nodding his head vigorously. For several miles, they glided through the worst of the traffic before pulling off for lunch at a Mexican restaurant.

After they'd ordered, Cash asked the small Mexican lady what town they were in. She answered something in Spanish. Cash tried to say it more plainly, but she went into the back of the restaurant.

A moment later, a manager appeared. "Yes, sir. You have a question?"

"Yeah, no big deal. I was just wondering where I'm at."

The manager looked perplexed. "You are here," he said seriously.

The brothers finished their meal and walked outside as two old, Mexican ladies were approaching the restaurant. One of them wore a sweeping, blue sunbonnet and the other carried an umbrella.

"Too much sun, ladies?" Cash asked.

They looked at each other, and then one of the ladies replied bashfully. "Si. Mucho calor."

Cash wished them a good day, and the women said, adios, giggling to themselves as they entered the restaurant.

The interstate next led the brothers on a dull parade through the unbroken suburban ramble of West Covina, Pomona, Ontario, Rancho Cucamonga, Fontana, Colton, Redlands—all fused together at the foot of the San Bernardino Mountains. Traffic finally thinned beyond Beaumont, and the brothers were relieved to be freed from the frantic tension of so many cars and signs and exits. They had entered a new barren terrain, riding past Palm Springs and Indio and then skirting the boundary of Joshua Tree National Park. Then on through a wasteland as their brains began to wander into the most perfectly random thoughts. How old would Grandpa be this year? Not all colors have words. Why did Sears ditch Roebuck? Nothing at all in that setting to distract their attention. Just miles of sand and scrubby bushes and the drone of their engines.

Across the Arizona border, they pulled into the town of Quartzsite and parked their bikes in front of a McDonald's. They looked back toward where they'd come and saw the sun low on the horizon, the sky huge and pink.

"How many miles have we made today?" Charley asked.

Cash put it into his phone. "Three hundred and thirty-nine."

"That's really good, right?"

"Most we've done so far."

"Do you wanna keep going?"

"I don't know. How you feeling?"

"My shoulder's getting a little sore, but I could keep riding."

"Well, we gotta be sure cause the map's not showing another town for over seventy miles."

"We are in the desert."

"I'd really like to make it to Phoenix. Bet they've got a hostel."

"How many miles to Phoenix?"

"Another hundred and thirty."

"That's still a long ways."

"Let's eat and see how we feel."

Once their meals were ready, they brought them to a plastic table and sat down.

Halfway through their burgers, Charley leaned in close to Cash and whispered, "That old dude's weirding me out. He keeps staring at me. And like, smiling."

"What old dude?"

"Behind you. In the corner."

Cash swiveled around. An old man in a wheelchair was indeed staring at them. As soon as Cash met his eyes, the man spoke.

"Those your bikes outside?" he asked.

"Yep."

"They're real nice bikes. Suzuki makes some real nice bikes. I have a Honda Shadow at home in the garage. Don't ride anymore though."

"I'm sorry to hear that."

"Huh? What's that?" With a rapid twist of his head, he threw his ear at the brothers and cupped it with his hand.

"I said, I'm sorry to hear that."

"Oh, yes. Yes, it is too bad. I fell out of the back of a truck going fifty miles an hour and learned you can't crawl along the pavement that fast. Him and I aren't friends anymore."

Both brothers had stopped eating.

"Where you riding to?" the old man continued.

"Maybe Phoenix tonight," Cash said. "We're not sure. But we're ending up in Florida."

"Hmm? What's it now?"

"Florida. We're going to Florida."

"Say again?" He threw his ear at them once more and then decided to roll over to the edge of their table. "Did you say Florida?"

"Yeah. Florida."

"Long ways. Good luck to you both."

The brothers watched him play with his hands, which were stained a ghastly white. The old man noticed them watching.

"They're stained from the rocks. I'm a rock hound. I dig 'em up and sell 'em to people who make jewelry and all kinds of stuff from 'em."

"I see."

"I make money from it. I do alright."

"I'm glad to hear that."

"What's it?"

"I said, I'm glad to hear that."

"Mmm. Yeah. That's why my hands are like this." The old man continued to rub his hands together and then suddenly he stopped and looked straight into Cash. "I have a few friends around, you know. Well, I guess you'd call 'em acquaintances. I got a few acquaintances."

When the brothers finished their meals, they said goodbye to the man. As they left, they saw him wheel his chair back into the corner.

Outside, the sky had purpled, and the sun was now sinking ever dimmer behind the red-rock horizon.

"Well, what do you think?" Charley asked. "Ride on?"

"Hell, yes."

They gassed up and went on, their headlights growing more powerful in the darkening dusk. Both shoulders of the highway were cluttered with a disastrous amount of blown tire shreds, an unending litter of the stuff that gave the brothers something to dwell on. Black night came, and the red rock hills were now just another layer of black upon the star-wealthy sky. The brothers watched their odometers and counted down the miles to Phoenix, feeling propelled by a sense of mission. Even in the best conditions Charley's bike could only hold seventy miles an hour, and they had not passed a car since California. Occasionally, a semi would advance, the brothers watching its headlights gain steadily until it finally switched lanes and whizzed past with a sound like a mortar shell missing them narrowly.

On and on the desert went, until way out there the electric haze of civilization became visible. Soon enough, they encountered the dim orange lights of the suburbs and finally Phoenix itself with enormous dealerships along the highway containing thousands of cars all reflecting the white gleam of floodlights. Traffic herded on and off cloverleaf overpasses, and the brothers took an exit and came to a red light in the midst of the desert megalopolis.

Cash used his phone to guide them to another hostel in a neighborhood bordering downtown. The hostel was in an ordinary one-story house, clean and inviting. An animated young woman in exercise clothes checked them in and asked where they had come from.

"Santa Barbara," Cash told her.

"Don't shit me."

"I'm serious."

"I don't believe you. Not with that little bike I saw him pull up on."

"Really, we did. We left this morning."

"Well, do you have a hostel membership card? Ah, never mind. I'll give you guys the discount after that feat."

After they'd found their beds and had their evening showers, they went out and sat in chairs in the front lawn. Surrounding them were hedges adorned with string lights, and a young man in glasses was playing acoustic guitar on the porch. On the other side of the lawn, a group of travelers sat around a table playing a board game that seemed to involve a lot of gesturing and clapping laughter.

"I'm going out tonight," Cash said.

"I figured."

"You'll be fine here. I bet these guys will let you play with them."

"Can't I at least try and sneak in with you?"

"No way. I don't want you messing up my mojo."

"Ooohhhh. Look out ladies. Cash is on the prowl."

"How does my hair look?"

"I don't know. It looks like hair."

Cash stood.

"Don't wait up for me," he said as he walked away.

Despite having traveled one-fifth of the American continent that day, Cash felt the good juice running through him. At Roosevelt Street he waited for a speeding truck to pass and then crossed with brisk strides toward the towers of Phoenix. A few blocks along, he passed a yard full of kooky statues and lawn art and a colorful bus with the words FEED THE UNICORN painted on the side. The next block he came upon a house with a bright green porch light and a lawn full of vegetable crops. A young man and woman sat among rows of squash and green beans, while another man stood talking to them from the sidewalk. Cash stopped alongside them, and the woman smiled and said, hey, as a guy rolled out of the alley on a skateboard propelled by an attached sail. Behind him another following on a bicycle with a sidecar.

"You look lost," the woman said.

"I guess I'm in sensory overload right now," Cash said.

"New to town?" the guy on the sidewalk asked.

"Just got here an hour ago," he said as he caught sight of the ziplock bag the guy was holding, in it at least an ounce of marijuana.

"Don't you worry about having that out so visibly?" Cash asked.

The guy shrugged, and Cash decided to walk on. Around the corner he came to a bar, but he felt too immersed in the zaniness of the streets to go in yet. He kept wandering and soon began to hear what sounded like feverish drumming. He followed the sound until it led him to a derelict building that appeared to have once been an auto-body shop, one whole side of the structure now covered with a mural of sparrows in flight. The door was open, so Cash peaked into the darkness and saw two guys pounding drums while facing one another, both of them swaddled in a pulsing mess of Christmas lights. For several minutes, Cash watched them play with maniacal energy and intricate, exotic rhythms. Never once did the drummers look up or slow down even slightly. Directly next door to this was an immaculate Scientology building, and Cash watched people in suits and dresses milling about and shaking hands with formality. As Cash circled back to the bar, he felt mystified by Phoenix. There appeared to be no logic to the development of this city with so much land to spare. The ruins of abandoned buildings were all around its core, swanky apartments next to moldering vacant lots. All the cars were always speeding. Cash thought it some kind of vast and lawless free-for-all sprawl.

The bar he chose had been converted from a house, and it sat in the middle of a residential block. There was a five-dollar cover charge for the live music, and Cash paid the bouncer and went inside. At the back of the bar, the dance floor took up the space that had previously been some family's dining room, and against the wall a DJ was assembling his equipment. All around the house, groups of people sat talking around tables, and there was a solid line of patrons at the bar. Cash waited his turn, and when the bartender pointed at him he ordered a shot of whiskey and a porter. He took the shot and then strolled from room to room with his beer, looking at the abstract paintings that filled the walls. He thought he could maybe gleam some cryptic understanding of the artist's layered strokes, but after a dozen pictures the only meaning he had found was in the price tags.

Once he'd made a lap of the house, he went back to the bar and ordered another beer. From the speakers issued the shrill and troubling noise of a bow dragged across the strings of an untuned violin, and then suddenly the bar reverberated with bass. Tables began emptying as people made their way toward the dance floor.

Cash was watching the first dancers prance onto the floor when a short redheaded girl squeezed up beside him and ordered a vodka lemonade. Cash watched her stealthily, seeing first her hair, straightened to her shoulders and the color of an oak leaf the day it falls. Next her cleavage, shirt tight against the roundness of her breasts. Then her short, ruffled skirt, her smooth legs, not thin nor thick. And then lastly her face as she turned toward him with both hands on the drink. Cash smiled as they met eyes, and she smiled back and walked across the room and stood along the far wall with two other girls.

He finished his beer, and when the bartender returned he ordered another shot of whiskey. The bartender gave him a look, and Cash said, for the nerves. The redhead and her friends went to the dance floor, and Cash watched the three of them twist and giggle. He could not stop watching the way the girl was using her hips. Once, she looked up and caught him watching her, and he made a gesture that suggested there was nothing he could do about it. After a handful of songs, the girl went off to the bathroom. She didn't come back and didn't come back, and Cash thought maybe he'd scared her away. Then he turned, and she was beside him at the bar.

"What are you drinking?" he asked.

"You mean, you don't remember?"

Cash nodded the bartender over. "Vodka lemonade, please."

"Nothing for you?" she asked.

"I'm cutting myself off for a little bit."

She took her drink from the bartender and looked Cash up and down. "So, what's up with this jacket? Are you like a biker guy?"

"Something like that."

"Is that how you pick up chicks?"

"I don't know. You'd have to ask them."

"I'm surprised I've never seen you here before. This is pretty much my spot."

"It's my first time in Phoenix."

Cash told her about his trip to Florida and about his cousin's place and the job he had waiting for him. He told her about his brother running away from home, and it took him a long time to convince her that he wasn't making the story up for some kind of emotional advantage as she put it. Near the end of the story, Cash caught her friends watching them and looking intrigued.

"We got us an audience," Cash said.

"Oh, they're harmless."

"Sure."

"Well . . ."

"Would you like to dance with me later?"

"Why don't we dance right now?"

Cash took her by the hand and led her to the dance floor. He could feel her communicating something to her friends, but he didn't look back and stopped only once they were in the middle of the crowd. He turned to face her, and for a moment they each stood still amidst the jostle of bodies, his vision tunneled down to include only her. Then she stepped to him, and he put his arms around her waist, and they danced a close and consuming sway. Toward the end of the next song, she slipped around and put her ass into him and rocked it circularly. He thought if she continued much longer he'd have to ask her to stop if he was ever going to walk out of the bar, but she turned to face him again. They danced two more songs.

Afterwards, she introduced Cash to her friends and made him tell his whole story over again. When he was done, he asked if he could buy them all a drink, but the friends said they were leaving. Cash looked at her.

"Don't worry. I'm staying."

Once her friends had left, they both took another shot and then went back to the dance floor. During the third song, Cash asked if she wanted to go somewhere and she stopped dancing.

"What kind of girl do you think I am?"

Cash was stammering for a recovery.

"I'm kidding, man. Close out your tab. Let's go."

On their way out the door, she told him she wanted to meet his brother.

"You mean—"

"Yes, I want to meet your brother."

They took her car to the hostel. Cash thought he'd find his brother asleep, but Charley was still sitting outside with a handful of guys. In his hand was a beer.

"I thought you said he was eighteen?" she said.

"He is."

"Little rebel, isn't he?"

Charley did a double take when he saw Cash, and he tried to hide the beer.

"Just don't worry about it, ok?" Cash told him. "Brianne here wants to meet you."

She approached him as he shrunk into his seat. "Your name is Charley?" she asked.

"Yeah."

"Hi, Charley. I'm Brianne."

She held out her hand, and Charley took it briefly and weakly and sat back again.

"Your brother says you're a runaway. Is that right?"

"I guess."

"Well, what do you think of Phoenix so far?"

"Warm."

"How about California? That must have been a beautiful ride."

"Yeah."

"Did you see San Francisco?"

"Yeah."

"What did you think of it?"

"It's nice."

Cash cut in. "What's the matter with you, Charley? You meet a pretty girl and you turn all monosyllabic."

"It's alright," Brianne said. "So, Charley, I know I'm a little weird about this, but, well, my brother died when he was the same age as you. Had nothing to do with motorcycles, but he was the same age, and I just want you to be careful. I just wanted to meet you and tell you to be careful. Ok?"

Charley nodded.

"Don't give him any more beer, guys," Cash called as they headed back to the car.

She lived on the bottom floor of a townhouse near the University of Phoenix which she said she shared with a friend from college. Inside the door, a tawny cat greeted them, and she bent down and stroked it.

"This is Thomas," she said as the cat went over and rubbed its head against Cash's calf.

She led Cash into her bedroom and flipped on a soft desk lamp and then looked up at him with anticipation. He pulled her to him and they kissed. He ran his hands down her sides and squeezed her ass and pulled their groins together. He was walking her backwards to her bed when she stopped him and patted his chest once.

"Wait right here," she said.

Cash heard her padding up the stairs as he sat on the end of her bed and looked around the room. The floor was messy with discarded clothes, on the walls were a map of Italy, a framed diploma, a photo of her running a marathon. Next to her desk, there was a short bookshelf, and on top of this, two more pictures sitting at a lean. The first photo was of a young, thick-necked soldier looking very proud in his uniform. The other, a photo showing this same man standing behind Brianne with his arms around her, both laughing into the camera. The frame the shape of a heart. Cash was studying these as she returned.

"I'm guessing this ain't your brother," he said.

"I'm sorry," she said. "I should have put those away."

"He still around?"

"It's a long story," she said as she put the pictures in her dresser.

"I'd like to know."

"He's in Afghanistan."

"When's he coming home?"

"I don't know. He doesn't . . . Listen, can't you just be happy getting laid?"

He smiled, and she came to him again, taking the back of his head as she kissed him. She pulled him into the bed and unbuttoned his shirt and then went for his belt.

"I hope you know I don't feel good about this," he said.

"Will you just shut your mouth before I change my mind."

The brothers were seated at a booth in an IHOP fifteen miles south of Phoenix. A pregnant waitress, heavy with child, brought them two coffees. Cash emptied into his mug a creamer and a packet of sugar and gulped it two-thirds empty, as hot as it was. Charley giving him silent, knowing looks.

"You've been looking at me like that all morning," Cash said, his face puffy with carousing. "Will you just say what you're gonna say already."

"How come you look so tired?"

"Why do you think?"

"Oh man," Charley erupted with a clap. "I knew it."

Cash stared at him levelly and unamused.

"How many times did you guys do it?"

"Nine times, Charley."

"Nooo. Maybe like five though, right? What kind of positions did you get her in? Did you do this one?"

As Charley humped back and forth, he pretended he was holding a girl's ankle above his head with one hand, while spanking the side of the table with the other.

"That doesn't even make sense," Cash said.

"So, you didn't do it then."

"Cut it out."

"This is their favorite."

"I'm serious. She's bringing our food over."

Charley settled down as their waitress came over and set their plates in front of them.

"Anything else I can bring you guys?" she asked.

"We're all set," Cash said, and the waitress waddled back to the kitchen.

While lifting his eyebrows, Charley angled his thumb at her and said, "She knows what I'm talking about."

"You need to get laid. I mean, bad. Desperately."

"I've gotten laid."

"A handjob don't count, Charley."

He looked at Cash with his fork and knife both up and at the ready. Then he burped and cut into his pancakes.

After they'd eaten, Cash fortified himself with a third cup of coffee, and then they saddled up and rode southeast through Tucson and into a cactus country teeming with prickly pear and saguaros. For some time, they traveled parallel to a yellow Union Pacific train, overtaking it so slowly they read most of the legible graffiti spray-painted on the boxcars. After the town of Willcox, five motorcycles came booming up from behind, the riders helmetless and in formation, their beards and hair and American flags all wind-whipping as they cruised past with macho panache. Near San Simon, they stopped to rest on an overpass and looked all around them. They could see twenty miles in every direction, and there was nothing nowhere in that desolate cyclorama except a gas station and the tiny, squalid town beyond.

"Why would anyone want to live here?" Charley asked.

Cash lacked even a hypothesis, and they rode on into New Mexico. Between Lordsburg and Deming, they passed a sign announcing the Continental Divide, and soon after, another night fell upon their riding. The highway had seemed flat enough, but they were up above four thousand feet, and now in the dark and the desert chill, they each began to tremble. On a little plateau, they stopped to put on their sweatshirts, while to the east below they saw the shimmery glow of Las Cruces against the silhouette of the Organ Mountains, the moon like it was perched on the shoulder of the highest peak.

"I'm getting really sore," Charley said.

"Almost there, bud. About an hour to El Paso."

Charley groaned and hung his head.

"You need a little shoulder rub to keep you going?"

"It's not my shoulders. It's my ass."

"Saddle sore?"

"Yeah."

"Well, you're on your own there."

Cash smoked a cigarette while Charley walked around pounding his backside and saying, wake up cheeks. When Charley was ready, they rode south around Las Cruces and then crossed the Texas border, running along the Franklin Mountains and into El Paso. In town, the highway briefly sidled up to the Rio Grande which looked incarcerated there flowing through its concrete channel and caged by border fences. Beyond those were the shanties of Juarez.

After some searching, they found a cheap hotel in a venerable, brick building downtown. The lobby was silent and musty with the smell of a décor that hadn't been altered in some decades, its overlarge emptiness amplified by the mirrored walls. The front desk was unattended, and Cash dinged the counter bell which echoed until a man with a crooked mustache and floppy gray hair came out of a locked side door and checked them in.

The room they were given was on the third floor, and they took the stairs creaking at every step to a murky, dim hallway that seemed charged with an aura of poorly concealed doom. Inside the room, the furnishings looked even more antique than the lobby, and aside from the miniature television, it could have been a set piece for a black and white movie. Charley pointed out the sink which dripped without remedy.

"You get what you pay for," Cash said.

"Listen to it. Plop. Plop. I won't be able to sleep."

"Nine hundred miles the last two days. You'll sleep."

Right then, an overhead pipe groaned something horrible. Their gazes went up to the ceiling and back to each other.

"I'll get some earplugs," Cash said.

Charley sagged onto one of the beds and said, "You know how Dad always says to trust your instincts?"

"Yeah."

"Mine say run."

"You'll be fine. I'll only be gone a couple hours."

"You're leaving me here by myself?"

Cash walked the first four blocks without seeing a single moving car or pedestrian, and nearly every storefront was thoroughly barred and shuttered. Suspicious quiet. Only the hush of the distant highway and the clink of a chain against a flagpole. Cash walked on in search of a bar feeling as spooked as he could ever remember. He scrutinized the darkness of an alley and then as he faced ahead again he heard something coming at him. Fists clenched, he spun around only to realize it was a cardboard box beating against a dumpster.

When he finally came to a few dive bars in a row, he went inside the first one and ordered a whiskey to calm himself down. The bar was a typical midweek scene of locals shooting pool and singing karaoke. Cash was sipping a beer when he noticed the guy on the next stool looking at him funny. He had the appearance of a half Mexican, half Italian, his long black hair slicked with pomade.

Cash turned to him. "Why are you looking at me like that?"

"You look like somebody, man. Yeah, you do. You know who you look like? You look just like Nick Cage, man."

"You mean, like Nicholas Cage?"

"Yeah, man. Nick Cage. Anybody ever tell you that?"

"No."

"Just like him, man. Whoa!"

He said his name was Benny and that he'd been an actor in Los Angeles for several years, once working alongside Al Pacino. He listed some of the movies he'd been in, and though Cash had never heard of them, he thought Benny might have been telling the truth.

"What actor would you say I look like?" Benny asked.

Cash thought about it for a moment while Benny presented himself theatrically.

"Christopher Walken," Cash said finally.

"Walken? Really? Wow. Most people say Johnny Depp. Chris Walken, huh. What makes you say that?"

"I think it's the way you talk."

"I always liked Chris Walken," he said before gathering himself for an imitation. "Five long years he wore this watch. Up his ass. Then he died of dysentery. He give me the watch. I wore this uncomfortable hunk of metal up my ass two years, and now, little man, I give the watch to you."

"Pulp Fiction."

"Chris Walken, huh. You really think so?"

Cash hadn't noticed it at first, but he saw now that Benny was quite drunk. He kept saying, JD, JD, and the bartender would come and top his shot glass with Jack Daniels. And he could not get over the notion that Cash thought he resembled Christopher Walken. They were in the middle of a discussion about Juarez when Benny interrupted Cash to ask if he really, truly, believed he was like Walken. Later, Benny had moved on, telling Cash about how he and his girlfriend were having problems, only to suddenly stop and say, "Chris Walken. Now why would you say that?" Drunk as he was, Benny continued tossing back shots of whiskey until he was stuttering like an imbecile.

"Hiya. Um. Hey, do you, I mean, hey Carl—"

"It's Cash."

"I know who you is Carl is like Cash. What I need is, maybe a phone, because my girlfriend. Needs to call my girlfriend."

"You want to borrow my phone?"

"Yes. That's it what I'm saying."

Cash passed it over. Benny tried dialing the number, but his fingers wouldn't cooperate. Cash dialed for him and passed the phone back. Benny listened as he wavered on his stool, but there was no answer.

"Maybe it'd be better to call her tomorrow."

"One more time. How do I do this? Where does the numbers go?"

Cash paid his tab and turned around as Benny lost his grip on the phone, nearly dropping it into the pint of beer he had tucked into his crotch.

"I have to leave, Benny."

His bleary eyes seemed not to comprehend.

"Can I get my phone back?"

Benny made a petulant sound and then slapped the phone into Cash's hand.

"Nice to meet you, Benny," Cash said as he stood.

Benny merely bobbed his head and looked into his beer.

Cash went into the bar next door where a Mexican band was playing covers of pop songs from a mezzanine shelf above the entrance. Cash ordered a beer and his phone rang.

"Hello?" he answered.

A shrill flurry of Spanish came through the line.

"I'm sorry. No habla espanol."

"Donde esta Benny?"

Cash hung up. He listened to a few songs as the band alternated between English and Spanish and he found them surprisingly good.

Between sets the band came outside while Cash was smoking, and he went over and chatted with them. He told them he thought they were very talented and asked why they only played covers. Didn't they have any original songs? Of course, they did, the guitarist answered, but there was no money in that. People only wanted to hear songs they could sing along to. Cash disagreed and said he'd buy the whole band a round of shots if they would play one original song. They said it was a deal, so Cash bought them all a whiskey and then the guitarist bought everyone another. An hour later, Cash was drunk again. In the middle of a song, he waved goodbye to the band and staggered back to the hotel.

At the door to the room, he pulled out the key and dropped it onto the carpet and picked it back up. Then he put it in the keyhole, but it wouldn't turn. He was jiggling it when a woman's voice called out for him to go away.

"What's going on in there, Charley?"

"Go away," the woman called more urgently.

"Open the door, Charley. She can stay but open the door."

Cash heard another door squeak ajar behind him and he turned. Charley was peering through the crack. Cash faced the door again.

"Very sorry, miss. Wrong room."

Cash followed Charley inside and fell face first into the bed. After a moment, Charley asked him if he had a drinking problem, but he was already asleep.

They had been riding for less than an hour when Cash pulled off at the town of McNary and turned into the first gas station he came to. He put his bike on the kickstand and went and lay down in the yellow grass of a median. Charley walked over and stood next to him.

"What's the deal?"

"I'm tired."

"It's not even noon."

"I know."

"We've barely even started."

Cash looked up at him and then rolled his head to the side and closed his eyes. He took a deep breath and groaned it back out.

"This is because of your drinking. How are we gonna make it to Florida if you're like this all the time?"

Once Cash finally picked himself up off the ground they rode past the town of Sierra Blanca and into a headwind. They had been riding a steady sixty-five miles an hour which already made them the slowest vehicles on the freeway, but as they continued east the wind increased and Charley's bike lagged to fifty. Cash slowed back to him and waved him onward, but Charley shook his head and held the speed. Traffic was screaming by them now, and semis were struggling to get over and pass them in time. Like this they rode into the town of Allamore where they gassed their bikes.

"You've gotta pick it up, Charley. It's dangerous to ride that slow."

"I'm trying."

"Pin that accelerator all the way back."

"I have been. This wind is killing me."

"Isn't this what I told you about that two-fifty? It's too small in the pants."

"Well, we're in Texas now. What do you want me to do about it?"

"We need to get off this freeway." Cash brought out his phone and scrolled over the map. "Okay, this looks good. This should work for a while."

"What?"

"Map's showing another highway that'll get us as far as San Antonio. Doesn't look like it'll lose us too much time. The next town is Van Horn, and we turn off for it there."

Highway 90 was a straight and narrow two-lane road, and it took them through a parched brown scrubland. The wind kept up, and they were still holding at fifty, but the cars were so infrequent now that it no longer mattered how fast they rode. The few vehicles that did come the other direction were mostly pickup trucks driven by men wearing cowboy hats. Almost without exception the men would put a hand up hello as they went past. Through the tiny town of Valentine a dog was sniffing along the shoulder of the road, and an old woman collecting her mail watched them go with real interest. Thirty miles later they went through the small commercial district of Marfa and then into a new rocky hill terrain, dodging tarantulas that scuttled across the highway. In Alpine they gassed up and rode on trying to make the most of what little daylight remained.

They were going along the Glass Mountains and watching gusts of wind ruffle through the tall grass when they passed a sign warning them to watch for antelope. Cash looked up beyond the sign and immediately saw two pronghorns loping toward the distant hills. He pointed them out to Charley and then he felt his bike sputter and catch and sputter again. It continued sputtering for several miles until finally it snorted out a backfire and died. Cash downshifted and brought it to a stop along the highway. He tried starting it back up, but it only whined and coughed. Charley came up alongside him.

"You just filled it with gas."

"So obviously that isn't it."

"What do you think?"

"I don't know."

Cash looked off to his left and saw two more antelope, a doe and a fawn, unmoving and blended so well against their backdrop that he'd nearly missed them at thirty yards.

"Look at those two," Cash said.

Charley aimed his forefinger at the antelope and said pow, and then they all turned toward the sound of two motorcycles roaring at them without mufflers. The doe went bounding across the highway while the fawn watched its mother cross and then looked back at the motorcycles as they kept barreling on. The bikes were only yards away when the fawn finally made a dash for it. Cash winced for the collision, but he saw the fawn leap off the road and the motorcycles zoom on.

"Don't be like those guys," Cash said.

"The antelope or the bikers?"

"Don't be like any of them."

Cash tried the bike again, but it wouldn't start.

"You'd think those guys would have stopped for us," Charley said.

"They were obviously in a hurry for something."

"Can you imagine if they had hit that fawn?"

"Yeah. I can."

Cash hit the ignition again, and the bike started. They both shrugged and then took off riding again as the prairie night bloomed a starry blue-black. Toward them a train came alighting the tracks, and they turned to watch it pass, seeing the shadow of a man go clacking away in the caboose. Even from such a distance they made out the pinpoint orange as he inhaled a cigarette. As they came into the town of Marathon, Cash's bike began sputtering again. He lost his throttle, regained it, and then the bike died in front of a bright and festive restaurant.

"Did it die or are we stopping?" Charley asked.

"Looks like both."

"You wanna wait and see if it'll start again?"

"No, I don't. If it's gonna keep dying on us, then this is a better spot than camped out with a bunch of rattlesnakes. Besides, I'm tuckered."

They went into the restaurant and waited for the middle-aged hostess who was talking on the telephone with her back turned. After she hung up she turned to face them with a smile and two remarkable breasts. Large and strikingly perky for her years.

"Lookin' for some dinner, hun?"

Cash finally made the proper eye contact and said, "No thank you, ma'am."

"What can I help you with then?"

"Well, we were hoping you might know of the cheapest place we could stay around here. We're on a tight budget."

"Boy, did you come to the right gal. My old man runs a hostel on the other side of town."

"No kidding. I never would've guessed there'd be one way out here."

"Oh, you two are gonna love it."

"Awesome. How do we find it?"

"I'll take you. Chuck, hold down the fort for a few minutes, will you? I'm gonna take these guys over to the hostel."

They went out to the bikes where Cash explained their predicament. The hostess had him push his bike into a gravel lot behind the restaurant and said somebody at the hostel could take a look at it.

"So, which of you is taking me over there?" she asked.

"You mean on my bike?" Charley asked.

"I ain't walking."

"I'll do it," Cash said.

"But it's my bike."

"I'll do it."

Cash saddled up, and the woman kicked down the passenger pegs and got on behind him. Charley held his helmet out for her, but she declined.

"I put too much effort into this hair."

"You ready?" Cash asked.

She squeezed her breasts into his back and wrapped her arms around his chest and told him to go straight across the train tracks. They made a few turns through the town's small neighborhood and then went down a dirt road until it ended at the guesthouse which sat at the edge of the prairie. The building appeared to have been constructed from some sort of clay, and its roof was white and cylindrical and looked like the cover of a pioneer's wagon. Its walls painted turquoise and maroon and covered with ornate designs. In front a sign that read La Loma Del Chivo.

"What does that mean?" Cash pointed.

"The hill of the goat," she answered.

"I don't see any goats around."

"That's because we ate 'em. Take a look around. I'll be back in a minute."

Cash went around the side of the guesthouse and found an external staircase which led him to a balcony overlooking the empty miles. On a wall there someone had brushed the words MALLS AND MALLS OF DESERT IN EVERY DIRECTION. Cash took the stairs back down and strolled around the hostel grounds, finding the bathroom housed in its own richly decorated building and then another clay structure shaped into a squat dome that looked like a residence for hobbits. He was standing before this dome and regarding it quizzically when the woman returned.

"What's this one about?" he asked.

"That's where Susie lives."

"Okay."

Afterwards, she guided him down a gravel path until they reached another building which she said was their headquarters of sorts. They got off the bike as a guy came walking around the side eating an apple.

"Quetzal," she said. "Do you mind following us back to the restaurant in the truck? This guy and his brother could use some help with their stuff."

"Sure thing," he said, holding his hand out to Cash.

"Quetzal?" Cash said as they shook.

"It's my Mexican name."

Despite the name, he was a white American with a shaved head, a solid physique, and a latent sense of malice made more immediate by a network of tribal tattoos that encompassed half his face. At the restaurant he helped load their things into the bed of the truck and then went and had a look at the motorcycle.

"You know much about bikes?" Cash asked.

"No, but Cliff does. He'll be back the day after tomorrow. How far you riding?"

"Florida."

"That's a good piece. Where you coming from?"

"Washington."

He looked at Cash and nodded his head.

"Intrepid."

Quetzal stopped first at the guesthouse where the brothers stashed their belongings and then took them back to the headquarters. Inside, several guys sat around a heavy wooden dining table covered with beer cans and slices of homemade pizza.

"This is Mike," Quetzal said, gesturing to an old hipster in his sixties. "He lives here and pretty much runs the place."

"Welcome," Mike said deep and languidly and looking like a redheaded gnome. His beard long and styled into twin fangs. His ear lobes drooping from where they'd been abandoned by gauges, and through the bottom of his nose a brass bull ring.

"Thanks for having us, Mike," Cash said. "We've stayed at a few hostels now and this is . . . Well, this is something else."

"That it is."

Charley nudged Cash's elbow.

"What?"

"You know," he muttered.

"No, I don't know."

"I'm hungry."

"Say, guys. Is there a store open this late where we can pick up some cheap eat?"

"Plenty of pizza here," Mike said. "Have at it."

"Ah, we don't want to impose."

"Just throw me a buck or two if you feel like it. Eat up."

As the brothers ate their pizza they became acquainted with the others around the table. One of them was a student in Austin who came over occasionally for the company. Another a young laborer helping out around the hostel. And the last a middle-aged man named Leroy who spoke with a subdued Texan drawl.

"So, Quetzal," Cash said between bites. "How did you come into your name if you don't mind me asking?"

"My wife gave it to me. She's Mexican. Half the year I work in the States and save up my money, and the other half of the year I live with my wife and kids in Mexico."

"Which country do you prefer?"

"Life is better in Mexico. Don't get me wrong, things aren't perfect down there. The poverty you see sometimes is astonishing. But then again, there's a lot of poverty in America too. The difference for me though is that down in Mexico people really look out for each other. Their communities are so strong. If a family is going hungry, then their neighbors will bring them fish or chicken or vegetables. I don't worry about leaving my family because I know the neighbors will look after them. And when I am in Mexico, my neighbors know that I will do the same. Americans are dog eat dog. Americans think that if you are poor, it's because you are a failure. And people feel disgraced by that. In America there is so much loneliness. So much isolation. In Mexico everyone is poor, and yet there is so much more happiness there."

Cash was digesting everything he'd heard when Leroy leaned forward and said, "Quetzal here is a lot wiser than he looks."

"How about you, Leroy?" Cash asked. "What do you do around here?"

"I work for a billionaire who owns a ranch down toward the park."

"A billionaire? How'd he make his money?"

"Oil man. Friends with the Bush family. I've met both the

presidents down there. Old Cheney comes along sometimes. I do just about everything you can think of for this guy. There was some talk of the local school closing down not too long back, and he calls me up and tells me to make sure it don't happen. I asked him, how do you propose I go about doing that, and he just says, figure it out. That was the whole conversation. I wish I knew what my job was."

He chewed on this for a minute and then said, "Mike here, he's the star of the show. He was a professional musician in Austin."

"I was just a damn busker," Mike said.

"You made a living playing music," Leroy said. "Ain't that a professional?"

"I'd like to hear one of your songs," Cash said.

"I think I'm too drunk."

"Come on, Mike," Quetzal said.

"Think I'm too drunk."

Everyone continued to coax Mike until he finally went and got his guitar. As he was tuning the strings a small white dog emerged from under the table and began pawing at Mike with excitement.

"Watch this," Leroy said. He pulled out a mess of dollar bills and handed a few ones to each of the brothers. "Just watch."

Mike commenced to strum the guitar with his fingers while picking the strings with a thumbnail grown long for that purpose. It was a sweet simple song he played. Love's confusion. His voice husky but not without grace. When he finished the song, everyone clapped. Leroy told him to pick it up a little on this one, and Mike increased the tempo. For just one guy and a guitar he really filled the room up with music. Leroy took Mike's hat from the table and set it upside down next to him like he was still a street performer and then sat back down and held a dollar bill out between his legs. The dog had been following all of these proceedings and when he saw the money he snapped to attention, trotting over and taking the dollar politely between his teeth. Then the dog turned and dropped it in the hat.

"That's how he got 'em in Austin," Leroy said.

Leroy then stood up and held another dollar three feet above the ground. The dog positioned itself underneath and then stood up on two legs and twirled around and around. Finally the dog leaped up, snatched the dollar in its teeth and dropped it in the hat. Mike played several more songs while they all fed the rest of the dollars to the dog who appeared to be indefatigable when it came to money. Mike strummed one last rapid flourish and then took a thirsty drink of his beer.

"Thought I was gonna be famous for that last one," he said.

"What do you think of all this, Charley?" Leroy asked.

"It's way better than school."

"Charley, you wanna hear a parable of mine?" Quetzal asked.

"What's a parable?"

"It's like a lesson in the form of a story."

"Okay."

Quetzal looked around to make sure everyone was paying attention. "So, the story goes that there was once a Buddhist monastery which had a great master and many devoted disciples . . ."

"I remember this one," Leroy said.

". . . and each day before meditation the disciples would create separate cubicles for themselves by hanging white sheets from the ceiling. They believed the cubicles helped them to focus on their meditation and allowed them to delve deeper than they ordinarily would. The only problem was that the master had a pet cat, and the cat loved to play around with these sheets. This, of course, was distracting to the disciples, so after a few incidents, the master put the cat in the closet before their meditation. This served a dual purpose as punishment and also to avoid interference—"

"Boy, you've really dolled this thing up, haven't you?" Leroy interrupted.

"It's more fun this way. Anyways, this went on for many years. Each time before meditation the master would put the cat in the closet, and they'd begin. Then one day the master died. His greatest disciple became the new master, and now it was his responsibility to put the cat in the closet. Then a few years later the cat died, so the new master had to go out and find the monastery a new cat. For hundreds of years this went on, with new masters and new disciples and new cats, but the tradition remained the same. Before meditation, the cat went in the closet. Finally, after about a thousand years of this, one of the disciples asked the master why it was necessary to put the cat in the closet. The cat didn't even like to enter the monastery, and it was hardly a nuisance. The master wasn't even sure himself, so together they went and read through all the ancient texts, many many volumes, until they finally found the texts written by the original master of the original cat, and they discovered the only reason he put the cat in the closet was because it ran around annoying his disciples. There was never any reason for getting all those other cats just to stuff them in the closet."

"Bravo," Leroy said.

"So, what's the moral, Charley?" Cash asked.

Charley looked around the room, shrugged, and said, "Don't just take somebody else's word for it, I guess."

Outside the guesthouse the next morning, Cash found Mike and Charley facing each other in lawn chairs, each with a guitar. Charley was imitating Mike's strumming technique with some success, but he was getting the chords all wrong. Mike told him to hold on, and he repositioned Charley's fingers on the frets.

"Like that," Mike said. "You see the difference?"

Charley strummed it once.

"Sounds like music now, don't it?"

Cash stepped out into the sunlight and he realized it must have been close to noon. Mike told him there were eggs and toast there, so he fixed himself up a breakfast in the open-air kitchen as the performing dog came begging for a scrap.

"Say Mike," Cash called. "Does this guy Cliff really know his motorcycles?"

"I imagine he'll be able to diagnose it at least."

"And you're sure he'll be back tomorrow?"

"You're forgetting that pinkie finger again, Charley. Tomorrow? Sure. Just took a little trip down to Mexico, but he'll be back."

"Charley, what are you gonna do today?"

"Learn to play like Mike."

"Then get that pinkie down," Mike said.

"Well, I feel like riding. You mind if I borrow your bike for a few hours?"

"Where you going?" Charley asked.

"Wherever. Just exploring."

"You oughta take a ride down to the park," Mike said. "Go see Big Bend."

After he'd eaten, Cash saddled up and rode south, feeling clumsy on his old bike. Though now the last week of October, it was nearly ninety degrees, and Cash unzipped his leather jacket to let the wind rush through him. He passed several lonely, arid ranches and wondered how much somebody would have to pay him to run a herd of scrawny cattle over that land. He figured you couldn't stuff that much cash in Charley's pack as big as it was. When he came to the entrance booth for Big Bend National Park, he stopped and paid the five-dollar entry, and a woman handed him a map of the park which he stowed under his jacket.

He rode on expecting sights worthy of an admission fee, but to him the landscape seemed just as barren and bleak as it had before. He thought it about as lively as Mars, and not so different in looks neither. The earth all cracked and caved and fissured into arroyos. Not a drop of water anywhere, and from the looks of things there hadn't been one in a long while. He eyed sinister looking stands of lechuguilla, some of them flowering stalks ten feet high, and all of them sharp enough to bleed a man woozy. A roadrunner came out from behind the spiny sticks of an ocotillo plant jerking its head about with spasmodic contemplation, and then nimbly sprinted along the highway with its tailfeathers erect. Straight ahead, the dusty heap of Chisos Mountains grew with his progress under the threatless white of a few tattered clouds. Finally, at the first real intersection in seventy miles, he arrived at Panther Junction and pulled into the gas station.

At the pump he was looking around for a credit card console when a stocky man wearing a blue Forever Resorts uniform approached speaking with friendly gruffness.

"Gotta come inside to pay," he said.

Cash followed him into the store and handed him his debit card. The attendant put the card in the groove of a wooden box and pushed a button for pump three.

"Doesn't look like you guys are quite caught up to the twenty-first century yet," Cash said.

"Got nobody to compete with, so the bosses figure why bother."

"Sure is quiet out here."

"Tell me about it. We had a TV over there in the corner, but this other guy who used to work here wouldn't do nothing but sit on his ass watching it, so they took it away."

"You grow up here?"

"Hell, no. I'm from Maryland. Came out here with a girl and now I'm stuck for a while."

"You like it?"

"It's alright."

Cash looked out the window and saw a group of what looked like wild boars ambling toward the pumps. The leading member bit the edge of a green window washing bucket and spilled it over.

"You might have a problem," Cash pointed.

"Javelinas!" the attendant exclaimed.

He raced around the counter and out the door, stomping and shouting for them to get. Startled, the javelinas hackles went up, and they ran clopping single file across the road and away into the desert.

"Ahh, they got the bucket," the attendant said.

He went back in the store and returned with a jug of vinegar.

"You wash your windows with vinegar out here?"

"It's cause of them javelinas. The rangers won't let us use normal suds cause they'll drink it up and poison themselves. They are the bane of my existence. Down in Mexico they marinate javelinas in coca cola, but we can't touch the bastards."

Cash unlocked his tank and began gassing his bike.

"They got some predators at least?" Cash asked.

"Panthers get 'em."

"You really got panthers down here?"

"Same thing as cougars. Down here they call 'em panthers."

Cash was locking down the gas cap when the station phone began ringing.

"Gotta get this," the attendant said and went jogging inside.

Cash started up the bike and took off west. A moment later, he looked back to see the attendant lifting his free hand. Cash waved him a farewell.

Outside the park, Cash came into the ramshackle town of Terlingua looking improvident there within that scorched waste of the desert. Meandering he drove down a dirt path that passed along an old-time cemetery. The graves disorderly and covered over with stacks of rocks which held pinned wooden crosses all warped and blackening with age. Past this he parked in front of a large adobe building that announced itself as the Terlingua Trading Company. Overhanging the entrance was a long and wide porch under which people were taking shelter from the sun and tapping their feet to the rhythm of a fiddler and a banjo player. Cash bought a sandwich and a beer and then leaned against a porch post listening to the music. An old man with a scraggly beard and a lazy eye produced a bottle of hooch and offered it around the crowd to much admiration. When the bottle came around to Cash he took a swig and passed it back to the old man.

"That tastes pretty damn good."

"Made this here from sotol. You ain't gonna come acrost it too many places. Tell you that much."

"Appreciate you sharing then."

"I like to make friends. Hell, I'm friends with everbody includin' the devil himself. He and I jus' don't hang out that much anymore."

"Nice to meet you. I'm Cash."

The old man took his hand. "Donald P. Cunningham the fourth."

"The fourth?"

"And my son's the fifth. Why change a name if it's been workin' for you?"

"Could get confusing at a family reunion."

"Confusing? It simplifies things. That much less to remember."

"You live here? In Terlingua?"

"Came here thirty-seven months ago on vacation, and I'm still on vacation. I live way back in a cave over . . . Well, over that ridge there. Fixed it up real nice like. Don't got running water or 'lectricity and that's the way I want it. Some damn buracrat came snoopin' aroun one day tellin' me I had to get up to code, and I toll him, I said, how you gonna make me pull an egg outta my ass if I ain't a hen? He came by one more time, but I ain't seen him in a long while."

"He must have found bigger fish to fry."

"That's what I'm a'guessin."

"Well Donald, I'll trade you a beer for another drink of that sotol."

"Make it a Lone Star and you got yerself a deal."

Cash took what he considered a fair swig and then went in the store and bought two more beers. When he returned the fiddler was all flinging elbows, and a few men were swinging their ladies around with flourishes to match the music. The banjo player sang something about the Terlingua porch, and a beer-raised cheer went through the crowd. Cash stayed on drinking and mingling as the sun drooped into Mexico leaving a crimson and indigo wake. After full dark, the musicians packed their instruments, and people began heading for home. Cash swallowed the last of his beer and then saddled up.

He rode back toward Marathon singing to himself the last tune he'd heard and feeling not drunk, but not necessarily sober. He was watching out for cops, but there weren't any cars anywhere. A ways along, he looked up and uttered a little moan and stopped in the middle of the highway. Centered there in the loftiest of all lodgings was the Milky Way. Its billionfold brilliance looking like a celestial suture all stitched together with stars. He'd known about it since he was a schoolboy, but he realized then that the knowing of a thing and the seeing of it could be as radically different as not knowing it at all. He stood there gazing for a full minute and then he saw the red and blue lights.

The cruiser pulled up behind, and a heavyset Hispanic officer got out and walked alongside him.

"Your bike break down on you?"

"No, sir."

"Then are why you stopped here in the middle of the road?"

Cash pointed at the sky, but the officer didn't even bother to look up.

"Sir, have you been drinking this evening?"

"I had a couple beers in Terlingua."

The officer had Cash follow him the two miles back to the gas station where he checked his driver's license and the registration on the bike. The officer asked why he was so far from home, and Cash explained his story, leaving out the details about Charley and his other motorcycle. The officer scribbled in his notepad and then said he needed Cash to take a field sobriety test. First he shined his flashlight in Cash's eyes, and as he was doing this he said he could smell the alcohol on his breath. Next he made Cash walk heel to toe in a straight line, and Cash made it thirty yards without faltering. The officer asked Cash to recite the alphabet and then he asked him to say it backwards which he did without error. The officer then took out a breathalyzer.

"Do I have to blow?"

"You have the right to refuse, but if you do it's within my rights to take you to jail. Most judges are gonna look at a refusal as an admission of guilt."

Cash thought it over for a minute and then agreed. He blew, and the officer jotted the figure down and had him blow again.

"I'm gonna be taking you in to Alpine," the officer said.

"What'd I blow?"

"Turn around please," he said as he uncinched handcuffs from his belt.

"What'd I blow?"

"Point O eight three."

"What about my bike?"

"It'll still be here," the officer said as he guided Cash into the back of the cruiser.

The door closed shut, and Cash's head fell back and stayed there. A moment later the driver's door opened, and the officer slid in and started the cruiser.

"I'm gonna need to make a phone call," Cash said.

In the morning he was taken from the jail to a bright red courthouse and led into a small wood-paneled courtroom. The bailiff showed him where to sit and Cash looked around at the observers feeling as though he were in a movie. In the corner the arresting officer was sitting in his uniform. Cash caught his eye and the officer looked away. Soon after, a stout and motherly blonde woman came out of the court chambers and the bailiff called, all rise. The judge took her seat smoothing out her robe and then looked at Cash.

"You don't need to keep standing."

"I'm sorry ma'am. I've never been in a courtroom before."

"Well, that's a good thing."

Cash sat as the judge leaned over and had a hushed word with her assistant who passed her several documents. She flipped through them momentarily and then sat back in her chair.

"Cash Dawkins. Is Cash your given name?"

"Yes ma'am."

"Alright Cash, first off I want to know why you've declined to have representation."

"I figured if I'm guilty why waste my money on a lawyer."

"Are you aware of the ramifications a DWI conviction can bring with it?"

"Yes ma'am."

"I have reviewed the evidence against you as provided by Officer

Martinez, and before we proceed I would like to read you the police report and see if you believe everything to be accurate."

Slowly she read through the report, stopping now and again to get Cash's confirmation, which he gave on every aspect. When she was finished she set the report aside and took off her reading glasses.

"I'd like to hear it from you why exactly you were stopped in the middle of the highway?"

"It's gonna sound silly."

"I'm listening."

"I stopped to look at the stars."

"They don't have stars in Washington?"

"Not like out here they don't."

She smiled and then caught herself.

"You are twenty-two years old. Is that right?"

"Yes ma'am."

"And are your parents aware of this trip you're taking across the country?"

"Yes ma'am."

"Did they give you their blessing?"

"My dad told me I was man enough to make my own decisions about things. My mom was real nervous at first, but she came around at the end."

"And what's your plan for when you get to Florida? Do you have a place to stay? A job lined up?"

"I've got a cousin out there who's gonna let me live with him. He says he can get me work in a restaurant."

"Do you have much money to live on?"

"Not much. Enough to get me to Florida and that's about it."

She watched him for a moment.

"I've got a daughter the same age as you. If she was making a trip anything like what you're doing I think I would just be mortified."

She took a sip of water.

"I take these DWI cases very seriously, son. We see far too many people killed and maimed by drunk drivers around here. On a motorcycle it's almost like suicide if you want my opinion. Can you imagine the mournfulness your mother would have on her plate if you died in a crash? Have you ever considered that?"

"Yes ma'am."

"But it didn't convince you to stop from riding intoxicated."

"I guess not."

"This is an unusual case," she said. "I'm going to take a few minutes and return with my decision for sentencing."

The bailiff called, all rise, and the judge went into her chambers. Twenty minutes later she returned.

"Cash Dawkins," she said. "Please stand."

He pushed his chair back and took a deep breath.

"As I said, I consider this to be an unusual case and I'm going to make an unusual ruling. In fact, I'm giving you a choice in the matter. Your first option is to take the standard sentencing for a first time DWI conviction. That means five days in jail, a two-thousand dollar fine, ninety days license suspension, eighty hours of community service, an alcohol and drug evaluation, and completion of a DWI education class. Option two is reducing your charge to reckless driving which will be contingent—"

"Your honor," Officer Martinez interrupted, leaping to his feet. "You're being too lenient. This is clearly a DWI. He's not even contesting it."

The judge had been trying to stop him with her hand.

"Officer Martinez, I respect your opinion, and if you still feel strongly about it in the morning, you know where to file your grievance. However, this courtroom is my domain. Now sit down or I'll ask the bailiff to remove you."

"Yes ma'am," he said sitting.

"As I was saying, option two would reduce your charge to reckless driving. This means no jail time and a two-hundred dollar fine. All the rest of it is the same including the ninety days license suspension and the eighty hours of community service. Are you paying attention, Cash?"

"Yes ma'am."

"This reduction is contingent on you completing the terms of your punishment in the state of Texas, preferably in Brewster County."

"How am I gonna do that?"

"I just made a phone call to the General Manager of Forever Resorts down in Big Bend. He says he's got a couple openings he needs to fill. A recycler and a gas station attendant, I believe he said. Just about every ranger down there could use a volunteer, but I'll make another call if you can't line it up on your own."

Cash had the look of somebody whose world had suddenly switched orbits.

"Do you know why I'm giving you this deal?" she asked.

"No ma'am."

"I'm offering it because I don't believe a big fine and a jail term are going to do you any good. I believe you'd simply hold a grudge against me and the state of Texas and that as soon as your five days in jail were up you'd be on your way again. My experience with non-resident DWI offenders is that most of them skip out on the service part and a good number of them end up with warrants and extraditions and it'd be a shame to see that happen to you. Besides, it seems to me that what you need most is to be slowed down for a while. I understand that you're eager to get to Florida, but you committed a serious crime in this state. In this state. And for that I believe you owe Texas something. I'm recommending Big Bend not only because that's where you were caught driving intoxicated, but also because I believe in what Theodore Roosevelt started with the National Parks. I believe in what they stand for and I believe in the effect they can have on a young person like yourself. Now, it's certainly in your rights to pass on this deal, but it's this court's belief that service to one's country is far better compensation for reckless behavior than hefty fines or jail time combined. But it's your decision, son. Take a moment to think it over."

Cash got a ride back to Marathon by a crew-cut border patrol agent in plainclothes who let him out at the hostel.

"I'll meet you back here at two-thirty," the agent said. "Sounds like Tommy wants to fill those positions right away so I'd get your stuff packed."

Cash nodded and the agent rolled down the gravel drive as Charley emerged from the guesthouse.

"Are you a free man?"

"Far from it."

Charley came up and appraised his brother at arm's length.

"You look worn out."

"Jail isn't exactly a restful place. I had the craziest dreams."

They took a seat and Cash recounted everything that'd happened from Terlingua to the courthouse. Then he explained the bargain he'd agreed to while Charley chewed on a toothpick. A few people from the hostel came around the corner laughing about some joke and when they saw the brothers hunkered down with the gravity of their situation they stopped laughing and walked away.

"How long will you be stuck here?" Charley asked.

"If I've been a good boy they'll reinstate my license after ninety days."

"They can really force you to work here?"

"It was weird. The way the judge went about it. She made the whole deal seem like it was my choosing."

"What'll you do for work? Where are you gonna live?"

"That's what I'll be finding out this afternoon."

"What about me?"

"You need to head home, Charley. There's no reason you should be getting dragged into this whole ordeal with me."

Charley was chomping the toothpick all around his mouth as a sinewy man with a beard and long frazzled brown hair approached.

"You the boys with the bike trouble?"

"Among other things," Cash replied.

"Well, hop in the back of that truck there and let's go have a look at her."

At the restaurant Cliff got out and walked around the motorcycle.

"Nice color to it," he said. "I always liked these Intruders. Fast little fuckers."

Cash explained how it had been sputtering and that it seemed to die and start again at random. Cliff asked for the keys and he tried firing it a few times. Then he knelt down and removed the side cover.

"Yep," he said.

"What?"

"See this here?"

"Yeah."

"That's your fuel filter."

He removed a four inch tube and held it up to Cash's face.

"See all that black crud in there?" he said jiggling the tube around.

"Yeah."

"There's your problem. It's stopping the fuel from getting through."

Cliff cleaned the tube with a single swift blow and then reattached it. He squeezed the clutch and gave the ignition a thumb and the engine fired right up like nothing had ever happened.

"Unbelievable," Cash said.

"How much do we owe you for your help?" Charley asked.

Cliff looked from one brother to the other.

"For two minutes of work? Nah. I won't charge you nothin."

Cash put his hands over his face.

"Lost my freedom to a damn clog."

"Buck up, son," Cliff said. "It's better than losing it to a woman."

Charley followed them back to the hostel on the Intruder and the brothers thanked Cliff and then went inside the guesthouse. Cash found a couple grocery bags folded up near the entryway and he sat on the edge of a bunk stuffing them with his belongings.

"What do you say I split the cost of a flight with you?" Cash said. "One-way can't be too expensive."

"I'm not leaving."

"I'm putting my foot down on this, Charley. Look, you did real good. You had yourself a big adventure and now it's time you get back home and finish up with high school. Don't worry about the motorcycle. I gave it to you fair and square and I'll honor that. Soon as I find someone to sell it to I'll mail you the money and you can pick up another one."

"I don't care about the bike."

Cash stopped packing.

"You're my brother," Charley said. "That means we're in this thing together."

Cash tried to say something but Charley went on.

"You didn't leave me behind. You didn't leave me, so now I'm not gonna leave you."

He'd said it with such a tone of finality that it left Cash speechless and he just sat there rubbing his knuckles.

"It's not like this is the worst thing in the world. I mean, I kinda like it out here."

Cash lifted his head.

"Well, Charley. Looks like I've stranded you in the desert after all."

The border agent let Cash sit up front with him in his truck and they chatted as though he hadn't just been convicted of a crime. A few miles past the gas station they took a left and the road began to climb and wind its way into the basin of the Chisos Mountains. They passed a large wooden sign reading *BEAR AND MOUNTAIN LION COUNTRY. SPECIAL REGULATIONS APPLY. CHECK WITH RANGER*. Cash pointed at the sign.

"Is that something I should be worried about?"

"Nah. Well, not too much anyways."

"You seen any panthers?"

"Only once. It was about a month ago. I was driving down there by PJ…"

"PJ?"

"Panther Junction."

"Sounds fitting."

"It was real early in the morning. Pitch black. I was about fifty yards past the gas station when a deer goes sprinting across the road in front of me. So I slam on the brakes and right on this deer's tail is a panther chasing after it. There's a lot more to this place than you'd think on a first impression."

As they climbed higher and deeper into the basin the terrain began to show a surprising lushness. The flora greenly thickened with bushes and shrubs and for the first time a considerable number of trees. Pines and junipers grew along the road and seemed to clamber up the rocky slopes until they could no longer draw sustenance from the craggy terrain that encircled the basin entire. The border agent pointed out a congested little campground and then they swung around past the Chisos Mountain Lodge and parked outside the restaurant.

"I appreciate you helping me out like this," Cash said.

"Oh, I don't mind. I'll take any excuse that gets me up here."

"It's a lot nicer than I'd expected."

"Yeah, it's a pretty special place. Look over there. Way over there. You see where it looks like there's a V cut into the rocks? They call that the window. Lots of times the sun sets right down in that groove. Fact I'll probably just order some dinner and stick around for it. Anyways…"

He took Cash's hand and they shook.

"You seem like a pretty good kid to me. Maybe just try not to be so dang conspicuous next time would be my advice. Lotta times I think young people get in trouble not so much because they committed a crime as because they appear to have a disdain for common sense." He nodded to a little building annexed to the restaurant. "Office is right over there. We'll be seeing you."

Cash walked in the office and stood there hugging his bagged possessions. A woman with short blonde hair swiveled toward him in her chair.

"And who might you be?"

"I'm Cash Dawkins."

She rocked back and smiled at him.

"So you're the one the judge sent us."

"Yes ma'am."

"Don't call me ma'am. It makes me feel old."

"Alright."

"My name's Karen. You can call me that. Go on and set your bags down."

Over her shoulder she shouted, Tommy, and from the next office a man's voice shouted back, yeah.

"Cash Dawkins is here."

"Send him in."

A skinny and energetic man with sunglasses resting atop his thin blonde hair met him at the door and shook his hand and told him to take a seat. Then he went around the desk where he stayed standing.

"I've got scores of things to do today, Cash, so I'm going to keep this short. First off, I don't particularly care what you did that got you here. All I'm concerned with is whether or not you can get your job done. I had two guys up and leave me for Vegas without any notice and they've put me in a bind. I'm hurting for a recycler, but I need another gas station attendant even worse. If I put you in the station down in PJ can you handle the customer service part of the job? Dealing with people all day?"

"Sure. I had to do some of that working for my dad."

"Are you any good with numbers?"

"Better than average."

"That's good. I'm getting sick of these guys screwing up the accounting every night so that Karen has to spend an extra hour—"

"At least an hour," Karen called.

"At least an extra hour putting it back together."

"Where will I live?" Cash asked.

"Since you'll be working in PJ we'll put you down there in the new dormitory. Rent is two dollars a day which we'll deduct from your paycheck. Those come every two weeks. Karen will set you up with all the paperwork, uniforms, bedding. I need you to start training tomorrow. Eight a.m."

"Alright."

"Okay, good. Now I gotta see what happened to this shipment."

"Just one thing, Tommy."

"Yeah?"

"I know somebody who can fill that recycler position."

Karen walked him into the dormitory's common area as three middle aged Mexican men turned to look at him from the couch. He nodded to them and then surveyed the clean and white-walled dwelling. In the corner a dining table and next to it a standard kitchen where another Mexican man was working on a stew. Karen led him down a hallway and into the first bedroom on the left where there were two twin-size beds on opposite sides of the room. Cash chose the one under the window and she set down his bedding.

"You'll be rooming with Jordan," she said. "He gets here in a couple days."

"Why not my brother?"

"The recycler works up in the basin. It's more convenient for him to live up there. Don't worry, you guys'll see each other plenty."

She held out a book and Cash turned over a Spanish dictionary.

"These guys don't speak much English," she said.

Once she was gone Cash arranged his few things in the closet and then made his bed and laid on the firm mattress. From across the hall he heard the toyish wheeze of an accordion and soon the music was accompanied by a raspy and disharmonious voice singing lyrics he could not understand. Cash stared at the ceiling. Feeling like he was well on his way to becoming someone other than himself.

He thought he would take a nap but the stew had filled the dorm with such an irresistible aroma that a hungered curiosity got him up to have a look. In the kitchen an effeminate old Mexican was ladling stew into bowls for the others. After they'd all been served the cook gestured toward Cash.

"You like a food?"

"Yeah. I like food."

The cook filled him a bowl of the stew and he took it saying gracias.

"What's your name?" Cash asked.

"Jose."

Cash flipped through the Spanish dictionary.

"Um. Mucho gusto?"

"Si. Mucho gusto. You speak a Spanish?"

"No. Only, uno, dos, tres. Cuatro, cinco, seis."

Jose smiled and then ladled himself a bowl. He found them each a spoon and directed Cash to take a seat with them in the living room. On the television a busty black-haired woman was on her knees sobbing and jabbering a hysterical soliloquy. The men were all engrossed with whatever drama was taking place and when the show cut to two women in bed together they all went, oooohhh, and one of the men slapped his leg so hard he splashed stew on the floor to the tsking of the cook. Cash supped a tentative first spoonful of the broth, and the spice and pepper of it made his tongue hop.

"This is really good," Cash told the cook. "Mucho mucho tasty."

"Yes. There is more. Please."

By the time Cash was midway through his second bowl he was nearly sweating with the heat of it and he fanned himself in an exaggerated way. The men were all laughing with approval and the one named Chuta whose English was the best came up and patted him on the back.

"That's good. You eat alots of hot peppers you learn Spanish very fast."

After dinner Cash went out on the concrete porch and lit a cigarette. He took a few drags and then saw a group of javelinas come around the side of the building and nose up to a trash can. He had just moved to shoo them away when he heard a man shriek a HEEEYAWW. The javelinas scattered and the redheaded man from the gas station walked into sight.

"Hey, what are you doing here?" the man said.

"I'm your new gas station attendant."

"Wait. Huh?"

Cash told him the whole story and when he was finished the redhead unzipped his backpack and removed two shot glasses and a half gallon of whiskey.

"I'm Joey Cain," he said. "May as well start getting acquainted."

He poured them each a shot.

"Rich and Rare Canadian," Cash said.

"I call it blah blah."

"Why that?"

"Cause it makes you stay up all night going, blah blah blah blah," he said talking with his hand. "Ok, cheers."

"Actually I've been forbidden from it."

"Forbidden?"

"By the judge."

Joey held his hands out and looked around to show there was nobody watching.

"Not on day one at least."

"I'm taking 'em both then."

He took one shot after the other and then made an ugly grimace.

"So Joey, are you one of these avid outdoorsman types?"

"You kidding me? I'm from Maryland."

"What does that got to do with it?"

"Ok, I'll tell you a story. Why you won't ever find me backpacking. I knew this lady once who was a writer for some travel magazine—"

"Which magazine?"

"I can't remember. It's not around anymore. Anyways, this one time she took an assignment to hike the Appalachian Trail for a couple weeks. She was supposed to go with a friend of hers but the friend dropped out so she decided to go alone. So when she's out there hiking she takes tons of pictures, you know, to go along with the article and when she gets home she has them developed. And when she gets the pictures back and starts looking through them she realizes that a bunch of the pictures were taken of her. While she was sleeping. And not just one night. Multiple nights somebody had followed her in the woods and snuck into her tent and took pictures of her. Creeps me out. So now Joey Cain says fuck camping."

"Maybe she just made up the whole story."

"Why would she do that?"

"You said she was a writer. Isn't that what they do?"

Joey disregarded him with a wave.

"Besides my back and knees are too messed up from all my years as a bricklayer to be climbing up the side of a mountain. I prefer it down here with my blah blah."

"The brick business sounds like a tough one."

"Hell yeah, it is. Try carrying around two fifty-pound buckets of mortar all day long and see how you feel. Crawling up and down ladders with the stuff. That's part of the reason why I'm here. My body started breaking down on me. I had to get out before I wound up on disability. But I miss it sometimes. I was an artist with mortar. Started working for my father's business when I was six. I'm telling you, I was born with a trowel in my hand."

"Must have been painful for your mother."

Joey glared at him and then broke into a smile.

"You're alright, man."

It was very quiet in the store and they were staring at cans of refried beans. A short Hispanic man with a trace of an accent pointed at the cans.

"What is wrong with this picture?" he said.

"I don't know, Manny. Is there supposed to be more of them?"

"No. Look."

He took the first can off the shelf.

"What is the expiration date?"

"April eleven. Of next year."

He replaced it and then took the can farthest in the back.

"Now read this expiration date."

"October sixteen."

"Of this year."

"So it's expired."

"Yes."

"So we should throw it out."

"Yes, but that's not the point. These cans aren't being rotated. New cans go in the back, not the front. You see? If the new cans go in the front then the old cans stay in the back and they expire. You see? Everything in this store must get rotated. I tell the other guys all the time. I tell them, you must rotate, but they are too lazy. They just put things in the front and then we have waste."

A brass bell dully jangled for the door and they went and stood behind the register while a couple did their shopping. When they were finished the man dumped an armload of goods on the counter and the woman added a few more. Cash lifted the items one at a time, manually typing them into the register and then loading them into a brown paper bag. He got to a box of tampons.

"There's no price on this one, Manny."

"Tag must have come off. Let me go check the others."

Cash smiled at the couple and the woman looked away with embarrassment.

"Eight-fifty," Manny called.

Cash typed in the price and hit a button to show their total. The man gave him a fifty dollar bill and he dinged open the cash register and made him his change. As they were leaving Cash saw Charley ride up to the pumps on the Intruder. He watched him search around for the credit card console and then he walked inside and handed Cash his card.

"I'll take a fill up on number two, sir. And clean those bugs off my windshield while you're at it. I wanna keep my nice new bike looking spiffy."

"How's it going, bud?"

"Oh, you know. Excited to start my career as a garbage man."

"Recycler, Charley. It's much more prestigious."

Charley looked around the store.

"So this is you, huh?"

"This is it. Slinging gas and microwave cheeseburgers. Hey, did you talk to Mom about all of this yet?"

"Yeah, I called her this morning. She says she blames you for everything."

"Those were her exact words?"

"Actually it was a lot worse than that. I think if she doesn't see us for Christmas she's gonna throw a conniption fit."

The brothers turned at the sound of a tanker truck rolling

up out of the calm and it lurched to a stop alongside the holding tanks. Manny came out of the storeroom and pressed buttons on a machine that printed a gas report. He was just tearing the slip of paper off the machine when the brass bell jangled.

"Goddamn if you ain't got the skinniest sumbitch pull in here."

A burly old man with a face like he'd just been drowned and a swinging gut where all the water must have went.

"How y'all doin today?" he said.

"Doing good," Manny said. "How about you?"

"Just fine. Livin and breathin. You got me my ullage count there for unlead?"

"Yes sir. Ullage reads two thousand five hundred and seventy-seven gallons."

"Twenty-five seventy-seven and I'm comin with twenty-five hunerd. Oughta fit her just tight."

"Where's Dwayne at today?"

"At home sicker'n dead. Somebody wanna get them cones out for me?"

"Cash, grab those orange cones from the back," Manny said. "Once this young man here fills his motorcycle put those cones all around the pumps so customers know they have to wait."

"Manny, this is my brother Charley. He's our new recycler."

"Hey, great. Nice to meet you. Now let's get those cones."

"Gotta run," Cash said. "I'll take care of that gas for you."

Once he'd arranged the cones Cash watched as Manny undid the lock to the holding tank and unclasped the hatch. The driver unsheathed a twelve foot measuring stick from the side of the truck and walked over with it and an oil grubbed container of baby powder. He had a great swollen lip of tobacco and he spat an oily splash of it on the concrete and then lowered the measuring stick into the tank. Once he hit bottom he raised the stick up, sprinkled baby powder on the topmost portion that was wet with gas and lowered it again. This time when the stick came out there was a line the gas had eaten clean through the powder.

"Eighty-six even," he said. He took the fueling tube and clamped it tight to the tank and then slammed some levers on the side of the truck. As the tube began contorting with the flow of fuel a pack of kids emptied out of a van and Manny followed them into the store.

"You new here?" the fuelman asked Cash.

"First day."

"Likin it?"

"It's not bad. Just getting used to being out in the middle of nowhere."

"Boy, this ain't the middle of nowhere. It's the end of nowhere. But it's got its upsides. In the city you don't hardly even know your next door neighbor, but out here you know everone for hunerds of miles. I been lotsa places so I know this here is good country. Good people."

"Where else you been?"

"I was in the Navy for some years so that got me around just about everwhere. Began my time by serving on an aircraft carrier during Vietnam. People tell me I'm not supposed to say this, but I had a great time over there. Us boys had lots of fun. Lots of dyin to be sure, but lots of fun. Those old aircraft carriers… Whoo! Most dangerous job in the world workin on one of them, but it's a beautiful dance, boy."

"I've seen video of a helicopter falling off the side of one of those carriers."

"Yup. That happened. I saw ever kind of shit happen on those suckers. I mean everthing."

He spluttered another spat on the concrete and then wiped the dribble with the back of his hand and cleaned it off with his jeans.

"Boy, I'm famished. Why don't you get me one of them cheeseburgers heated up while I finish."

Cash went in and put a cheeseburger in the microwave as Manny called for him to come get some more practice on the register. He rang the kids up for their chips and soda and then another young couple placed on the counter a carton of eggs and a box of tampons. After they'd left the store Manny turned to Cash and whispered.

"I know two guys who aren't getting laid tonight."

Cash went down the hall reading the names and titles labeled on the office doors. When he came to the one that said Wildlife Biologist he knocked twice and a very tall man with glasses swung the door open.

"Cash Dawkins?"

"That's right."

"I'm Raymond Skiles," he said tapping his nametag.

"Nice to meet you, Raymond. Can't help but notice you've got that nametag upside down."

"Oh. Yes, I see. I'm a little out of it this morning. It's usually my day off."

From a pile of folded uniforms Raymond found Cash a pair of cargo pants and a tan khaki shirt with a National Park Volunteer emblem sewn onto the breast pocket. After Cash had changed his clothes they loaded a park service truck with shovels and spades and measuring sticks and then drove to Rio Grande Village. The radio was on quiet and a newscaster was reading headlines from yesterday's news. When the newscaster mentioned something about the weather Raymond turned the volume up and when the newscaster went on to discuss foreign affairs he turned it back down.

"Not much to a weatherman's job in West Texas is there?" Cash said. "Hot and dry. Hot and dry. I don't see how the plants can make it."

"Oh, it's really amazing the schemes evolution has come up with in the desert."

"Like what?"

"Lots of these plants have what are called germination inhibitors. That means their seeds will lie dormant for years and years waiting until enough rain falls to bypass those inhibitors and trigger their development. Desert plants are patient. Take that plant there. The one that looks like it's got a big asparagus spear growing up out of it. That's a lechuguilla plant. They'll grow for as long as thirty years before they bloom, and they only ever bloom once. All those years it's storing up nutrients, and then when it's got enough it grows that bloom stalk and shortly after that it dies."

"For a wildlife biologist you sound like you know an awful lot about plants."

"Got to. If you don't understand the plants the animals are eating then you can't understand the animals. Take the lechuguilla, for example. The javelinas gobble them up, but for cattle or sheep they're toxic. Their stomachs never evolved to handle them."

"Seems like people aren't too fond of the javelinas around here."

"It's not the javelinas fault. People around Panther Junction are so bad about keeping their garbage that the javelinas learned how to get an easy snack. The problem is when they get aggressive. A few years back there was an employee who kept her little dog outside on a leash. She had built a kennel for it out of this wire fence but one day she went away for a few hours and when she came back the javelinas had broken through the fence. All she found of her dog was that leash and a pile of bones. They hung a picture of it up in the basin so people would know how dangerous they really are."

In Rio Grande Village they first visited a large pond surrounded by giant river cane. "This is nice," Cash said as they walked out onto a series of floating platforms.

"This is a beaver pond. They built all of this. Without the

beavers it would hardly look like anything. What we do out here is take depth measurements of the water."

"Make sure those beavers are doing their job?"

"No, we're not worried about them. What we're worried about are ranchers."

"Ranchers?"

"Underneath this whole area are aquifer springs. Not just under the pond but the whole area. The thing is nobody knows just how extensive these aquifers spread. It could be lots of miles. That being the case a rancher outside the park might have access to this same water source and if he had it in mind he might just dig enough wells to pump this whole aquifer dry."

"No more beaver pond."

"That's right. A single rancher could destroy this whole habitat. Hypothetically. We don't really know. But that's where the depth measurements come in. We need to gather enough data about the water levels in this area over a long enough time that if a rancher did start pumping us dry we could take our data into court and prove the rancher was causing the water loss."

"And the court would make him stop."

"That's the hope."

They made a dozen different measurements all around Rio Grande Village and then Raymond drove them to another much smaller pond enclosed inside a chain link fence.

"This is a special man-made pond we built for some of our Gambusia fish. They look pretty much like minnows, but they're an endangered species. In the whole world they only exist in a few aquifer ponds here in Big Bend. So that's another reason we make our measurements. We had to build some of these man-made ponds because the Rio's been flooding in recent years and invasive fish species have been spilling over and devastating the Gambusia population."

"Why don't you just stick them in an aquarium?"

"We've done that with some, but the government's given us a grant to protect and preserve their natural habitats. Or as close as we can come to it. Some biologists believe you take a fish out of its habitat for long enough you might not have the same fish anymore. Or at least you might not have the same habitat. There's all sorts of biological synergy at work that we don't have a clue about yet."

Raymond led Cash down a dirt path to a brick cistern.

"This cistern traps the aquifer water as it rises out of the earth. We built a pump and a pipeline to shuttle the water from the cistern to the pond so the Gambusia have plenty of water. Problem is the pipeline's starting to give out on us."

"I see now where the shovels come in."

"So what we're going to do today is start digging a new trench that'll house the new pipeline."

Raymond shut off the pump and they began heaving dirt and sweating in the eighty degree sun. Between grunts Raymond said, "I sure appreciate you giving us so much of your time. Not too often we get such devoted volunteers out here."

"I wouldn't make too big a deal of it. Not like I had much choice in the matter."

"What do you mean?"

"Didn't the judge talk to you?"

"Sure. She said you were looking for volunteer opportunities."

Cash planted his shovel in the ground.

"Opportunities? That's all she said about it?"

"Yeah, I just figured she was using her reputation to help out a relative or neighbor or something like that."

Cash leaned against his shovel laughing.

"I must be wrong then."

"Sorry, Raymond. I guess I should tell you the judge ordered me to do this. It was part of the deal for getting my DWI reduced to reckless driving. Don't get me wrong. I'm enjoying the experience, but it definitely wasn't my choice."

"Why the heck did she choose me?"

"Maybe she's a wildlife nut."

Raymond reached down into the trench and removed a few big rocks.

"Well, I'm still glad to have you."

They dug for another half hour and then Raymond ran the back of his hand across his slick brow and said it was time for lunch. He switched on the pump and the trench began to mud and then fill up with water.

"Well, now, shoot."

"What happened, Raymond?"

"I cut the old pipe open with the shovel."

Alongside the gas pumps Cash and Joey were tossing a ball they'd crafted from duct tape. Joey told him to go deep and hurled a long throw. Cash sprinted after it and when he came to the end of the pavement he leaped over a cactus and caught the ball with one hand and then went hopping through a maze of shin daggers.

"Yeah, buddy. Looking like Willie Mays out there."

Cash jogged back and tossed the ball.

"I was a little league All Star. Couldn't hit for shit, but I was a great fielder."

"That just gave me an idea."

Joey went inside the store and returned carrying one of the lacquered lechuguilla stalks they sold as walking sticks for fourteen dollars.

"Baseball bat," he said.

"Step up to the plate."

"No curveballs."

"How could I throw one? There's no seams on a tapeball."

"No curveballs."

"Just stand against that wall there."

"Throw it nice and easy."

Cash tossed him an overhand lob and Joey swung and missed. He tossed Cash the ball and Cash threw him another lob. Joey swung and missed.

"Hit the thing, Joe. You coulda done practice swings without me throwing it."

"Shut up."

Cash tossed him another and this time Joey nicked the ball and it dribbled to a stop halfway between them.

"Maybe you're just no good with the changeups. Let's try a fastball."

Cash wound up and flung a sidearm pitch. The ball hit the wall before Joey had even swung. Cash threw another fastball and Joey stepped away from the ball flailing wildly.

"You almost hit me."

"Quit crowding the plate."

"There isn't a plate."

"Alright. Here comes a slow one."

Cash tossed him an easy pitch right down the middle. Joey swung and missed.

"You don't have much hand-eye coordination, do you?"

"You try it then."

Joey passed him the walking stick.

"I can't believe we get paid for this," Cash said. "It's like recess."

"That's what they do in China."

Joey spit on the ball and delivered his pitch with a herky-jerky motion. Cash hit the ball and sent it zipping between Joey's legs.

"Lucky," he said retrieving the ball.

This time Joey threw it much harder and Cash spun at the high inside fastball and connected with a crack. The ball went soaring into the desert. Joey watched it go and then looked back to see Cash holding only half of the walking stick.

"I thought you said you couldn't hit?"

They heard cars and turned to watch a border patrol cruiser pull up to the pumps followed by a ragged old Ford truck driven by another border agent. In the bed of the truck a heap of something was covered over with tarps. Cash went in and turned on pump three and then collected the errant half of the walking stick.

Joey approached one of the border agents.

"Hey John, how you doing today?"

"Fine."

"What you got hiding under those tarps?"

The agent said nothing.

Joey moved to lift the corner of the tarp and the agent's hand went to his gun.

"Back up."

"Whoa. What the hell?"

"Back up. In fact, I need both of you to stay inside the store until we've left."

They went inside and Joey clutched Cash by the shirt.

"It was weed under there. I saw it."

"You think?"

"You saw him go for his gun, didn't you? I'll bet they snagged some Mexicans trying to run that truck across the border."

Cash turned and looked at it.

"Can you imagine how much that truck must be worth right now?"

Joey was speculating on what he would do if he had that much money when Cash interrupted him.

"Who is this?"

A tall blonde girl wearing a Forever Resorts uniform was approaching the store.

"That's Emma," Joey said. "She's a receptionist up in the basin."

"So that's the one my brother told me about."

She came in and said hi to Joey and then turned to Cash.

"You must be Charley's brother."

"That's right."

"Him and I have been hanging out a lot. He's a funny guy."

"I'm surprised he even talks to you. He's usually pretty bashful around girls."

"It took him a few days to come out of his shell, but now he's a hoot. Everybody loves him up there. Well, I've gotta run. I'll just take twenty on pump two. Nice to meet you finally."

When she was gone Cash turned to Joey.

"She's a fox ain't she?"

"I would eat the corn out of that girl's ass."

"Excuse me?"

"I would eat it up. You hear me, hoss. Eat it up."

The forest they climbed was of pinyon pine and juniper and they were lucky to have the dappled shade because even at that elevation it was over eighty degrees. Loose rocks shuffled with their steps and a few hidden birds were twittering in the trees, but loudest of all on that steep switchbacking trail was the huffing and panting of the brothers. Leading them was Emma. Taller and fitter than either of the brothers, her strides were long and brisk and unrelenting. Cash soon called out stop and he dropped to the flat of a rock and sucked in the mountain air.

"Again?" she said.

"I'm going dizzy."

"We're almost to where it flattens out."

"Just let me catch my breath."

"Smoker. You get what you deserve."

"Charley, you just gonna let her lecture me like this?"

While the brothers rested and drank water Emma showed them a rock wall she sometimes practiced free climbing. Other than a few crevices and some minor protrusions it was a sheer twenty foot slab to the upper ledge.

"You want to try it with me?" she asked Charley.

"Let me watch you do it first."

"How about you, Cash?"

"I prefer my bones unbroke."

"Don't you know you can't fall off a mountain," she said.

"What?"

"It's from a book I'm reading by Jack Kerouac. He says that you can't fall off a mountain. It's a Zen thing."

"I believe some people at the bottom would've disagreed with him on that if they'd had the chance."

"It's supposed to be literary, not literal."

"Tell her, Charley."

"He hates books."

"I abhor them. That's a fancy word, right?"

She looked disgusted.

"But I like them," Charley said. "I just read Catcher in the Rye. When we were in Santa Barbara I told Cash—"

"Ok, watch my route now, Charley."

She turned and grappled with the first handhold and then pulled herself up and began to deftly ascend the rockface.

"I don't think your friend Emma likes me very much," Cash said.

"She likes you."

"But not very much."

"Well…"

"Go on."

"She did say she thinks you're cocky."

Cash snickered.

"She said that you don't walk. You strut."

"I'm sure there's more."

"She called you a ruffian."

"A ruffian, huh?"

He sat appraising the term.

"I can live with that. So tell me…"

Cash leaned in and lowered his voice.

"You two been getting it on?"

"No. We've just made out a couple times. I felt her boobs."

"Were they magical, Charley?"

"Pretty nice."

They heard Emma shout, "Look at me you wusses," and saw her standing atop the ledge with her hands on her hips in a graceful pose of triumph.

"That girl could kick your ass, Charley."

"She'd kick yours too."

"She might."

Emma scrambled up another forty feet and then went out of sight behind a ridge.

"I will admit it though, Charley. She is pretty. Wish I had a prospect."

"There's no cute girls down in PJ?"

"Well, it depends on how much plaque you consider reasonable on a girl. How much upper lip hair you're willing to overlook. We've been here for what? Three or four weeks? I've already started lowering my standards. Question is just whether the bar drops low enough by the time we leave. Funny thing is, I can't decide if I want it to or I don't."

"I found a porno magazine somebody left in my closet. You want it?"

"Gonna pass on that one. Besides, you'd better hang on to it in case things don't work out with Emma."

She had come back over the ridge and now was beginning to ease her way down the slab. Cash's eyes were fixed on her ass which looked ripe through the tightness of her shorts. He looked over at Charley and saw that he was watching the same thing.

"You lucky shit," Cash said.

After the last of the switchbacks the trail leveled out as Emma had said and they entered a meadow of yellow waist-high grass. Cash held out his arms and palmed the stalks which slipped through shooshing. They went around a bend and a rabbit hopped out onto the trail and looked about for its next move. Emma removed her camera and clicked a few shots as Cash heard something rustling in the brush to his right. He looked over and saw a big black head. He nearly asked them what that dog was doing loose, but then he realized what it was and said, oh shit.

Twenty yards off the black bear lumbered out of the brush and swung its head at them. Cash put Emma and Charley behind his arms and they began to backpedal.

"Don't run," Emma said.

Cash stopped and waited to see what the bear would do. It stared at them. Then after a few moments the bear turned and plodded up the same trail they had been hiking. Cash let it get fifty yards ahead and then he shouted, move it bear, and it doubled its pace. Once the bear had disappeared off the trail Cash noticed that Emma was gripping his arm with one hand and holding out a canister of bear spray with the other. Charley was giggling with the adrenaline.

"Anybody need to change their underwear?" Cash asked and Charley patted his backside like there was actually a chance. "I won't blame you guys if you don't wanna go on with me, but I need these service hours."

"We'll be fine," Emma said. "Let's all just talk really loud for a while."

They began walking as Charley shouted, "So brother, what did Raymond assign you today?"

Slowly and even louder Cash shouted, "That's a great question, Charley. Our mission for today... Are you listening, bear? Our mission for today features this special GPS unit which Raymond attached to the top of my pack. I say this GPS is special because it will be recording our route. If Emma there can keep us on the right path, not to mention falling off the mountain..."

Charley mimic shouted, "The mountain."

"… then Raymond will be using this data to make more precise maps. Isn't that right, bear?"

Emma shouted, "Hey, boo boo."

Cash continued shouting, "I imagine Raymond will use this data for other things as well, but I think he dumbs stuff down for me when he explains it." And then he sang with a lilting holler, "Because I'm just a ruffiannnnn."

She shot him a glance.

"Sing it with me, everyone. It's fun. Sing, aaa rrruffiannn."

Charley looked back and forth between Emma and Cash.

"Nobody," Cash went on. "Alright then. Emma, why don't you lead us in a song of your choosing."

Emma began singing the Star Spangled Banner but the song soon dissolved and for the next twenty minutes they meandered through a new forest of oak while improvising a rowdy and nonsensical offensive against the ears of the bear.

Cash sat at the poker table fiddling with a stack of chips atop the green felt. It was the weekend before Thanksgiving and there were eight guys playing in one of the immobile trailers that served as employee housing. All of them were drinking beer and whiskey except Cash who was halfway through his second Coke.

The action came around to Cash and he peaked at his cards and saw the king and queen were still there. On the table the communal cards were a king, a queen and a nine. All of them hearts. Cash checked and across the table Joey pushed forward a bet. Cash and one other called. The dealer turned over another king and again Cash checked and called. The final card was a two of spades. Cash checked once more but this time when Joey bet he raised him. Joey studied Cash's face and then he studied the board.

"Hell, I don't know why I'm even thinking about this," he said finally. "I've got the nuts."

He called the raise and showed an ace high flush. Cash flipped over his full house. One of the men guffawed and smacked the table.

"The nuts you say? More like a kick in the nuts."

Joey took a swig from his half gallon of whiskey.

"I don't care. Poker's just an excuse for me to drink."

"Everything's an excuse for you to drink," Cash said.

"I need as many as I can get," he said and took another swig.

The dealer gathered up the cards and shuffled. He was firing the hole cards around the table when Charley burst into the trailer and took Cash's arm with excitement.

"I gotta tell you something," he said.

"So say it."

"Come outside with me for a minute."

"I'm in the middle of a hand."

"Come on. I gotta tell you now."

"Jesus, Charley. This better be good."

Cash folded his cards and wagged his finger at the table.

"I have a photographic memory. I'll know if there's chips missing."

Outside the trailer Charley looked around to make sure nobody was listening and then he said, "I lost it."

"Lost what?" Cash said but then he recognized the gleam in his brother's eye. "You went and got your cherry popped didn't you?"

"Yep."

Cash pounded his brother's chest with both fists.

"You a man now. And what a girl to lose it to. It was Emma right?"

"Duh."

"So tell me about it. Did you use that move you showed me at the IHOP? Did you spank her, Charley? Did you make her scream?"

"She pretty much just pounced on me."

"Took control of the whole thing for you, huh?"

"Yeah. Seemed like she was drunk."

"How do you feel?"

"Really relaxed."

"And tell me, Charley. How did she feel? You know."

He twiddled two of his fingers together and made a trilling whistle.

"Like ripples of velvet, right?"

Charley just stood there grinning with the recollection as Joey opened the trailer door.

"It's your turn again, dude. You playing or what?"

"Don't fold me. I'm coming."

He turned to Charley.

"I'm gonna remember this night for the rest of my life. The day my kid brother lost his virginity. Alright, get on back up there and show her you're not just a one trick pony."

The poker game went on for hours. Joey was the first out and then one by one the rest of the guys lost their money and stumbled home. At two in the morning it was down to just Cash and a scrawny man named Dale. He was a campground host in Rio Grande Village and he was very drunk.

Dale pushed out a big bet and sat back with a cocky grin. Cash took a long time thinking it over and then he called with the last of his chips. Dale flipped over a six and a nine of spades. He had caught a gut shot straight on the river and he leaned forward and raked the chips in laughing.

"Amazing," Cash said.

"I told you how good I was. Didn't I tell you?"

"More like amazing that you would stay in that hand so long. You had nothing."

"I knew the seven would come. I have great instincts. Because I am a great player. Because I am the best."

"Let's keep playing."

"I'll take your money all night."

Cash opened his wallet and saw it was empty.

"I'm out of cash. Will you loan me a twenty?"

"Sure. I can always use an extra twenty bucks."

He winked at Cash and then spit tobacco into an empty beer bottle. Cash watched him shuffle with drunken clumsy and he could not believe the mound of chips Dale had stacked on the felt before him. That so much luck could swing in the favor of one who deserved it so little. Dale drank two more beers and the game went back and forth for another hour. Cash wanted to continue but he'd been up since six-thirty that morning and he couldn't stop yawning. He won a small pot and then said he was finished. He counted his chips.

"There's thirty-six bucks here, Dale. Minus that twenty you loaned me and I get sixteen dollars back."

Dale looked up with his eyes rolling around like marbles in a game without rules. He shook his head and slurred.

"I don't owe you anything."

"It's simple, Dale. I have thirty-six in chips. I owe you twenty. That means I get sixteen bucks out of your cash there."

"I already beat you. I already won all the money. I always win all the money cause I'm the best."

"You might be the best, Dale, but you still owe me sixteen dollars."

"What are you even talking about, man?"

Cash explained it to him one more time and Dale got up to leave. Around him was the wall, the couch and the table and Cash stood to block his only exit.

"You owe me sixteen dollars."

"I don't owe you anything."

Cash's voice began to rise.

"Give me my money, Dale."

"Get out of my way, man."

"Then give me my money."

"Let me go."

Dale tried to charge past and Cash pushed him back into the corner. He hadn't used much force but Dale was so scrawny and drunk he stumbled backwards, tripped over a chair and knocked his head against the side of the table. When he stood up a little trickle of blood ran down the side of his forehead. Cash imagined himself wearing an orange court jumpsuit and he let Dale dash outside and into the next trailer. A minute later a hairy man naked except his boxers pushed him out the door.

"Don't ever come into my place again," the man screamed.

Cash ran over and pinned Dale against the side of a trailer with his forearm to his chest.

"Why are you doing this? Just give me my money."

"You're crazy, man. Let me go."

"Just give me sixteen dollars."

"I don't owe you any money."

"Why are you lying?"

He tried to squirm out of Cash's grasp but he was too weak and Cash pushed his forearm harder into his chest.

"Just reach into your pocket and give me sixteen dollars and I'll leave you alone."

"I thought I knew you, man."

"How could you know me? You just met me today."

"I'm gonna get you fired for this."

Again Cash released him and Dale scurried into another trailer. Moments later the door flung open and Dale's bony body was sent crashing into the railing. He looked back with bewilderment as the door slammed shut, bang. Cash thought this was the moment to quit but he was so overcome with loathing that he followed Dale back into the trailer where they'd been playing poker. In one of the bedrooms Cash watched as Dale tried to rouse a man from sleep but the man feigned like he couldn't be woken. Cash stood with his back to the room's only door.

"Now you're trapping me?"

"Yes I am."

"You're gonna hold me hostage?"

"Until you give me my money."

Dale scanned the room and then picked up the sleeping man's phone. He dialed 911.

"Yes. Yes, I've been attacked. And now he's holding me hostage in a bedroom. Yes. I've been assaulted. You need to send the rangers. This guy's crazy. I'm in trailer forty-one in Panther Junction. Big Bend, yeah. He's right here in the room with me. He attacked me. He threw me against a table. I have blood gushing out of my head."

Cash listened as he embellished the story and then snatched the phone out of his hand and walked outside.

"Hi. This is the other guy. I'm not holding him hostage. I'm not even in the same room with him anymore. He provoked this entire thing by trying to steal my money."

Dale stood aside watching him.

"I didn't attack him. He pushed me so I pushed him back. He only knocked his head because he's too drunk to stay on his feet."

The operator told Cash to stay where he was at and to leave the other man alone. The rangers were on their way and they'd get both sides of the story. Cash hung up and slapped the phone into Dale's hand. Then he sat on the curb and waited.

He was back in court that Wednesday and this time he sat without being asked. The judge faced him looking stern and unforgiving.

"Cash Dawkins."

"Yes ma'am?"

"You know what I ought to be doing right now?"

"No ma'am."

"Shopping for turkeys. Playing with my grandchildren."

"Yes ma'am."

"If I had any evidence that you'd been drinking last night I would be dissolving your sentence reduction right now. That notwithstanding I'm charging you with disorderly conduct. This one comes with another two-hundred dollar fine."

"But your Honor. Why do I deserve this?"

"Because you caused a disturbance the other night."

"I didn't cause it. Dale caused it by trying to steal my money. Well, not try actually. He did steal my money. He still has it."

"Yes, but you became physical with him. You should have told him you were going to report it to Tommy and left it at that."

"So what you're saying is the next time somebody tries to steal something from me I should just let them do it. Say, I'm gonna tattle on you, and leave it at that?"

"It was sixteen dollars. That's not quite worth getting into trouble for."

"It was the principle, not the money."

"I understand that."

"And Dale gets away scot free?"

"Dale will be receiving the same punishment as you."

"Still, it really feels like I'm getting screwed here. A guy steals from me. He falls down and hurts himself because he's so drunk. I didn't punch him. I didn't assault him like he says. All I wanted was my money and now I'm getting fined two-hundred dollars on top of it all."

Cash was fuming. He took a deep breath.

"So what am I supposed to learn from this?"

"I guess you need to learn to pick your friends better."

"I've barely been here a month. I'd just met the guy that night."

"Stay away from poker then, I guess. In fact, you're on thinner ice than you think because gambling is illegal in the National Parks."

"There were eight other—"

"Just be quiet. I understand why you feel you're getting a raw deal on this, but you're demonstrating a pattern of recklessness. And it's such a shame too because I see what kind of potential you have. Others do too. Raymond and Tommy both told me you've been doing a great job for them. You're a confounding young man, Cash."

She leaned forward and put out her finger.

"Now I want you to listen good to the next thing I'm about to say. You're almost halfway through your probation. If I hear about you getting into any more trouble in the next seven weeks, and I mean anything, then I'm going to come down on you as forcefully as the law allows. Are we straight on that?"

"Yes ma'am."

"Good. Now get out of my sight."

Cash was shaken awake and he looked up at Manny.

"What are you doing sleeping?"

"Huh?"

"You're late."

"Ah, damnit. I forgot I picked up that shift for Joey."

"Yes, you forgot. Hurry up and get your clothes on. I'll start opening the store."

In five minutes Cash was out the door and running the road to the gas station. The sun was just rising in the east and it backlit the Sierra Del Carmen mountains and made them appear like a pale purple jawbone. At the end of the road he took the shortcut trail through the desert and when he looked off to his left he saw three mule deer running parallel to him at thirty yards.

His first customer of the day was a mangy looking man wearing an Arkansas Razorbacks hat who came walking in with a limp.

"Do ya'll have a stirefom izjiss?" he asked.

"Have a what?"

"Stirefom izejist."

"No, we don't have that. Wait, what are you asking for?"

"A styrafoam izechist."

"Oh, an ice chest."

"Uh course."

"No, we don't carry those. Sorry."

"It's alright. I figger'd it."

"You from Arkansas?"

"Yip. What about yerself?"

"Washington State."

"Ya, you soun funny."

His next customer came in and gave Cash forty dollars for gas. There was nothing useful to be done so Cash stood outside and watched the man fill his tank. When he was finished pumping the man went around the side of his truck. Cash shouted, hey wait, but the man began driving with the nozzle still stuck inside his gas tank and it ripped the hose off the breakaway and then fell onto the ground. When the man realized what he had done he slowed his truck for moment and then sped away.

Cash was reattaching the hose as Charley rode up.

"Where you off to this early?" Cash asked.

"I came down to see you."

Cash started to tell him about the strange morning he'd been having but he stopped when he realized Charley wasn't paying attention.

"What's the matter, bud?"

"It's Emma."

"Don't even tell me you got her knocked up."

"No."

"Thank God."

"I don't know what's going on with her. She won't even let me touch her anymore."

"I thought you two were regular love birds."

"So did I. And then all of a sudden it just stopped."

"She must've said something about it."

"Well. She always said she thought I was too young for her, but then what… I mean then why…"

"Why was she pouncing on you?"

"Yeah."

"Sounds like she just wanted to get frisky. I wouldn't let it eat you up. You should feel lucky she chose you. I mean that girl could've had anybody around."

"But I love her."

"Oh man. Were you guys saying that to each other?"

"No, but that's the way I feel."

Cash came over and put his arm around his brother's shoulder.

"Buddy. Buddy. You gotta see this thing for what it was. You and her had a nice little fling, but that's all there was to it. You and I are going to Florida. I mean we're down to the last week."

"I'd been thinking of staying here."

"To be with her?"

"Yeah."

"Buddy. You got way over your head on this one."

"Why doesn't she care about me? Why doesn't she care I love her?"

"The first one's always the hardest, Charley."

"Why's that?"

"Cause it's the only one you think will never end."

It was Superbowl Sunday and their last night in Big Bend. Inside the girls dormitory there was a party and most of the employees were there. Cash had been freed from his probation and he sat outside on the patio with Chuta drinking whiskey.

"Soon I retire to Mexico," he said. "You must a come and visit me. We go drinking and have dancing and big partying. Maybe a little…" He held one nostril closed and swung his head with a sniff. "You come to Mexico and we kill good time."

"I promise, Chuta. One day I'll come see you in Mexico."

"You hava my phone number," he continued. "You calla my house and you saya, Chuta, Chuta, I am in Mexico and I come and I picka you up and we hava party and my wife will a cook for us."

"I'll do it, Chuta."

"You are a nice young man. I will a miss you."

"I'll miss you too, Chuta."

"Now I know you must a watch your football so ok. No more goodbye. Just one more drink of whiskey together."

Inside the dorm, Joey was screaming at the television and Cash found Charley hovering over the chips and dip.

"Big day tomorrow," Cash said.

"You're all good with the judge?"

"Free and clear. That lady is a funny bird. She told me to come say hi if I ever make it back this way again. I actually think I would."

"I changed the oil on the bike this afternoon. And cleaned the chain."

"Did you check the tire pressure?"

"No. I forgot."

"It's alright. We'll do it in the morning."

"I can't believe we're really gonna be on the road again."

"I know. Seems like it's been ages already doesn't it?"

Charley's eyes had wandered away from the conversation and Cash followed his gaze to where it rested on Emma. She had a glass of red wine in her hand and was dancing in the hallway with two of the waitresses. Cash rubbed the back of his brother's head.

"I'd say it's just the right time we left."

"Yeah."

When the football game was over Joey said stupid and threw an empty beer can at the television. A lady yelled, bus is leaving, and the basin employees gathered their things and shuffled out for their ride.

"What time we meeting tomorrow?" Charley asked.

"Let's call it nine. We better get an early start if we wanna have any chance at San Antonio."

"Alright, see ya at nine."

"Alright, bud. Get some rest."

Charley looked back at Emma who was pouring herself a fresh glass of wine and then he walked out to the van. Cash turned to her.

"You're gonna miss your ride, girl."

"I'm staying down here tonight," she said.

She took a sip of wine and lifted her eyes to his with a look that both troubled and stirred him immensely.

Joey motioned for Cash to have a smoke with him and they

retreated to the patio. A cold front had blown down the plains from Canada and Cash zipped his leather jacket against the wintry chill. Each of them lit up and the heat and smoke of their exhalations showed as big tumbling billows.

"I've got a farewell gift you," Joey said.

He reached into the pocket of his jeans and passed him a small black switchblade.

"It's a knife," he said.

"I see that."

"Try and open it."

Cash undid the lock and then turned the knife over a few times looking for the spring mechanism. He pressed all about the knife but it wouldn't open.

"Dummy," Joey said. "Push right there."

Cash pressed at the corner and the blade flung out four inches.

"I'm sure this isn't legal."

"It's not. One of my buddies gave it to me a while back. He was a knife collector. I'd forgotten all about it but then the other day I was going through my stuff and found it at the back of my drawer and I thought, there's a lot of crazy fucks in this country. Cash might need this switchblade."

"That was very thoughtful of you, Joey."

"Remember. It's one of those last resort things. But if you've got to use it then go all the way. Stab 'em in the heart. Stab and twist. Oh, and don't forget to lock that puppy down before you put it in your pocket. I forgot one time and nearly cut my whangdoodle off."

"You oughta come out and visit us in Florida," Cash said.

"I couldn't afford it."

"If you cut your smoking and boozing in half you'd have the money inside a month. Or better yet you could just come with us. We'll stuff you in Charley's backpack. Chubby as you are I bet you'd fit."

"I'd asphyxiate myself with farts."

Cash sprayed out the mouthful of beer he'd meant to swallow and then laughed coughing as Joey slapped him on the back.

When he finally settled down Joey said, "You guys ride safe out there, okay."

"We will, Joe."

"I'm serious. I had a buddy in Maryland who got killed riding his bike."

"That's a shame."

"Closed casket, hoss. You hear me?"

"We'll be careful."

"Alright, let's go back inside and drink some blah blah. It's so cold out here my nipples are about to puncture holes in my shirt."

Emma was sitting at the kitchen island with the few stragglers leftover from the party. They all talked park gossip while Cash indulged in his alcoholic liberation with a fervor of beer. He couldn't remember a time when the mere act of drinking felt so vital. Ninety days without a drop he realized his tolerance was not what it had once been, and soon the room was fuzzy at the edges. As he continued to drown his inhibitions with beer he found himself telling bawdy and forgotten tales of his past with a charisma that brought Joey to tears more than once. He had missed this magic of liquor.

In the middle of one of his chronicles he noticed Emma had taken his leather jacket from the back of his chair and was now wearing it around the room. She tilted back the last of her wine and then came around the island. Cash felt her lift the back of his shirt and run her fingers along the small of his back. The pleasure of her feel made him close his eyes. When they opened he looked at Joey and saw he was lost in a drunk neverland.

"Take me for a ride?" she whispered in his ear.

He was thinking nothing. The girl behind him was beautiful and he simply felt the hunger of those many days he'd gone without. He motioned for her to follow him outside and she sat behind him on the motorcycle. He fired the bike and took them down the road and when he came to the gas station he stopped.

"They never asked for the keys back," he said.

He opened the door and then locked it behind them. At once they were together, her mouth pressed to his, their hands going everywhere. He stopped her.

"Where is this coming from?" he asked.

"I liked you the first time I saw you," she said. "You're so cool."

He thought to question her further but she looked so delicious there he realized he didn't have the slightest care. He removed her top and her bra and she smiled to say yes. She lifted his shirt off him and they went around the corner into the grocery room. In a few moments all their impediments had come undone and they were naked among the merchandise. Cash spun her around and bent her over among the boxes of energy bars and packaged donuts. As she felt him she moaned and sent snacks spilling to the floor. Their names cried out and echoing in the gas station dark.

The cold front that blew in the previous night had lingered through the morning and the brothers were bundled up in as many layers as they could manage. It was forty-five degrees and that was disregarding the wind chill. Even excepting the cold, it was not a charming sort of day. The sun was somewhere swinging along its low February arc, but its exact locale was murkily diffused by the overcast gray. Their bodies stayed reasonably warm but neither of their gloves amounted to much and it wasn't long before all twenty of their fingers were throbbing cold.

Thirty miles north of Panther Junction, Cash stopped for Charley who had pulled to the side of the road. Charley tore off his gloves and immediately shoved his hands down his pants, gripping the inside of his thighs.

"This is crazy," Charley said. "It was eighty degrees the day before yesterday."

"It's these plains. Nothing to stop the cold from blowing south."

"Screw the plains."

"You tell 'em."

"God, my hands hurt."

"How's that warming method working out for you?"

"Better than nothing."

Cash took off his gloves and put his hands down his pants. Alarmingly cold. Charley removed one of his hands and stuck his fingers in his mouth.

"You just had those in your crotch, dude."

Garbled by fingers he said, "You think I care?"

After ten minutes of this they resumed riding and despite the conditions Cash was glad for it because it meant he didn't have to talk. That morning he had seen that Charley knew nothing, but it didn't make him feel any better. He despised her for what she had done to them. He despised himself for being so weak. Fort Myers Beach was seventeen-hundred miles away and Cash thought that was an awfully long distance to haul a secret.

Twenty miles along they stopped again to warm their hands, and then once more in Marathon where they gassed their bikes. Afterwards Charley rifled through his pack and produced two pair of white socks. Cash watched as he pulled a pair over each hand.

"You sure that's gonna help?" Cash asked.

"No. But I know the gloves aren't doing the job."

East on Highway 90 the landscape appeared as inhospitable as any they'd yet seen. Dingy, drab and desolate. Like land that only ever took and never gave back. Perhaps on a more clement day they could have seen its finer qualities, but bearing that painful cold it was simply a portion of earth to be joylessly travailed. As his hands began to throb again Cash tried doing exercises to liven them up but the movement was only distracting so he resigned to suffer it like part of his penance. Cash looked in his rearview mirror and thought Charley's sockhands resembled two limp bunnies.

They stopped again near where the town of Longfellow had once existed. Cash brought out his pack of cigarettes and then decided it wasn't worth it. Charley had his hands down his pants again, socks and all.

"What's the next town?" Charley asked.

"Sanderson."

"Then that's where I'm quitting."

"It'd be nice to get as far as Del Rio, don't you think?"

"I don't know Del Rio. I don't care about Del Rio. I'm quitting in Sanderson."

Cash had fantasized this day of re-embarking for so long he didn't want to believe it could be spoiled by the difference of ten degrees Fahrenheit, but he realized he was of the same mind as Charley and when they came into Sanderson they rolled down Oak Street looking for a cheap hotel to hole up in for the night. They'd made one hundred and twenty-two miles and it seemed like a lot.

In the musty single-bed hotel room they cranked up the thermostat as high as it would go and wrapped themselves in colorful quilts like a pair of garish mummies. Cash made a pot of coffee and when it was finished dripping he poured himself a cup.

"I'll take a coffee," Charley said.

"Proud to see your hot chocolate days are over."

Cash left his black and watched as Charley filled his with two creamers and four packets of Splenda.

"I like coffee now."

"No, you like sugar."

Charley shrugged and Cash paced the room.

"What the hell are we gonna do with ourselves today? It's only two o'clock."

"We could look around town."

"I think we saw the whole thing already."

"I've got a deck of cards in my bag."

"Get 'em out."

Still wrapped in their quilts they sat cross-legged on the bed as Charley shuffled and dealt a hand of gin rummy. Cash drew a card and then set it on the discard pile.

"You excited for Florida?" he asked.

"I don't know. I haven't been thinking about it very much."

"I have."

"Is Cousin Spencer still gonna let us stay with him?"

Cash chuckled.

"I think you're old enough now to just call him Spencer."

"Whatever."

"Yeah. He says it's gonna work out better this way actually. Better that we're coming now than three months ago. Spencer said the tourist season really kicks off in the next few weeks."

"What kind of jobs will we have?"

"Something in a restaurant. Guess we'll find out when we get there."

Charley drew a card and studied his hand for a full minute.

"Good god, Charley. Will you make a play already."

"What's your hurry? We have all day."

Charley analyzed his options one more time and finally discarded.

"Are you gonna miss Texas?" he asked.

"No," Cash said as he drew. "I had some good times, but no. How about you?"

"Me neither. I'll just miss Emma."

His eyes went to Charley.

"What?" Charley said.

"Nothing."

"What? Why'd you look at me like that?"

"I'm just surprised to hear you say that after the way she treated you at the end."

"She really was a nice person. She left me a note this morning before she went to work that said she was sorry about the way things turned out but that she'd like to visit me in Florida sometime. That'd be cool, right?"

Cash was scowling and shaking his head.

"Charley, you need to forget about that girl."

The next morning they rode marveling at the world's capriciousness. The sky as big and blue as a map of the ocean and only clouded by little islands of white. By noon it was fifteen degrees warmer than the warmest it had been the day before. Past Langtry they crossed the bridge soaring over the Pecos River where it had dug itself a deep canyon in the bareness before the Rio Grande. Then soon after Comstock the Amistad Reservoir which shone a blinding aqueous shimmer beyond the old train trestle.

In Brackettville they lunched on fast food burgers and fries and afterwards Cash went to the restroom. A man in a cowboy hat was using the urinal so he pushed open the stall door and saw a gaunt old man squatting over the toilet with his pants around his ankles. The cowboy looked up without surprise and politely said, excuse me. Cash let the door swing shut and backed up to wait for the urinal. The man shook himself and zipped up and turned to Cash.

"Frankie there's a little touched."

"I saw the lock looked good."

"He never uses it. I bet he's not even taking a shit. Frankie? Frankie?"

"Yeah."

"Don't you know not everybody considers it an honor to see your pale legs humped over that porcelain."

"Lock don't work."

"Yes it does, Frankie."

He went in the stall and locked it and unlocked it and came back out.

"He's a little touched," the man said again. "Frankie's a regular in our congregation so I try to look out for him. My mama raised me to be a good Christian but she never explained that this would be a part of the bargain. Suppose the faith wouldna seemed as attractive."

Cash took his place at the urinal.

"I want to hear that lock now, Frankie."

After a moment there was some shuffling and then the click of the lock.

The rest of the day's ride on 90 was unremarkable and unmemorable, and they entered the beltway of San Antonio during rush hour realizing they had somewhat forgotten just how many people can live in one place. No longer were they immune from the frenetic pressure a city wreaks on its citizens, and Charley was forced by traffic to give his bike as much throttle as it could muster. Cash led them exiting into downtown and once they'd gotten their bearings they rode to a hostel on Pierce Avenue.

They'd heard of the famous river walk and they went through the neighborhood searching for it and then followed it downtown as the lights along the canal began to intensify with the coming night. Never before had either brother seen a river look so tamed and urbane the way the city crowded up against the concrete banks and created in the water a colorful and glitzy reflection. Hauling tourists, the river boats passed with gentle wakes and rippled the river into a kaleidoscope of commerce. Boisterous fat families wearing the colors of their football teams trundled into restaurants with their bags of souvenirs. Outside on the patios, mariachi bands flocked to the tables of diners who showed any interest in the pageantry of their performance.

Cash wanted no part of the gimmicky chain restaurants so they took a staircase up to the main level of the city and went into a simple soup and sandwich shop.

As they were waiting in line Cash said, "It's weird to be back in the city isn't it? Kind of overwhelming."

"I was thinking the same thing."

"This river walk is really nice but I can't stand most of these people. They look so damn soft. Like big lumps of dough. Just chitty chattering about every stupid thing."

"You mad about something?"

"I'm not mad. I'm just… Well, I don't even know what I am. Guess maybe if you spend enough time in the desert you see people's obnoxiousness more clearly. I mean imagine what would happen to these people if they ever had to fend for themselves. Power just went out permanently or something crazy. Not ten percent of them would make it. Half of them can barely walk. Just buying shit and stuffing their faces. That's all they know."

"What are you getting at, Cash?"

"Ignore me. I'm just ranting. Your turn to order."

After they'd eaten Charley asked if he was coming back to the hostel with him.

"Nah. I just want to be alone for a little bit tonight."

"You mean you don't want me around."

"Well… Look, I'll meet you back there later."

"Are you sure nothing's wrong? You've been acting kinda weird the last couple days."

"What do you mean?"

"I don't know. Just weird."

"Got a few things on my mind is all."

"Like what?"

Cash swallowed.

"Like that. You're acting weird right now."

Cash rose and dumped his garbage in the trash.

"I'll see you back at the hostel, bud."

He took the staircase back down to the canal and ordered a beer in the first bar he came to. Outside on the patio he couldn't help but notice the two strawberry blondes and he took the empty table next to them. Beauty to make him ache. He shifted his chair so he could glance at them casually and he liked everything he saw. He wanted to talk to them but he didn't know how to start. Finally he laid his arm over the back of his chair and said the first thing that came to his head.

"Are you girls from around here?" he asked.

With a tone of hostility one of them said, "Excuse me?"

"I just asked if you girls were from around here."

"Oh. I'm sorry. I thought you said something else."

"What'd you think I said?"

The girl laughed.

"I don't wanna say it now. I thought you were being lewd."

"Guess I need to enunciate better."

"We both go to school here," said the other. "How about you?"

"I'm just passing through for the night. My brother and I are riding our motorcycles across the country."

"That's awesome," said the first. "I've always wanted to do that. I ride a Gixxer."

"Bad ass chick."

"You have no idea," said the other. "She was in the Marines."

"Dangerous bad ass chick."

The girls were very interested in his adventure as they called it and they asked him many questions about the places he'd seen and about Charley. Always the girls were curious about Charley. The runaway. He told them about the night ride in the redwoods and that he'd never been more certain he would crash. He told them about Highway One and Phoenix and El Paso and they kept asking for more. When he got to explaining about how he'd ended up in Big Bend for so long the girls both agreed that he should write a book about it all someday. Then they leaned in to have a secret conference and concluded it by nodding their heads.

"We're taking you with us," the Marine said.

"Come on now. Drink up," said the other.

They led him around the corner and then up several flights of stairs to a club that looked down over the canal. It was a warm night and again they brought their drinks out onto the patio.

"So do you girls have boyfriends?"

They both said yes.

"They're lucky guys."

"And they better not forget it," the Marine said.

The other girl was stirring her drink with her cocktail straw. She stopped and said she had a question.

"I caught my boyfriend looking at porn the other day," she said.

"That's not a question," the Marine said.

"I know that, Aubrey. I'm getting to it. Well, Cash, you're a guy. I assume you've had girlfriends before. Is that normal? Looking at porn when you're in a relationship. I mean, should I be worried I'm not enough for him?"

Cash laughed. He tried to stifle himself but he kept laughing.

"I'm sorry," he said.

"It's a serious question."

"I know. I'm only laughing cause you're more than enough for any guy. If he can't see that then he's clueless."

"Yeah, but what about the porn? If I'm more than enough like you say then what's he doing jerking off to some skank on the computer?"

"Is he a good boyfriend? Is he faithful?"

"He's a great boyfriend. I hope we have kids together someday."

"Then I wouldn't worry about it. I'll bet ninety-nine percent of the guys in this world have jerked off to another woman. I'd find it strange if your boyfriend didn't once in a while."

She looked off, stewing on it.

"Ok, I've got a question," the Marine said.

"Shoot."

"What's it like having a one-night stand?"

"You mean you've never had one?"

"Never."

"Me neither," said the other.

Cash looked back and forth between the girls.

"You two are serious?"

"We've always had boyfriends."

"So really, Cash. What's it like?"

"It's exciting. You see somebody that you think is attractive and you just cut to the chase."

"You mean, cut out the chase."

"You could say it like that. Hard to generalize one-night stands though. They're all different."

"You've had a lot haven't you?" the Marine said excitedly.

"What's a lot?"

"I'd say more than five."

"Then yeah, I've had a lot."

"Tell us about the last one you had."

Cash snorted and then thrummed his fingers on the table as the girls watched him.

"Alright, I'll tell you the story," he said. "And what I'm wondering is does it make me a bad person."

The girls made ooohing sounds and leaned closer.

He told the story slowly and with great detail in the way people will when they know they have a rapt audience. All along the way they stopped him for interjections and clarifications and they would not let him continue until they were satisfied they'd understood everything thoroughly. When Cash explained the part about how heartbroke Charley had been they looked truly saddened. Then he told the last part and he tried to censor it for them but they wanted to know all the most carnal details. The Marine girl said it was making her kind of hot. Lastly he told them about the card Charley said she had left him the final morning and the other girl exclaimed, that bitch.

"She's using Charley to get to you," the Marine said.

"I'm gonna be all the way out in Florida."

"Sounds like you impressed her."

"What a bitch," the other repeated.

"But I don't get it," Cash said. "Why would she wait so long to come on to me? Why would she use Charley like that?"

"I'd say she was intimidated by you. She was probably afraid you'd reject her."

"She did invite me to go hiking with her one time. I thought she meant all of us but…"

"She was trying to get you alone."

Cash sat back and took a drink of his beer.

"So. The question is, am I bad person?"

"You're not a bad person," the Marine said. "I mean she came on to you. And you were drunk and you hadn't gotten laid in how long? Three months. That doesn't make you a bad person. Not good. But not bad."

"There's one more thing," Cash said. "It's been eating me up."

"Do you tell your brother?"

"Yeah."

The girls looked at each other to verify their feelings and looked back at him.

"I think you know you have to."

Texas goes on forever. At rest stops now Charley would ask to see the map, shaking his head despondently at the tedious progress they were making along Highway 90. He also seemed to have lost patience with his tremendous pack and he was constantly adjusting the straps and repositioning the pack on the seat behind him. When they stopped for lunch in the town of Eagle Lake, Charley leaned his pack against a garbage can and tore through it looking to shed weight. In the trash went his towel and his water bottle. A book. A shirt. He analyzed the value of the porno magazine he had found and then rolled it up and packed it.

Cash meanwhile was busy formulating the words that might exonerate him in his case before Charley. Words that could be truthful but not damning. He hadn't found them yet. When Charley was finished they went into a Mexican restaurant and ate tacos together in an awkward and heightened silence, each of them nursing the worst of their situations.

If there was a city to lift their spirits it most certainly was not Houston. They were miles yet from the skyscrapers when they hit gridlock and the brothers rode slowly through the blight of that populace reading the signs for distraction. Furniture Land Clearance Sale. New Go-Karts & Bumper Boats. Southwest Collision Center. Texas Car Title & Payday Loan. NY Sen. Chuck Schumer Insulted Houston. Properties all along the freeway were draped with American flags and defended by barbed wire. In the melee of vehicles Cash took the wrong exit for the Route 90 detour and then he missed the road that would have taken them back. In the end it took them more than two hours to get through the city.

Beaumont was where they decided to spend the night and they searched for the cheapest hotel they could find, finally pulling into a parking lot advertising rooms for twenty-nine dollars. Inside the office, the receptionist was absent and a large black man sitting in the corner smiled to show a mouth of gold teeth.

"My girl be back in a minute," he said. "She'll check you in."

Cash told the man about their long and misguided ride through Houston and he nodded with empathy.

"That place is godawful. You know what they say about Houston? They say, life's too short to live in Houston. I spent enough time there, I know that's true. My brother tried to get me to move back there after I got out of prison and I told him forget that. Told him I'd already wasted five years in the slammer. Wasn't gonna waste no more time on no Houston."

"What prison were you in?" Charley asked.

Cash looked at his brother with incredulity but the man seemed unfazed.

"Served my time in Texarkana. Not a bad prison if you got to be in one."

"Did you ever try to escape?"

Cash doubled down on his look.

"You a sneaky little FBI agent or something?" The man chuckled. "Nah, I never tried to escape. It wasn't all that bad. You know Adrian Peterson?"

"You mean the football player?"

"Running back for the Vikings. Yeah. Well me and his daddy were prison buddies. I've known Adrian since he was this high."

A skinny white woman walked into sight behind the counter

saying to the man, "The police say I can't press charges because I assaulted him." Then she noticed the brothers and turned to them with a professional tone. "How can I help you, gentlemen?"

The room they were given reeked of cigarette smoke and every piece of furniture was somehow chipped or cracked or bent. Charley opened the door to the bathroom and from it came a cacophony of toilet gurgles and pipes rattling their metallic anguish.

"Now I'm excited for Florida," Charley said.

They went out for another cheap fast-food dinner which neither of them had much enthusiasm for. When they'd finished their meals they talked some about the day's ride and then they just sat looking out opposite windows. Cash opened his mouth hoping the words would go tumbling out but nothing came. He tried again.

"There's something I've got to tell you."

Charley turned to him.

"I've been thinking about this all day and I still don't know how to say it except to just say it. The last night in Big Bend I had sex with Emma."

Charley stayed perfectly motionless. Then the tempo of his breathing rapidly quickened and he stood up clutching his tray with both hands. Cash was ready to block his advance but instead Charley spun around and began smashing the tray against the back of a chair. All the workers had turned to watch him with gawking confusion. Cash stood up and approached cautiously. He was about to intervene but Charley stopped and as he took another step toward him Charley suddenly wheeled around and threw his fist into Cash's eye socket. Cash stumbled backward and Charley dove at him and got both hands around his neck as they landed onto a table which overturned and sent the brothers toppling to the floor with a clatter of falling chairs. Cash felt his head hit the tile floor, and entangled the brothers went rolling and grabbling at each other for position. Charley was outweighed by thirty pounds and it wasn't long before

Cash had his brother's arms and legs corralled in what otherwise would have looked like an erotic embrace, the two of them panting just as heavily as if it were one.

"Give up," Cash was saying between breaths. "Give up now."

Charley was still struggling to jerk free as a man who'd been eating a cheeseburger in the corner came over and said, "I watched the manager call the cops. I'd get out of here quick if I were you two."

Back in their seedy room Cash waited for his brother to return. Outside the restaurant Charley had raced away on his bike and Cash had thought it wise to let him be, but now two hours had passed and Charley was not answering his phone. Cash paced from wall to stained wall as he repeatedly opened and closed the switchblade. He had just smoked a cigarette ten minutes ago but he lifted his pack from the bedside table and went outside for another. Down at the back end of the hotel Cash saw a police cruiser parked in front of room 121 and an officer questioning a woman at the door. Then he noticed through the windows of the cruiser the black two-fifty motorcycle parked at a lean. He sighed with relief and walked down the parking lot.

As he approached the cruiser he heard the officer asking the woman, "You're sure you don't know where I can find Mr. Adams tonight?"

"I already told you," she said. "I never heard of him."

The officer struggled to remain patient.

"Ma'am, we know you've been associated with Mr. Adams. If you continue to lie to me you're gonna find yourself in some serious trouble. Now I'm gonna ask you one more time. Where can I find Mr. Adams?"

As Cash drew even with the room the woman lifted her head and met Cash's eyes with a look like she was seeking his guidance. From behind the cruiser Cash heard the woman say with resolution, "I don't know him."

Charley's bike was parked outside room 125 and he knocked twice. He heard the bed springs squeaking and then the door opened to the end of the chain lock.

"Leave me alone," Charley said

"I just came over to give you this."

Cash removed the switchblade from his jacket and held it out in his palm like a peace offering. Charley only stared at it.

"Take it quick before this cop sees. Take it."

Charley took the knife.

"You press right there at the—"

"I know how it works."

"Good."

For a long moment they stared at each other through the six-inch slit and then Cash nodded and went back to his room.

Cash woke wondering how his pillow could be causing him so much pain. Then he sat up and felt the lump on the back of his skull and. remembered the fall he'd taken in the restaurant. Groggily he went into the bathroom and flipped on the light. In the mirror the underside of his eye showed purple and swollen. After he was dressed and packed he returned his room key and poured two cups of bitter hotel coffee. At room 125 he kicked the door twice and Charley opened it wide and stood there evaluating Cash's face.

"You like your handiwork?" Cash asked.

"I don't feel bad about it."

"Rub the back of my head," Cash said. "Gently."

Charley felt the lump.

"I beat you up pretty good, didn't I?"

"You did alright. Just don't be expecting a stranger to hold back anything on you."

"One of those coffees for me?"

"This one's about half sugar. Probably still gonna taste like shit though."

Charley took the coffee and went inside to finish loading his pack. Cash was waiting outside for him smoking a cigarette when the door to the next room opened. A middle aged man came out and stretched and then noticed Cash.

"Say, you wouldn't have any rolling papers would you?" he asked.

"How many do you need?"

"One or two. Just enough to roll a joint."

When Charley was ready the brothers saddled up and headed for the highway. They had spoken no more of the fight. Nor of Emma. Over the Sabine River they rode into Louisiana and watched the land turn swampy and dank. Beyond the town of Sulphur they came upon a SWIFT semi-truck and saw that someone had fingered an alternative acronym into the dirty film on the rear doors. SURE WISH I'D FINISHED TRAINING. When they passed they saw the driver singing with much animation to the radio. Lake Charles was next and they took the bridge gazing down at the ten-story casino and the two gambling riverboats and then went on through the Cajun heart of Louisiana.

They rode into New Orleans just before sundown and checked into a hostel in the Garden District, five blocks from the Mississippi River. After their customary showers the brothers brought their toiletries back into the dormitory. Cash changed into his nicest clothes while Charley was pulling on his simple black t-shirt.

"Why don't you put on your nice button up," Cash said.

"What for?"

"For New Orleans, buddy. Can't have you looking like a slouch tonight."

"Are you saying you're inviting me out with you?"

"That's what I'm saying."

"You're gonna sneak me into the bars?"

"I'll try."

"You don't have to do that."

"I want to."

"You really want me to come?"

"Yes."

"Are you just doing this because you feel bad?"

"Charley, you sound like a woman right now. Just put on your nice shirt and let's roll."

On the next bunk over a small handsome guy was sprawled out on his bed and reading a magazine. Cash leaned toward him.

"Say man, you know the best way to get to the French Quarter?"

The guy looked up from his magazine and spoke with a British accent.

"I'd hop on the streetcar if I were you."

"And how do we find that?"

"Heading there meself. I can show you the way."

"Yeah, that'd be cool."

"Pardon me for asking, but what happened to your eye, mate?"

Cash thought about it for a moment.

"Just had a little accident."

Along with the Brit, the brothers picked up a chubby young Aussie and the four of them took the antique looking trolley downtown. On the ride, Cash asked about the Brit's story and he explained that after college he'd gone into finance for several years.

"I was in a venture capital space. Specializing in debt. Later I joined a leveraged finance group at a bulge bracket bank and . . ."

He noticed their stares.

"You have no idea what I'm talking about. I'm sorry. I start rattling this stuff off like I'm back in London. Basically, I was a money whore and I gave it up a few months ago. My plan now is to just travel the world for as long as the money lasts. If I'm real frugal I might make it a year."

Cash whistled.

"Damn, boy. You must've been hauling in some dough."

"I did well. People back home thought I was crazy for leaving, but I just couldn't do it any longer."

"What'll you do once you get back to England?"

"That's what I intend to find out. All I know is that I hate finance."

The streetcar let them off at Bourbon Street and they strolled their way through the throngs of tourists. Charley was obviously enchanted by New Orleans and he was swinging his head up and around everywhere like he wanted to capture it all. "I've never seen anything like this," he kept saying. A woman went past sipping alcohol out of a foot-tall lime-colored container and the Aussie pointed and said, "I want one of those things." When they found a vendor the Aussie bought four and passed them around.

"They're called hand grenades," he announced. "Isn't that great?"

Down Bourbon Street they continued. Charley looking paranoid now as he sipped his drink.

"Stop that," Cash told him.

"What if a cop sees me?"

"How's he gonna know you're underage if he does? Look, you just gotta be cool. If you see a cop, don't look at him. But don't not look at him either, you know what I mean?"

"No."

"Okay. Instead, why don't you pretend you're twenty-one already. No reason for a cop to stop you. You're twenty-one."

"But I know I'm only eighteen."

"Work with me, brother. In fact, take a couple big sips of that drink. Summon some swagger."

Charley sucked and gulped and did it again.

"This is the easy part," Cash said. "Hard part's gonna be sneaking you in."

The Brit suggested they might have more luck getting Charley into a bar somewhere off Bourbon Street so they began wandering through the French Quarter. Crowds of people everywhere. One herd of tourists huddled around a raving middle-aged woman as she called out to the rooftops summoning the wayward spirits to show themselves. Down the street forty people queued up outside a shop advertising gumbo. They kept walking until they came to Frenchmen Street where there was a string of bars all hopping with live shows. Cash scouted out each of the joints while the group waited at the corner and he came back saying they all had bouncers.

"May as well try whichever one looks best to you guys," he said.

They chose their target based on the most appealing music, a well-lit bar with a jazz band and plenty of people bouncing their heads to the jaunty rhythm.

"How's this gonna work?" the Brit asked.

"You guys just go on in," Cash said. "I don't wanna get you in trouble."

"Ah, come on, mate. I don't care if they catch us. We're not coming back here again."

Cash looked to the Aussie and he shrugged to say he didn't care either.

"Alright then, here's what we'll do," Cash said. "I'll go first from the left side and try and get the bouncer to turn away from the door while he's checking my ID. You two guys go next and just stand there on his right, shoulder to shoulder. Charley, you duck in behind and use them as a shield. Hopefully the bouncer won't even notice you at all. As soon as I get him to turn for my ID, you go for it, Charley. Got it?"

"Got it."

"What happens if he doesn't turn for you?" the Aussie asked.

Cash thought about it.

"Drop your ID," the Brit said. "Make it look genuine and he'll look down at it."

"Yep. That'll work. Charley, it's on you to time this right. And don't run in. Just take a couple long steps until you're in the crowd."

"And what do we do if this plan goes to shit?" the Aussie asked.

"Run away."

Charley was grinning.

"This is fun," he said.

Cash waited until the bouncer was distractedly texting and then signaled for them to move. Each of them played their positions as they'd planned, but Cash had a gut feeling it wasn't going to work. Several paces out the bouncer suddenly stood up from his stool and ran away down the sidewalk. Cash motioned for Charley but he was already inside. The three of them watched the bouncer cross the street and continue running.

"That was weird," the Brit said.

Just inside the entrance the band stood atop a low stage and played a frolicking high-tempo jazz led by the drummer and the pianist. The bassist was wrapped around his instrument as he bobbed his head dripping sweat. The saxophonist provided the hooks and flairs. Every once in a while an elderly man at the corner of the stage would raise his trumpet and join the sax for an exclamation mark or two and stand still again. The band then shifted down a gear and only the drummer played to allow space for a solo. Cash expected the saxophonist to step forward but instead it was the old trumpeter who did. As he raised the trumpet his eyes closed and he took a deep inhale. His first blow burst out like a sudden feral barrage and all around the crowd people were applauding and sharing looks of astonishment. The old man smiled and winked at someone or everyone and then followed his initial salvo with a stream of brassy vigor that befitted a man one-quarter his age. When he was nearly finished he signaled to the others and they picked up on their refrain as the old man drifted back to the corner of the stage.

Cash was beside himself.

"Can you believe that guy, Charley? He must be eighty years old."

A man standing in front of Cash turned and said, "He's eighty-four."

When the band finished their song the crowd cheered and hooted and several people went up to shake the old trumpeter's hand as the band broke down their equipment.

Next on the stage was a young and all-black band that played tight and easily digestible songs. They were all talented musicians, but their songs lacked any real improvisation. Every tangent to the main flow seeming contrived and premeditated. Best of the group was the tall and muscular saxophonist who riffed with great speed and precision but who always gave up his turn before he'd taken his listeners anywhere. It was evident that he was bored with the music and several times when it was another player's solo Cash spotted him checking his smart phone. The band was fine to listen to if music was just pleasant sound, but Cash believed he knew better and he herded the group on to another scene.

Drunk now, they went down Bourbon Street as the Aussie began insisting they visit a strip club. They stopped out front a club advertising free entry, Charley's eyes big with excitement.

"Alright," Cash said. "We'll give it a shot. Charley, you take my ID. After five or ten minutes one of you two come back out and hand it to me."

"I don't have any one-dollar bills," Charley said.

"Just don't do anything but sit there until I get inside, ok?"

Cash watched as the three of them went up to the door and he was pleased to see the bouncer barely even looked at their IDs. Five minutes later the Brit returned.

"Let's not go in together," Cash said. "Pretend like you're using that ATM for a couple minutes."

The Brit walked off and Cash handed his ID to the bouncer who looked at the date of birth and looked at Cash and said, "Have fun."

Cash took the stairs up to the club and saw Charley and the Aussie sitting front and center before one of the stages as a well-endowed brunette sashayed toward them squeezing two handfuls of breasts together. As Cash drew near he watched Charley stand up and approach the stage holding out a ten dollar bill.

"Excuse me," Charley said. "Do you have change for a ten?"

Cash expected some sort of rebuke but the woman smiled and said, "Sure, honey." She passed Charley his change and he laid two dollar bills on the edge of the stage.

"Not like that," said the Aussie. "Like this."

He held out a dollar and the woman danced her way over to him, spun, and shook her ass. When she stopped the Aussie tucked a bill into her thong.

"Yeah, that was better," Charley said.

Cash took a seat next to them as a surly old Asian lady came over and asked him what he wanted to drink.

"Whiskey and water."

"What do you want to order for your friends?" she said. "They say only water, but it is two drink minimum so I must charge five dollars for water."

"Just get 'em each a beer."

"Okay, but you all must order two drinks or I must charge for nothing."

"Okay, lady. I get it."

Soon after, he felt fingers slide down the back of his neck and he turned as two dancers in bikinis came around and sat on the edge of their chairs. One of them trying to conceal her age with an overabundance of makeup. The other a young and pudgy black girl.

"What do you say to a dance?" the black girl asked Cash.

"Not right now."

She tried to pout but she was a poor actress and she knew it so she just sat there in silence for a while. The older dancer was more aggressive and she was hounding the Aussie. Cash heard her say she needed these dances to provide for her daughter, but the Aussie looked not one bit interested. He got up and took a seat on the other side of the room watching Sportscenter highlights.

"You know, you look just like Tom Brady," the black girl tried.

Cash laughed.

"And you're buddy over there looks like he's at home on the couch."

Cash looked at the Aussie slouched below the television and he laughed again.

"He does, doesn't he?"

"What's his deal?"

"I have no idea. He was the one that got us to come in here."

The girl looked at Cash more closely and said, "What happened to your eye?"

"I fell down some stairs."

"Oh, come on. I'm a stripper. I've seen a lot of black eyes and not one of them was because someone fell down the stairs. I hope the other guy got it worse."

"Look for yourself. There he is right there," Cash said pointing.

"Him? He's just a baby."

"No," Cash shook his head. "Not anymore."

"How did it happen?"

"Let's just say I got what was coming to me."

Cash could see her running through all the possibilities, but whether she was clairvoyant enough to know she didn't reveal. Instead she put her hand on his thigh.

"You sure you don't want a dance, sweetie? I'll make it special for you."

"I'll tell you what. That baby over there's my brother and it's his first time. I'll pay you to give him a dance."

"Boy, you must've done something pretty rotten to be buying him the dance when you're the one with the black eye."

Cash reflected on it.

"Funny thing is I think he's already over it. I'm the one that still feels bad."

He opened his wallet and gave the girl a twenty dollar bill.

"This should cover it, right?"

She took the money and then leaned in and kissed him on the cheek below his swollen eye.

"You're a nice guy," she said. "Just hang on a minute now. I'm gonna get Nateesha to double up with me and really give your brother a ride."

Nateesha was tall and thin and very black, and she along with the other girl led Charley to a padded chair against a mirrored wall. He looked back at Cash who held his hands out to signify he was welcome. When the next song started the girls commenced to strip and gyrate in a graceful unison and then took turns atop Charley's lap. He seemed not to know whether to grin or act unaffected. The girls then devised a way to straddle him at the same time, and as small as Charley was he looked like some gawky and immature new emperor becoming acquainted with the spoils of his inheritance.

From between Nateesha's legs Charley held out a thumbs up.

The brothers slept without stirring through all the morning commotion in the dormitory and they would have easily stayed down past noon had Cash's alarm not pierced his boozy stupor. After much bickering with his blankets Cash finally swung his legs onto the floor and lifted himself with unsteady legs. He felt not so much hungover as just plain drunk still. On the top bunk Charley had kicked and twisted his bedding into such disorder he appeared to have been dreaming of anarchy. Cash gave him a shake and Charley's eyes shot open with crazy alarm like a rabbit lying in the forest that had not heard or smelled the hunter until he was upon it. Charley groaned.

"I don't feel good," he said.

Cash passed him his nalgene and Charley took a sip.

"Don't get out of bed until you've drank that whole thing."

Once they were packed and fueled with coffee they rode out of New Orleans under a sky all whipped with the sort of white and freehanging clouds that could be named any shape depending on the person naming. I-10 took them across the eastern estuary of Lake Pontchartrain, the water glass placid and splotched with the clouds in depthless reflection. There was very little traffic on the freeway and for many miles they followed a semi through the marshy lowland of coastal Mississippi. Billboards advertised the casinos in Biloxi. Small unidentifiable rodents moldered on the roadside in their neverwaking pelts. A blue heron flapped across the freeway in laborious flight.

The brothers crossed into Alabama and shortly after came into the modest port city of Mobile. The George C. Wallace Tunnel ran them under downtown and under the ship canal with the sound of their engines reverberating. They resurfaced riding the Bayway viaduct along Mobile Bay, their motorcycles buffeting with the wind blowing off the Gulf. They'd been riding hard since New Orleans and they pulled off to rest at the Battleship Parkway interchange. Cash paced the gravel lot smoking while Charley threw rocks at a rusty oil drum.

"You know how close we are to Florida?" Cash shouted.

"How close?"

"Really close."

Charley flung another rock which flew over the top of the oil can and went skipping into the bay.

"Like today, close?" Charley asked.

"Like this hour, close."

"We've just about rode the whole continent, haven't we?"

"Just about."

"And you thought my bike would never make it."

Charley hurtled another rock and hit the oil can with a dull clang.

"Okay, we can go now," he said.

Beyond Pensacola they began the flat and monotonous ride through the pinewoods of the Florida Panhandle. Endless trees hedging the freeway and offering only the view of more freeway and more trees. In their rearview mirrors the brothers watched the sun dipping into the horizon as it slid along the spectrum from yellow to orange to red like an ember burning down to greater purity. At last light the forest wore the palest wreath of violet and then the night went black.

In Ponce de Leon they gassed their bikes and debated how much further to ride.

Cash said he wanted to make Tallahassee, but even as he was saying so he knew he didn't have the will to ride another hundred miles, especially in the dark. Lodging was almost nonexistent along 1-10 so when they came to Highway 77 they rode it up to the town of Chipley and then continued east on Highway 90 looking for a decent place to settle in for the night. Cottondale didn't look like much so they carried on. Cash could feel his concentration waning. He looked back to see how Charley was doing and when he looked forward again there was a deer captured in his headlight. He stomped on his rear brake and the back end of his motorcycle instantly swung out until he was nearly perpendicular to the direction he'd been going. As he slid he could hear the tires scraping against the asphalt, every atom in his body suddenly focused on staying on two wheels. He let off the brake and the motorcycle mostly righted itself. Lost to the headlight, the deer bounced once and took off at a sprint as Charley whizzed past Cash and then threw his head around. Cash's heart seemed to have temporarily forgotten its task and now it caught up for it with huge drumming beats. The whole thing had lasted about three seconds. They pulled over to the shoulder.

"Are you okay?" Charley asked.

"I'm fine."

"You almost hit that deer."

"Yeah, no shit, Charley."

The next town was Marianna and Cash checked them into a sixty-dollar hotel room along the main road. Around the corner was a Chinese Buffet and the brothers went in ravenous and looking to get their money's worth. A small lady appearing more Japanese than Chinese awaited them just inside the entrance and she led them with much nodding and gesturing to a table along the window saying, 'This way please. Yes. Come. Table is there for you. Yes. Please sit.'

It was an impressive spread for a ten-dollar buffet, and the brothers returned with their plates mounded over with fried rice, steamed vegetables, orange chicken, general tso's chicken, sweet and sour pork, crab legs and several cuts of sushi. They took their seats and watched each other's plates steaming.

"This is gonna be good," Charley said.

"Watch me make mine disappear."

They ate with great relish and very little small talk. An elderly Asian man, presumably the owner, approached near the end of their meal with his hands clasped behind his back and asked how everything was tasting. Charley chewed rapidly and hurried a swallow.

"This place is awesome," he said.

"Very good," the man bowed with obvious pleasure. "That is always what I like to hear."

They expected him to turn but instead he motioned to their helmets and packs which they'd placed atop the other chairs and leaned against the wall.

"You must be very brave young men," he said. "How far do you ride?"

Cash waited to see if Charley would answer and he did.

"Oh, we've come a long ways now, my brother and me. Do you know where Washington is at?"

"Of course. That is very far to ride. The capital is many many hours from here."

"No, not the capital. We rode from Washington state."

The old man looked at Cash and then back at Charley.

"This . . . No, this is too far. You must be joking to me."

"Lots of people say that. Don't they Cash? Lots of people don't believe it, but we sure did it."

Charley looked puffed up and proud and it made the old man smile to watch him.

"When I was a young man like you I have a... What do you call it? A small motorcycle?"

"A scooter."

"Yes. A scooter. When I was a young man in Japan I have a scooter that I ride around in the city so that I can carry groceries and these things, you know. One time I ride up into the mountains. Is it okay to tell a story?"

"We like to hear any story if it's about riding."

"It is maybe a long story so you tell me if you get bored. Yes? So in the summer one year I ride my scooter up into the mountains. For adventure. Like you. That day it was very hot in the city so I was only wearing shorts and a shirt. No armor like you. No boots. Only sandals. You see? I ride that day farther than I ever have ride before. I start to get very high into the mountains and it begins to be very cold. Even though it was very hot in the city it was cold in the mountains and then it begins to rain. I stopped then and I thought to turn around but I was close to the, how do you say it? The top of the mountain?"

"The peak?"

"Yes. Something like this. I was very near the peak of the mountain and I wanted to see it because it was very famous for its beauty and because there was a temple there. So I say to myself, I will keep going. I ride higher and higher and then it starts to snowing. Again I repeat, it is the summer. And it is snowing. And I am wearing sandals. But I cannot stop now because I am so close. I become like crazyman to see the peak and the temple. I am thinking that every corner will be the last and I will see the temple but there are more corners and more snow and it is so slippery that I have my sandals on the ground and I am using them like they are skis. You see? This is crazy. One time I fall and the scooter it almost slides off the mountain. I get wet and I start to shake and there is no other people traveling so I start to be very afraid that maybe this was a bad idea. Maybe this will become the worst thing. You know what I mean?"

"Like that you might die?"

"Yes. That I might die. But obviously this does not happen. Finally I go around another corner and I see the temple and I am happy. There are bigger words for this I don't know. I am very happy. I go in the temple and the monks they see how I have come to them and they wrap me in blankets and they give me soup and they tell me I must sleep the night there. So now that I am at the temple I am very happy that I did not quit. Later I am even more happy because they say the master of the temple would like to see me. I think that maybe he will tell me I am very brave for coming in the snow on the scooter. Skiing with sandals, like this. But instead the master tells me something different. That night the master tells me that I must not ride the scooter anymore. I ask him why. I am very young like you and I think maybe he has powers to know my future. I ask him if he has these powers and he says that he does not need them to tell me this. He says that I must not ride the scooter because anyone who is so foolish to ride a scooter up a mountain in a storm of snow will not live long enough to raise his own children."

At this the old man stopped.

"So that was your last time on the scooter?" Charley asked.

The old man's mouth pulled up into a smile.

"No. After this I ride for many years and it always was my favorite thing. After this I learn that no person knows what will happen to any other person. Even a master of a temple, he doesn't know. Maybe only one person knows what will happen, and that is the person who must decide to ride the motorcycle."

The brothers were hushed as they let the story sink in.

"I only say one more thing," the old man said. "My wife, she bake the chocolate cake herself. If you have any more stomach left you must try."

Once again they'd gotten a hotel room with only one bed and after dinner they reclined against the headboard side by side watching the end of a basketball game. Afterwards they waited for the local nightly news to see if there was anything worth knowing about the weather, but there wasn't. They learned there had been a rash of burglaries in Panama City and when it went to commercial Cash turned off the television.

"Cash?"

"Yeah?"

"Do you ever think that we might die on our motorcycles?"

"No," he lied.

"Even though you almost crashed today?"

"It wasn't that close."

"You were sideways at fifty miles an hour."

"I was in control."

"I don't know. I think it could happen, maybe."

"Do you think about this a lot?"

"Sometimes. Not a lot."

"I don't think it's good to think about it too much."

"Do you remember that night in the redwoods? When we rode through all that rain?"

"Of course."

"Did you ever think that we might have crashed that night?"

"I guess I did."

"Cause I know I did. I was really scared. And we just kept riding and riding because there was nowhere to stop, you know. I could barely see anything and even though I thought I might crash I had to keep riding."

"It was my fault, Charley. We could have stopped."

"It's okay. I'm not blaming you or anything. It's just . . ."

Cash waited.

"It's like there's some things you don't get to quit just because you're scared. Kinda like that old guy's story tonight. Even if you think you might die, you don't just quit."

"This isn't war. We're just riding motorcycles, Charley. You can quit whenever you want."

"Yeah, but what kind of person would that make you?"

"What are we even talking about here, Charley? Were you thinking about quitting?"

"No way."

"Then what are we even talking about?"

"I don't know. Hypothetical stuff."

Outside their room a car door slammed shut and they heard a woman cackle a hoarse smoker's laugh.

"Cash?"

"Yeah?"

"Well, I was wondering. I mean, I'm just wondering. Do you really not believe in God or do you just say that to seem tough or something?"

"What makes you ask that?"

"One time I heard you tell Tom that you didn't."

Cash just looked at the far wall.

"Well?" Charley asked.

"No. I really don't."

Charley nodded.

"I'm starting to wonder if I do either," he said. "But I'd like to believe I always could."

"I'm not sure that makes sense."

"I guess I just wonder if I might need it when I get older."

"Like you're gonna grow into believing in God?"

"It works that way for some people."

"I think it usually works the other way around."

Charley frowned with consideration.

"It is nice to think there's someone watching over us though, don't you think?"

"Just feels a little cheesy to me."

"Well. I think I'm not gonna make a decision on that one yet."

"Good," Cash said. "Now are there any other hypothetical questions you'd like to ask me before I shut off this light?"

"No."

"Okay good."

He pulled the brass chain and the light expired. Within moments he felt himself drifting into slumber.

"Cash?"

A moment later.

"Cash?"

"What?"

"There's a fly in the room somewhere."

"Please go to sleep."

"I can hear it buzzing."

They entered Tampa at sundown the day following. The sky gone raspberry pink and tangerine and the city awash in those colors. They'd been riding hard for hours and Cash turned into a parking lot so they could stretch their legs. Down the boulevard, cars hurried toward the towers of Tampa which seemed to rise higher each one after the other in a slantwise echelon. Cash brought out his pack of smokes and lit a cigarette. Charley pointed across the street.

"You see those?" he said.

"Yeah."

"Those are palm trees."

"I know it."

"Palm trees, Cash. We did it. I mean, we really did it."

Charley danced a giddy shuffle of celebration.

"Come here you maniac," Cash said.

He flicked his cigarette half smoked to the ground and wrapped his arms around his brother.

"We really did it, Charley."

From a passing truck full of teenage boys someone shouted at them, fags, and Cash held out his middle finger.

"Can't savor nothing in this world can you?"

"Who cares about them?"

"You're right. Who cares?"

Cash checked his phone.

"Well, it's six-thirty. What do you want to do?"

"How many more miles to Spencer's place?"

"About a hundred and forty."

"That's not so far."

"It's a good chunk though. We've already done three-hundred and some."

"I feel fine."

"After four months it's not like one extra day's gonna make a difference."

"We're so close. Let's just finish it off."

Cash thought about it.

"Spencer's not expecting us until tomorrow, but… Ah, what the hell. Let's do it."

He dialed for Spencer and after a number of rings it went to his voicemail.

"Charley and I are in Tampa, cousin. I thought we were gonna stay, but we decided we wanna finish this journey off tonight. Guess you must be working so we'll just cruise over to your place. It's six-thirty now . . . I'd say we'll get there about ten or so. Fort Myers Beach, baby! We'll see you soon."

Cash put his phone in his pocket.

"Hope he leaves his door unlocked."

They rode those final miles as though it were a victory parade, feeling like they'd at last conquered the continent. Which in a way they had. Four months and four-thousand miles they'd stowed their lives on those bikes, and now they were arriving. If never they'd known the euphoria of a great accomplishment they knew it now, and fatigued as deep down they were from so many days and hours of balance and concentration, their minds were reeling with visions of the fantastic and now present days to come. As they rolled through the February night, the tropical warmth seemed a ruffling and tangible reward.

They found Spencer's coul-de-sac long after ten and they pulled up to the dark house and parked in the empty driveway. Cash tried the front door but it was locked. He saw he'd received no call or text from Spencer. He called his cousin but again it went to voicemail. With their packs in tow they opened the gate at the side of the house and took the pathway around to the back. They stopped when they came to the swimming pool. A floating mattress and an inner tube there in the shallow end. Snorkeling gear strewn about the concrete pad. In the yard two bright yellow kayaks lay overturned and beside them was an inflatable party raft replete with beer cozies that they'd only ever seen in commercials. Beyond this ran the canal Spencer had spoken of and lining the canal were large pleasure boats and behind them many houses which bordered on being mansions. The brothers looked at each other.

"Looks like we got a water park in our backyard now," Cash said.

"And all the cool toys."

"Don't get all hysterical on me now."

"I'm gonna jump in."

"Let's just wait until Spencer gets home before we get too carried away."

Cash tried the back door, but it also was locked. He looked in through the windows and saw the big open kitchen and the nice hardwood floors.

"It's small compared to the neighbors, but it looks pretty damn slick in there."

"You sure it's locked?" Charley asked. "I have to pee."

"I'm sure."

Charley went and stood before some bushes and a moment later the leaves were splattering.

"Can you make that any quieter? I don't want the neighbors suspicious of us on day one."

"It just sounds like I'm watering them."

"It sounds like you're peeing, Charley. Hurry up."

Charley aimed his stream at the soil but it was just as loud and it did not stop.

"Jesus, dude. When's the last time you took a leak?"

"I like to hold it sometimes."

"Why would you do that?"

"To see if I can break my record."

"I'm not even going to spoil you with curiosity."

Cash took a seat in one of the cushioned lawn chairs and put his feet up. He closed his eyes and it felt wonderful. When Charley was finished he adjusted his chair so that it would recline farther and then sat alongside his brother. From the canal they heard the faint splash of a jumping fish. Then another. On the wall a thermometer shaped like a clock read seventy-two degrees and the brothers soon drifted to sleep.

Seemingly only moments later they awoke to the sound of a gigantic splash that most certainly was not a jumping fish. Cash sprang forward in the lawn chair as his cousin emerged from the turmoil he'd created in the pool. Spencer wiped the water from his face and stood shoulder-deep and grinning. Cash walked to the edge of the pool.

"We made it," he said.

"I see that. Looks like the trip got the best of you."

"Just resting the eyes."

"Like hell. You were both snoring."

Spencer looked off to Cash's side and nodded and Cash turned just as Charley gave him a shove into the pool. Cash toppled over slowly and he came up cussing at his brother.

"Goddamnit, Charley. My wallet was in my pocket."

"Ooops," Charley said.

Cash pulled himself out of the pool and went stalking after Charley who scampered around flinging his shoes and clothes into the grass. When Cash finally got to him, Charley was already down to just his underwear and he dodged Cash by leaping in on his own. Cash sat down at the edge of the pool and began laying his sodden dollars out to dry.

Charley swam over to Spencer who gave him a stylized handshake and said, "So how do you like my pad, little cousin?"

"It's alright."

"What? Only alright?"

"Well. If I'm honest I'm kind of disappointed you don't have a water slide."

Puzzled by the diss, Spencer looked toward Cash who was drying his debit card with a towel.

"He's kidding," Cash said. "You'll have to get used to a child's sense of humor."

"Cash thinks he's my dad now," Charley said.

Spencer looked between the two of them.

"You guys sound like you've spent an awful lot of time together."

"An awful lot," Cash repeated.

Spencer laughed and he splashed Charley.

"Guys, it's great to have you here finally. I can't believe you really rode those bikes all the way from Longview. Crazy. And guess what, Charley?"

"What?"

"I've got a couple surprises for you guys."

"Oh yeah? What are they?"

"You'll find out tomorrow. I'm taking you on a little field trip."

They sat on wooden benches in the small ferry boat listening to instructions from the captain. The brothers outfitted with flip-flops and flashy Hawaiian board shorts. Spencer pouring the contents of his flask into three red solo cups while the scruffy first mate demonstrated how to don the lifejackets. When these preliminaries were through the captain made some stale and hackneyed joke, waited for someone to laugh, and fired up the motor.

Once they were outside the harbor the captain accelerated and the boat began to grumble and shudder along the hull. Cash leaned over the gunwale and felt the salt breeze blowing against his face. It was one fine day to be out on the water, the sun beaming and the sky a pure blue yawn from Punta Gorda to the emerald Gulf horizon. The ferry then angled west and they began to follow a shimmering path of sunwater that shone like ten million diamonds in a great jeweler's glare. Pelicans had followed a school of fish into these mesmeric waters and they were everywhere plunging for food with the sound of many mini explosions. Cash observed three of the pelicans working in collaboration and he watched as they flapped up to a great height, banked around sharply and then swooped down, all in perfect formation. They were soaring without a wingbeat inches above the water when at precisely the same moment each pelican tucked its wings back, tilted forward and struck at their prey with terrific splashes. Bobbing there in the water, two of the pelicans lifted their beaks to the sky and sent the fish down their webbed gullets with spasming movements like they were retching.

As they approached the island the captain explained that they were about to enter Cayo Costa State Park. It was a very special place, he said. One of the few locations in Florida that was not for sale. There was no way to access the island except for boat and the few permanent residents lived without paved roads or an electrical grid. The captain said he considered himself a steward of Cayo Costa and he hoped those visiting would view themselves in the same light. Then, just before they docked, the captain reminded his passengers that though the island wasn't for sale, he and his first mate were, and on that cue the first mate gestured to their gratuity jar.

They were shuttled from the boat to the campground on a wooden trolley towed behind a park service truck, the road a primitive and rutted dirt track through a forest of palm trees. At the campsite they found Spencer's huge dome tent and much evidence of his friends, including bras hanging from a tree branch, but they were all elsewhere.

"Probably out kayaking," Spencer said. He tossed their bags in the tent and then asked, "Well, boys, you ready to hit the beach?"

"Cousin, we've been waiting four months to hear you say that," Cash said.

They took a sandy path to the ocean and soon came alongside a small lagoon. Charley sprinted toward it and when Spencer saw that he intended to jump in he screamed for him to stop. Charley was at the water's edge and he turned and held his hands up.

"Can't you read?" Spencer said.

"Read what?"

"That sign right there."

"What does it say?"

"That this lagoon you were about to jump in is full of alligators."

"Yikes."

"Stick to the ocean, okay."

When they reached the beach the brothers dropped their towels in the sand and bounded toward the ocean, leaping with shallow dives into the first rolling wave. Cash resurfaced with the taste of salt in his mouth and he swam arm over arm with powerful strokes straight into the sea deep. Once he could feel his heart beating he turned and floated on his back. The swells lifting him rhythmically as he stared into the sky. With his ears submerged all he could hear was a muted churning. The ocean warm as bathwater. He closed his eyes and without those prime senses the world seemed restored to embryonic simplicity. There was not one scrap of thought in his brain. Nothing but those swells. Endless rise and fall. He felt something almost electric tingle through him gently and he held it, savored it, knew it wouldn't last. The simplest bliss.

Then he opened his eyes and the world seemed somehow strangely real. He watched Charley and Spencer wrestling in the shallows. Saw a naked child scooping sand into a pile. The contrail of a jet hanging white across the heavens. He closed his eyes again hoping he could revisit wherever he'd just been, but it was gone now and he swam back to shore with a slow and easy pace.

Back on the beach they lay their towels out all in a row and let the sun dry them at its leisure.

Charley turned to Spencer and asked, "So what will my job be?"

Spencer winced.

"I'm sorry, bud. All I could get you was a dishwashing gig."

"Really?"

"I'm sorry."

"Crap."

Charley dropped his face into the sand and left it there. He groaned and then spoke into the ground.

"First a garbage man. Now a dishwasher. All the worst jobs for Charley."

He rocked his head some while mumbling indecipherably and then he sat back upright again looking terribly depressed. Sand stuck to his forehead. Cash and Spencer were both grinning.

"Is my misery funny to you two?"

"Spencer's pulling your leg, bud."

"You're gonna be a buser, not a dishwasher," Spencer said.

"You mean, the guys who clean the tables?"

"That's right."

"And fill waters and bring bread out and stuff like that," he said, his mood already looking much improved.

"Busers get a share of the tips, Charley. They make pretty good money."

"Like how much?"

"Fifteen bucks an hour. Maybe twenty on a really good night." Charley's eyebrows shot up.

"Impressed?"

"That's twice what I was making in Texas."

"How about me?" Cash asked. "Will I be a buser too?"

"Server."

"You mean like a waiter?"

"It's the same thing."

"What the hell do I know about waiting tables?"

"Jack shit, I'm sure."

"Does this GM know I've never waited before?"

"Hell, no."

"I'm not sure I'm comfortable—"

"Look. You wanna know what a guy told me when I was starting out as a bartender? He said, fake it 'til you make it. You think I knew anything about bartending before I got to Florida? Everybody lies to get their first big-money job in this industry."

"Fake it 'til you make it, huh?"

"They're gonna train you for four or five days anyway. If you can't pick it up by that time, then you're not the man I thought you were."

"It just seems stressful."

"It can be, but you won't mind the stress once you start making two hundred bucks in tips a night."

"No shit? Two hundred?"

"That's an average night where you'll be working."

"When's my interview?"

"Day after tomorrow."

"Goddamn, Spencer. I mean shit. I need a little time to prepare. Get my head right."

"All the good jobs'll be gone in a week, Cash. You wait, you're gonna miss out on the jackpot."

As Cash was thinking it over they watched an osprey dive at the nearby shoals and a moment later saw that a large silver fish was now struggling within the grasp of its talons. The osprey flapped with all its might but the fish was so large the osprey could not get it airborne and soon the waves had tossed both bird and fish to the beach. The osprey was still struggling when a young girl approached and the bird made one last desparate heave upward and then flew away.

"Alright," Cash said. "What do I need to know for this interview?"

"Lots of things, but seeing as how this place is the classiest joint on Fort Myers Beach you've especially gotta know your wine. The different winemakers, varietals, pairings. All that stuff."

"Why couldn't it be beer? Or whiskey?"

"Name me all the wines you know."

"Carlo Rossi. Sutter Home. Uh, something something Michelle."

"Chateau Ste Michelle is good. Those other two are shit. Do not, do not, do not mention either of those. Do not. What else?"

"That's all I know."

"Good lord. We've got some work to do."

"So I've got a question," Charley said. "Should I ask people if they want ice in their water or should I just assume that? Because I know some people like Uncle Randy hate having ice in their water so what's the right, you know, protocol?"

Spencer laughed but Charley wasn't interested in it being a joke.

"This is a skill position," he said. "I want to be prepared."

They stayed at the beach discussing the restaurant until Cash and Charley were nearly sunburnt and then they took the path back to their campsite. The girls had returned and the three of them were sitting at the picnic table drinking wine and listening to music from a boom box. They were all young and tan and quite pretty. Spencer introduced them as hostesses at his restaurant.

"Wrong," one of the girls said. She wore a bright pink swimsuit, ludicrously oversized sunglasses and a haughty expression. "Julie's training to be an expo now. And it's not your restaurant. It's our restaurant."

"Whatever you say. Just play nice with my cousins here. They rode their motorcycles all the way from Washington so they deserve it."

"Do your cousins have names?"

"That's Charley and this one's Cash."

"Your name is really Cash?" the girl asked.

"Last I checked."

"Did your parents like Johnny Cash or did they like money?"

"Wasn't either one actually."

"Then what was it?"

"My dad just thought it sounded cool."

After sunset they built a fire with palm fronds and chunks of rotting logs they'd snuck around pilfering from the forest. Charley whittled sharp ends into some sticks he'd found and they all roasted hot dogs over the flames. Spencer had diced some onion and now he doused the pieces in oil and wrapped them up in aluminum foil and set them to cook on the grill rack. Then he wrapped the buns in foil and set them alongside the onion. When everything was ready he slathered the buns with cream cheese and a layer of sautéed onions and passed them around, the girls taking them with great reluctance.

"This is a famous Seattle cuisine," Spencer said.

"I don't know," one of the girls said. "I don't think cream cheese and hot dogs belong together."

"That's because you're ignorant. Just try it."

The girl took a hesitant first bite. She began chewing and her eyes widened.

"Told you, didn't I?"

She swallowed her bite and said, "Holy shit, that's good."

When they'd finished their meal the girls cleaned off the picnic table and demanded they play a drinking game called kings.

"We didn't bring any beer," Cash told them.

"You've got rum and wine, right?" one of the girls said.

"We'll get pretty fucked up playing with the hard stuff, won't we?"

She looked truly perplexed.

"Isn't that why you came out here?"

Later that night, after most of the booze had been drunk, the group merrily staggered back to the beach and sat in pairs. Spencer and Cash with their arms around the bellies of two of the girls who sat before them. Charley and the other girl holding hands in the sand. Miles out on the horizon two ships twinkled like extravagant lost stars. The waves crashing loudly at regular intervals like the ocean was keeping time. A pipe went around from Spencer to the girls and the smell of marijuana was sweetly pungent in the air.

When the girl at Cash's lap was finished she held the pipe back over her shoulder, but Cash said no thanks.

"Charley and I might have to take a drug test soon."

She shrugged and said, "More for us, I guess."

"So how's the kayaking out here?" Cash asked her.

"Oh, it's amazing," she said. "We saw manatees today in this little like cove area. I love manatees so much. They let us get right next to them. I wanted to swim with them but Melissa wouldn't let me."

"What do you love about them so much?"

"They're just the most peaceful creatures. It's almost like they don't have a care in the world. That's the way I want to live my life. Just really free and peaceful. I've been reading a lot about animal spirit guides and there's so much that manatees can teach us about calmness and surrender. They have one of the most accepting spirits of all animals. I love that about them."

Spencer coughed from the pipe and when he got his breath he said, "That is the biggest load of crap I have ever heard."

"No, it's not. It's true. Manatees have very noble spirits."

"You believe in animal spirit guides? Are you fucking kidding me? You've been smoking too much of this pot. It's nonsense. It's new age nonsense."

"I can believe whatever I want Spencer, so shut up."

"Manatees are fat and slow and stupid."

Charley perked up.

"Like the tourists in San Antonio, right Cash?"

Cash chuckled and Spencer said, huh?

"Anyways," the girl continued. "We saw the manatees and we saw a water snake and some crazy birds I'd never seen before. Then we paddled over to the other side of the bay and we went swimming there for a while and then—"

"What?" Spencer interrupted. "You really went swimming in Pelican Bay?"

"Yes, Spencer. We went swimming. Do you have a problem with that too?"

"It's swarming with bull sharks."

"You're joking."

"Think about it. Do you remember seeing anyone else swimming in that bay?"

"Well . . . Oh my god. Oh my god. We could have been eaten. Oh my god, I'm freaking out now. Stacie, Melissa, we could have been eaten."

Spencer erupted into a high falsetto laugh distorted by the marijuana.

"Hey, Julie. Julie. Harness your animal spirit guide. It's acceptance, remember?"

He went on laughing and Melissa finally turned and clamped a hand over his mouth so that he'd be quiet.

"I'm really high," said Stacie.

Cash took a swig of wine and set it back in the sand.

"I'm really high," she said again, and then a moment later. "Did I just say that twice?"

The next afternoon Cash and Charley lowered themselves into a pair of rented kayaks and when they were situated Spencer gave them each a push and then thrust himself out after them. They were on the bay side of the island and they paddled out toward a simple aluminum skiff with a small outboard motor in which a man and his young son were fishing. When they approached Cash asked the man how they were faring and the man told his son to go on and show them. The boy opened a container and held a small fish aloft through its gills.

"What kind of fish you got there?" Cash asked.

The boy turned to ask his father and when he did the fish squirmed and the boy nearly lost it overboard.

"You better bonk that fish again," the father said.

The boy nodded and took up his little wooden fish whacker.

"It's a snook," the father said.

"What you baiting 'em with?" Cash asked.

"Shrimp. But it varies."

The boy had disappeared at the bottom of the boat, and they could hear him clubbing at the fish.

"Have you seen any manatees today?" Charley asked.

"Can't say I have. Though we haven't exactly been looking for 'em either." The father gazed down at his son who was still working at the fish and he said, "Quit torturing that snook now, son. Just whack him good right on top of the head."

"Well, good luck to you guys," Cash said.

"Yep."

The three of them paddled toward the dense and impassable mangroves which lined that side of the island. The roots of those tropical shrubs partially showing above the water like innumerable rib bones all white and elongated. A ways along, the mangroves opened into a cove they thought may have been where the girls had seen the manatees the day before and they paddled in with quiet shallow strokes, speaking with whispers and searching for air bubbles or huge white lumps in the water. They saw neither of these and when they reached the back of the cove they turned and then saw the dorsal fin of a dolphin slice through the water for a moment and disappear.

As delicately as they could they paddled toward where they'd seen it when another fin showed and then another and another. They were paddling closer when a massive dolphin much larger than their kayaks emerged only feet away, its back a slick blue-gray like a cloudy dusk in November. Then, as if it were performing for them, a baby dolphin the size of a carnival prize came out of the water upsidedown with its flippers splayed apart and its belly a pale and pinkish white. The calf submerged and then reemerged in the same goofy fashion with what very much looked like a beaked smile when another calf dolphin leaped onto the first and the two of them seemed to wrestle. All the while adult dolphins had been surfacing for air in twos and threes astonishingly close to their kayaks and neither Spencer nor the brothers had dared make a single paddle stroke toward the calves. Then all at once the entire pod disappeared and the last they saw them they were far outside of the cove.

Spencer turned around in the seat of his kayak.

"Welcome to paradise."

It was a short but congested commute from Spencer's house to the restaurant on Fort Myers Beach, hundreds of vehicles bottlenecking toward Estero Island. It was so warm and humid that the brothers rode without jackets to the interview, their shirtsleeves and collars flapping in the wind. When they finally reached the crest of the bridge over Estero Bay, and the whole sweep of the island presented itself for the first time, the brothers saw that their new home was just as magnificent as they'd always dreamed it would be. Beyond the strip malls and the white beach, parasailers were drifting in their portion of sky, and farther out, a sailboat was tacking the ocean's edge. Egrets and pelicans swooped all about their domain and Charley pointed out one unnaturally pink bird that flapped a high and solitary arc above the phalanx of hotels and condominiums which went on for miles and miles east and then south into Naples before washing out in a tropical blue haze.

When they arrived at the restaurant the brothers parked their bikes and hung their helmets on the handlebars and then took the stairs up to the lobby. Somewhat intimidated they crossed the waxed and glossy hardwood floor and were greeted by a cheerful pudgy woman awaiting them at the host desk.

"Lunch for two?" she asked.

"We're actually here for our interviews," Cash said.

"Fantastic. I'll go find Lawrence for you. Feel free to take a look around."

The dining room was tall and spacious and much fancier than any place they'd ever been invited to dine. Three tables of elderly guests were finishing a late lunch and a bald and muscular waiter in a baby blue polo shirt went from table to table smiling and nodding and then exiting for the kitchen. The far wall was open to the air and showed a view of the marina and the bay and the lush nature preserve in the distance. The tables were all set with polished silverware and blue napkins folded into the water glasses in a way that resembled perching birds.

"Well, here he is," the hostess called out behind them.

They turned and shook the General Manager's hand. He was younger than they'd expected and he wore a brash and impatient look. He tossed his wavy hair for no apparent reason and told them to follow him outside. Cash sat down across from the GM and Charley stood there wondering where he was supposed to go.

The GM nodded and said, "Just pick a seat over there, bud."

Cash passed him his massively fraudulent resume and the GM put on his glasses and skimmed over its contents. The restaurants Cash had listed were all authentic, places he could easily visualize, but the phone numbers belonged to Joey Cain and a friend from high school.

"What was this place The Masthead like?" the GM asked.

"Not nearly as nice as this spot, that's for sure, but it's one of the better restaurants in Longview."

"What kind of menu they got?"

"Standard stuff. Steak and pasta. Ribs. Chicken."

"We serve a lot of fish here."

"I saw that. Snapper, grouper, butterfish, scallops. I'm gonna look forward to trying it all."

The GM put down the resume.

"How good is your wine knowledge?"

"Not bad."

"Name me some of your favorite winemakers."

"Hogue. Hess. Robert Mondavi. Cakebread. King Estate."

"What do you pair with a steak?"

"A nice Cabernet. Maybe a Syrah."

"How about a white fish?"

"Chardonnay or Pinot Gris usually. Depends on what sauce your chef's using."

"Salmon?"

"Pinot Noir."

The GM then asked Cash to recall a situation where a guest of his was unhappy with their experience and what he did to rectify the situation. Cash paused for a moment, hoping his imagination would spark something, and then he remembered the dinner in Vancouver when his father had sent his steak back three times. He told the story from the perspective of the shell-shocked waiter and by the time he'd gotten through telling it, Cash felt like he had not only handled himself well that night in the face of his father's bluster, but that the assistant manager on duty had all but recommended him for a medal.

The GM picked up the resume once more and he tapped at the bottom of the page.

"I'm going to be checking these references," he said.

"Absolutely. They're gonna tell you how well—"

"Fine."

The GM sat back in his chair.

"Can you pass a drug test?" he asked.

"Sure thing."

He looked at Cash skeptically.

"I'm a Libertarian so I don't really care what you do in your free time, but you're gonna have to pass a piss test so there's no point in us going forward if you aren't clean."

"I don't do drugs."

"You're sure?"

"I would know, wouldn't I?"

"You just got to town, man. You don't wanna chill out for a while before you get going? Hit the clubs with old Spencer?"

"I want to work."

"When can you start?"

"Tomorrow."

"Come with me," he said.

The GM led Cash into his office where heavy metal music was playing from his computer. He handed Cash a form.

"Call this number, find the nearest office, and piss in a fucking cup for me."

"That's it?"

"What else would there be?"

Cash shrugged and asked, "How about my brother out there?"

The GM handed Cash a second form.

"You don't need to interview him?"

"Does he speak English? Can he lift twenty pounds without falling over?"

"Yeah."

"Then I'm not worried about it. It's not hard to fire a guy if they're not working out."

"Anything else I should know?"

The GM gave him a cool look signifying that his time could no longer be wasted.

"Just don't be a fucking hippy and you'll get rich here."

It was his third day of training and so far Cash had managed to arouse no suspicion about his total lack of experience. This evening he followed a bow-legged brunette named Donna who had been with the restaurant since it opened. She was brusque and professional and she seemed wholly intolerant of guests or colleagues who she felt were behaving improperly.

Midway through the shift, a couple sat in her section and she told Cash it was his table. He knew it had to happen eventually but even so his hands went clammy and he ducked into the server station and gulped down some coffee, clicked his pen a number of times. Then he nodded to Donna that he was ready and moved toward the table.

"Water pitcher," she said.

He stepped back into the server station and filled a pitcher from the tap, added a scoop of ice and walked across the dining room.

It was Friday night and there was not an empty table in the house. The din of conversation and clattering utensils sounding almost oppressive to Cash at that moment. Nearby, Charley was pulling dirty salad plates from a table of six and Cash envied the mindlessness of his position.

When he was at the table Cash lifted a water glass and the couple raised their eyes from the menus and smiled. As he filled the water he greeted them and told them his name. He set down the full water and then reached for the other glass which squirted through his slick fingers, slid along the surface and fell sideways, shattering across the table.

At once Cash felt naked and exposed.

"Oh, boy. I'm so sorry, folks. I'll get this cleaned up right away."

He didn't know whether to set the water pitcher on the table or the floor, whether to ask for help from the buser or clean the mess himself. His whole baffled thought process was plainly evident by the way he was juking about and the man leaned forward and very calmly said, "Just take it easy, buddy."

A moment later Donna was there with towels and a dustpan. She gave Cash the briefest frown and then cleaned the table as she made jokes about the quality of seasonal help. Behind her came a buser who exchanged settings and then they were both gone.

"Let's try this again," the man said.

Cash read for them the soup du jour and the evening's special from notes he had written in his pad and then took their drink order. Donna was waiting for him in the server station.

"What happened there?"

"The glass slipped out of my hand."

"You're lucky they're not the hoity toity type. You sure you're alright? You're shaking a bit."

"Too much coffee."

"Well, get it together, will you? That's my tip, you know."

Cash borrowed Donna's card and swiped into the computer terminal. He opened a new table from the map and hit the button for a glass of Syrah.

"What's he having?" she asked.

"Gin martini."

"What kind of gin?"

"He just said gin."

"You need to ask their preference. Beefeaters is fine for now. Right there. Hit that button to make it a martini."

Cash sent the order through.

"What operating system did you guys use at your last place?" she asked.

"I always forget the name of it."

"Was it aloha?"

"Yep. That was it. Aloha."

A small pugnacious waiter with the shadow of a beard and short gelled hair strutted into the server station followed by another young waiter with a square jaw and thick ropy arms. The two of them crowded up to Cash.

"Get a load of the new guy," the short one said in a Jersey accent. "Already breaking glass all over the guests. You sure you can handle this shit, new guy? Where'd you work before this? Fucking Chucky Cheese?"

The waiters laughed, and Cash simply stared at them.

"What? Are you tough?" the small one continued. "You a tough guy? Just gonna stare at me?"

"Look at his nametag," said the other. "He's from Washington."

"Fucking Washington. That's one of those homo states. Bunch of fucking queers out there in Washington. Drinking lattes in bed with their boyfriends."

"His boyfriend's out there busing my table right now."

"Oh, you brought him with you. What's your boyfriend's name?"

"He's my brother."

"You're banging your brother? Man, it's getting weird."

Donna had finally had enough and she said, "Don't you two have some work to do?"

"You're not the manager, Donna. I can stand here and haze this kid as long as I want."

Right then a paunchy man with a sagging face and unruly eyebrows appeared and the waiters straightened their postures and acted like they had some reason for being in the server station.

"It's Friday night," the man barked. "What the hell are we all standing around for?"

The small waiter mumbled something about needing a clean wine glass and the waiters headed toward their sections.

"Now let's sell some butterfish," the man hurrahed.

Once he was gone Donna said, "That's the owner."

"And those other guys?"

"Jeremy and Stu."

"They're like a couple of jackals."

"Just ignore them."

"That was like being in middle school again."

"Your drinks are ready."

Cash stabbed a pick through two olives and put them in the gin. Then he loaded the gin and the carafe of wine on a tray and carried it over to the table. He set the gin atop a cocktail napkin and poured the Syrah from the carafe to the woman's wine glass.

"Tell me," the man said. "Where are you all catching your snapper?"

"Out of the Gulf."

"And it's red snapper, right?"

Cash had not a clue but he said, "Yes, sir."

"In that case I'll try this butterfish."

"And for you ma'am?"

"Gosh. You're gonna make me make a decision, aren't you?"

"Get the scallops," the man said.

"All of it looks so good."

"Get the scallops."

"Well, I guess I'm getting the scallops."

Cash collected the menus and took the unused wine glass.

"I sure appreciate you folks being so tolerant of my clumsiness earlier."

"That wasn't nothing," the woman said. "I was a waitress for a while in my younger days and one time I broke a glass so that all the shards landed inside a woman's purse. I had to pick through it with tweezers."

"She's still doing stuff like that at home," the man said.

"What I always said about waiting tables was that you could either get away with being unfriendly or bad at your job, but you can't get away with both. You'll be fine, Cash. Just keep smiling."

Cash entered the order into the computer and fired it through and then he and Donna went in the kitchen. The hot line window was all full of food and the chef hurried around sprinkling garnishes and traying up the plates and hollering for runners. Two waitresses stepped up and took an armload of steaming appetizers. Cash pulled a loaf of sourdough out of the bread warmer and as he was cutting it he heard from behind him a man's voice saying, "God is great." Cash turned and saw the voice belonged to a stocky waiter with a crewcut and a joyous expression.

"God is great," he repeated. "Did you know that? He cares about us."

He hadn't been speaking to anybody in particular so nobody felt the need to reply and the waiter left as Cash and Donna and the chef all exchanged looks of amusement. Cash delivered the basket of bread to his table and then returned to the hot line where Donna quizzed him about the different entrees as the cooks slid them finished under the heat lamp. Several minutes later the same stocky waiter reappeared in the kitchen, now red-faced and scowling.

"I'd like to stab those people with a butter knife," he said.

"What's the matter, Roger?" Donna asked.

"People are assholes."

He cut himself a basket of bread and left the kitchen. Donna saw the wonder in Cash's eyes and she leaned in to his ear.

"Roger was a crack addict," she said in way of explanation. "He's in AA now. Works with his church. But I think he scrambled his eggs a bit too much."

When his table's food was ready Cash delivered the entrees which the couple said were excellent. After their meals they split a dessert and Cash dropped their check with relief that he hadn't botched anything else. The couple left him a twenty percent tip and he showed it to Donna and she said she'd let him have one more practice table that night.

It was a table of four, two middle-aged couples from Ohio. One of the men wore a Harley shirt and when Cash greeted the table he commented on the shirt and told them about how he and his brother had rode their motorcycles from Washington. The man with the Harley shirt had seemed disinterested in his story but when Cash returned with drinks the other man at the table told Cash that his buddy was jealous of him.

"It's true," said the man in the Harley shirt. "Always wanted to do something like that when I was your age."

"Why didn't you?" Cash asked.

"Things always seemed to get in the way."

He looked at his wife and back at Cash.

"This guy here is worth fifty-million dollars," the other man said. "Not too often a guy worth that much money is jealous of somebody. Think about that when you're going to bed at night."

Outside the club a portion of the beach was roped off and alighted with tiki torches which flickered with the murmuring breeze. Spencer and Cash sat at a picnic table smoking. The crash of the ocean equal to the bass line that throbbed inside.

Spencer tossed his butt in the sand and covered it over with his shoe.

"You hauling in the big bucks yet?" he asked.

"Made a hundred and seventy last night."

"Not bad, cuz. Any of the managers catch on to you being an imposter?"

"Don't think so. Some of my guests sure had a right to be suspicious though. The other night a guy asked me what kind of port we had. I told him I'd just moved to town so I wasn't exactly sure, but that I figured the longshoremen were mostly loading seafood and whatnot."

"You weren't joking?"

"No. But he thought I was. After he quit laughing he asked me again and that's when I knew I was in hot water. I told him I thought we were out but that I'd go check for him. Had to go in the bathroom and look it up on my phone. I blame it on you, you know. How were ports not part of my training?"

"I can't be held responsible for everything."

"You pushed me into this."

"Okay, then. Remember. A stout's not a fat lady, and her name ain't sherry or shiraz."

Spencer laughed and kept laughing and when he finally quieted down he said, "So Cash, this is kind of awkward for me but now that you and Charley both have jobs I was wondering if you guys could help me out a little bit with the rent."

"Seems only fair. How much you paying?"

"Fourteen hundred a month."

"Damn, dude. How you been affording that?"

"Working my ass off is how. I had a couple roommates but they couldn't keep a job so I had to give 'em the boot."

"Fourteen hundred is a lot of money."

"I know. That's why I was hoping you guys could maybe help me out."

"How much were you thinking?"

"Well, seeing as how I've got the master bedroom and all it wouldn't be fair to split it evenly three ways so how does a hundred bucks a week from you and Charley each sound?"

"That include utilities?"

"Sure. I'll throw those in for free."

Cash worked the math for a moment.

"Yeah, that sounds pretty reasonable."

"I was charging those other guys a lot more since it's my ass on the line here, but seeing as how we're cousins I'm giving you two the family rate."

"Let's shake on it then before you change your mind."

They shook and then gazed inside the club. Spencer licked his lips.

"Let's go find us some honey."

Inside the club the music was all grunts and swagger. Laser lights showered schizophrenic neon upon the dance floor which smelled of beer and sweat and cheap cologne. As large as it was the club was brimming with college kids there on spring break and Spencer began leading Cash around the periphery of the dance floor demonstrating for him how to troll for easy drunk girls. Soon they came upon two young bleach blondes wearing short jean skirts and dancing together with slow bored shuffles. Spencer leaned in to one of the girls and said something in her ear and she lifted her drink as way of an answer. Spencer leaned in again and the girl looked him long in the face and then appraised Cash. She looked at her friend and they shrugged and followed Spencer and Cash to the bar.

"Where are you girls from?" Cash asked.

"Wisconsin," one of the girls answered in her northern accent.

"And don't make fun of the way we talk," said the other.

When it was their turn to order Cash gave the bartender a hundred dollar bill and told Spencer the change was his. As the bartender was pouring four shots of tequila Spencer whispered something to him and the bartender eyed Cash and the girls.

"How much you want?" the bartender asked.

"Whatever's left of that benjamin."

The bartender put two fingers in his mouth and blew a loud distinctive whistle. A huge Samoan who had been leaning against a nearby pole perked up and the bartender fluttered him some hand signals.

"Meet him out front in ten minutes," the bartender said. "And don't be telling nobody about me. I've been feeling some heat lately."

The bartender swiveled in place to take another order and Spencer passed around the shots.

"You all down to party?"

Spencer made some phone calls and when they arrived at their house an hour later several cars were parked in the driveway and the front door was wide open spilling a raucous round of laughter.

The girls got out and stood waiting to follow inside as a raggedy man came slowly crutching from a house across the street.

"Busted," one of the girls said.

Spencer turned to look at the man and said, "What's happening, Murph?"

"Same old shit," he growled through lungs of emphysema. "Would say different day, but it feels like the same one over and over again."

"You ever get that settlement money?"

"Fuck no. I think this lawyer of mine is just stringing me along."

"You know what you call a hundred lawyers at the bottom of the ocean?"

"A damn good start."

"Come on over, Murph. I've got something that'll cheer you up."

In the living room a dozen people had formed a semicircle around the couch where a man wearing a wig of long curly black hair was playing Spanish style guitar. Spencer caught the guitarist's eye and gestured toward his bedroom and when the guitarist was finished with his song he stood up and passed the guitar to someone else. Cash and Murph and the Wisconsin girls followed and Spencer shut the door behind them. From his closet he removed a round glass mirror and Cash noticed a stack of twenty dollar bills which Spencer quickly slipped into a sock and hid under a heap of dirty laundry. He shut the closet door and set the mirror at the end of his bed.

"How much you score?" the guitarist asked.

Spencer tossed him the baggy and he looked it over and weighed it with his hand.

"Won't last long with this many people."

"It's enough to get us rolling."

The guitarist tossed the baggy back to Spencer and he dumped the small mound of cocaine onto the mirror and began breaking the few clumps into a fine powder. When he was finished with this he split the mound in half and divided that into six thin lines. Then he rolled up a five-dollar bill.

"Murph, would you like to do the honors?"

"Normally I'd wait to make sure you all aren't narcs first, but seeing how things are going for me I guess I don't got a whole lot to lose either way."

Murph took the five and stuck it in his nostril and snuffed it over one of the lines. When he lifted his head his bushy mustache was twitching and he was making a sound like he was snoring. Then he ran his finger along what little flecks and smudge of cocaine remained of his line and rubbed it onto his gums.

"I'm a little bit nervous," one of the girls said. "I've never done this before."

Spencer put his arm around her.

"You'll be fine. Just do exactly like Murph just did."

It took her and her friend each a few snorts to finish their lines and then Spencer passed the rolled up bill to Cash. He had thought he was going to decline but now after seeing both the girls do it he couldn't think of a very good reason not to so he knelt over the mirror and snuffed his first line of cocaine. A moment later it went trickling through his nasal cavity and down his throat and he couldn't see any pleasantness at all in the bitter numbing sensation. Then his heart took off in a stampede and his hands and his feet both demanded something to do and he asked if anyone wanted him to get them a beer. Spencer said to hold on just one second and when he and the guitarist finished their lines Spencer slid the mirror under his bed and they all walked out into the kitchen.

Charley was standing there at the counter and he had a look of ferocious curiosity. Cash passed beers around from the fridge and then he cracked one for himself and immediately drank it more than halfway empty like it was less than water.

"What were you guys doing in there?" Charley asked.

"Playing spin the bottle."

"I'm not a stupid kid, you know."

"I'll tell you later."

Murph crutched up to Cash and asked if he could bum a beer. His eyes madlike and commanding attention. Cash handed him a beer and then without the slightest prompting Murph began a frenzied and disjointed disclosure of all the various ailments and betrayals that had led him to his current station in life.

"I could have been famous, you know. Damned if it isn't true. I was on a flight once sitting next to this Berkeley AIDS researcher. A real pompous bastard if you ask me. Anyways, he told me he was trying to figure out why AIDS was afflicting so many blacks, gays and Haitians. Trying to learn what the commonality was there. And it didn't take me more than but a few seconds to figure it out. I told him, I'll bet it has something to do with the blood. You know what he said? He says, hmmm, that is a possibility. I pretty much forgot about it for a while and then one day I see this big news special about this Berkeley guy making a big AIDS discovery, and did he even mention how I put that thing about the blood in his ear? Course not. That's the way it is with these guys. That's the way the world works. You watch out. Now I'm just a broke old man with a busted leg and emphysema. I'll tell you something. Let me tell you something. A good man learns from his mistakes. But a great man learns from the mistakes of others. You go on and keep that one in your back pocket."

"You got any regrets in life, Murph?"

"Hell yes I've got regrets. I've got a whole treasure trove full of 'em. Any man who says they don't have regrets is lying through his teeth."

"You really don't think there's any way to live a life without regret?"

Murph squinted, drank the rest of his beer and clanked it down on the counter.

"I've gotta take a piss."

Cash figured he'd offended him in some way but he wasn't sure how and he didn't care to figure it out just then. He looked around for the Wisconsin girls and he noticed Spencer again had his arm around one of them and the other he saw chatting with a hipster in a tight plaid cardigan. He thought about it for a moment and then walked straight up and delicately cupped the girl's elbow.

"Hey, I want to show you that thing I was telling you about earlier."

He saw she understood the ruse and also that she had been waiting for him. The hipster looked completely blindsided as Cash led her outside to the edge of the canal. They sat down with their legs dangling over the water.

"I thought you were gonna be talking to that old guy all night," she said.

"Yeah, he kinda cornered me there for a while. Then he got interesting and then it just got weird."

"So what are you gonna show me?"

"You know, I hadn't thought it out that far yet."

She chirped a little bird's laugh and then said, "What do you do for work?"

"I'm a very bad waiter. How about you? You in college?"

"Yeah. Guess what my major is?"

Cash made an elaborate spoof of analyzing her features.

"Psychology," he said finally.

"That's incredible. Yes, I study psychology."

"Are you gonna be a shrink?"

"Ha. No way. I'm not that into it. I'll probably just wind up working for some stupid corporation."

"Making a boatload of money, I'll bet."

"I don't know. It scares me to think about." Right then a fish splashed in the canal and she said, "What was that?"

"Jumping fish."

"It wasn't an alligator."

"Hope not. Our toes are awful close to the water."

She swung her feet up and began scooting back.

"Take it easy. There's no alligators in this canal."

"I'm staying here."

She had her arms wrapped around her legs now and they shone milky white there in the moonlight. Her long eyelashes twittering against some small bug. She sensed him watching her and she turned and said, what.

"You're very pretty," he said.

Her smile was wry and defensive.

"You say it with such ease it makes me think you've had lots of practice."

"I just don't like wasting time stating the obvious."

"Oh my. A silver tongue on this boy. I'll bet spring break is like harvesting season for you and Spencer isn't it? Just waiting all year for the easy college girls to fly in."

"I wouldn't know. I just got here myself."

"You think that we're going to have sex, don't you?"

He didn't answer, but an hour later they were indeed naked in his bed. She was very shy now and she seemed somewhat embarrassed by her promiscuity. Cash spent a long time kissing her body from her neck down to her thighs and then back again to her breasts. As reserved as she was the pleasure she took from it was obvious enough. Her neck and face both blushing red and her breaths shuddering in and out of her. When he reached for the condom he expected her to make some meek protest but she only watched his every movement with a seriousness that was striking. She was no slut. And then they were moving together and it felt so good so fast he had to stop himself twice. She spoke not a word until he could hold himself no longer and then she said, please not inside of me.

When he was finished he tossed the condom on the floor and they spooned there as he caught his breath.

Then he heard her sniffling and he didn't want to trust his ears but she was in fact crying. He stroked her hair wondering what there was to say.

"I told myself I wouldn't do this," she said finally. "And I also told myself that if I did do it, I wouldn't cry afterwards. God, I'm such a woman, aren't I?"

"Did I do something wrong?"

"It's me. I'm fucked up."

"You don't seem like you are."

"I am. I thought I could handle it, but . . . I'll just tell you. I'll just . . ." She was crying again.

"You don't have to tell me if you don't want to."

"I had an abortion. It's so strange to hear myself say it. I never even told my parents. The last guy I was with, my ex-boyfriend, he got me pregnant and then he demanded I get an abortion and then he dumped me afterwards. Pathetic, right?"

"I don't think that's what I'd call it at all."

She rolled over to face him and wiped the tears away. Her mascara now streaked and sad looking.

"Are you okay?" he said.

"I think so."

He kissed her once on the forehead.

"Isn't it weird how people's lives converge like this?" she said. "Just random bodies bumping into each other. Never to be seen again."

Days later the east facing windows were full of that endless utopian sun and the brothers sat basking in it at the dining room table drinking coffee and orange juice. When Spencer was finished cooking he covered three plates with bacon and eggs and hashbrowns and toast and set them on the table. Cash said, Amen cousin, and shook salt and pepper over everything.

When they were nearly finished with their meal Spencer's phone began ringing. He looked at who was calling and his eyes goggled and he looked at the brothers and then stood up and walked into his bedroom. A few minutes later Spencer returned and he looked somewhat frantic.

"Hate to do this, but you guys are gonna have to split for a couple hours."

"What's the deal?" Cash asked.

"The owner's coming by. She wants to show the place to a potential buyer."

"But I thought you were renting it from her?"

"I am, but it's on a month to month basis. If she can find a buyer, she'll sell. Nothing I can do about it at this point."

Spencer was hustling around the kitchen now, taking their plates, clearing them into the trash, rinsing them, wiping the counter.

"You look stressed," Cash said.

"I have to get this place clean for her."

"She could've given you some better notice."

"Yeah. Well. See, I forgot about it. I'm a dumbass, I forgot."

"We can help you clean," Charley said.

"No, no. I got it. Well, okay. Actually, what you guys can do is throw all your stuff in your closets for me real quick. The owner wants it to look kinda empty. You know how they stage these things for the buyers."

"So just throw our stuff in the closets," Cash said.

"Yeah, and make the beds too, would you? Then hit the beach or whatever. But do it quick, guys. She's gonna chew my ass out if I don't get this done before they arrive."

The brothers did as they were asked and then went out and fired up their motorcycles. As they were riding away from the house they passed a red Mercedes convertible driven by a middle aged woman who appeared fond of hairspray and jewelry. They watched her turn into Spencer's driveway and park. The brothers made a left at the stop sign and rode as far as the bridge when Charley pulled over on the side of the street. Cash came alongside him and Charley shouted over the rumbling of their engines.

"I forgot my swim trunks."

"Damnit, Charley. We're halfway there already."

"Sorry. I just realized I threw them in the closet. It'll only take a second."

"Alright, I'll follow you back."

At the house they parked their bikes behind the Mercedes. Cash saw he'd left his Frisbee in the yard so he went to collect it as Charley walked up toward the porch. Cash bent over and picked up the Frisbee and then he looked in through the front windows.

"Charley. Stop."

"What?"

Cash stepped back out of sightline and he held his index finger to his lips for Charley to be quiet. Together they crept along the side of the house. Cash peered again through the window.

"Oh my god," he said.

"What? What?"

Cash was down on his knees trying to keep himself quiet as he buckled with laughter.

"Don't let 'em see you," Cash said.

Charley tiptoed to the edge of the window and peered in with one eye.

They were groin to groin against the dishwasher and Spencer had lifted the back of her skirt and was clenching her ass with both hands. Their tongues darting together like a pair of snakes.

"I see now why he wanted us to leave," Cash said.

"Why would he do that? She's so old."

"Guess he's trying to convince her not to sell the house."

Cash was polishing a wine glass in the corner of the dining room when he saw the bartender hobbling toward him. The bartender was young and looked like a Marine and he was dragging his left leg along the carpet. The foot was aimed perpendicular to normal and he made every step look agonizing. When he drew alongside Cash he paused before taking the three stairs up to the bar.

"What the hell happened to you?" Cash asked.

When the bartender turned Cash saw that he also had thick gauzed bandages on his right shoulder and forearm.

"Wiped out on the motorcycle," he said.

"How'd it go down?"

"My jackass friends. There was a bunch of us riding together last night doing wheelies and stuff. Nothing too crazy but then a cop starts following us and a couple of my buddies who've been in trouble before took off trying to shake the cop. It was stupid, I know, but the rest of us followed along. Going really fast. We were flying around this corner when the guy next to me wiped out and when he crashed he took my bike out with him and I went over the handlebars and slid across the road. The cop stopped for a second to make sure we weren't dead and then he sped away. I got scraped up pretty bad. They had to drain my knee with this huge needle. I can't believe I'm going through this again. I just finished recovering from my last crash."

"What happened to you that time?"

"I broke my back."

"Jesus."

"That's the second bike I've totaled. I'm done. I'm done."

"Shouldn't you be resting? I mean, no offense, but you look terrible."

"I can't afford to take any time off."

"You want some help up the stairs at least?"

"I've got it. Pain makes memory."

With gruesome labor the bartender lifted himself up the stairs and dragged his foot around to the back of the bar as the General Manager walked through the dining room calling out, Line 'em up, gang. Pre-shift. Line 'em up.

The staff assembled in the lobby and Cash took a seat next to Roger on one of the leather couches. Standing across from them were Jeremy and Stu.

"Hey Roger," Jeremy said. "Hey Roger."

Roger bent down and pretended to be preoccupied by tying his shoe.

"Your shoe's fine, Roger. Look at us."

"Roger, did you call that girl yet?"

Stu was shouting now.

"Roger. Roger. Roger."

He finally looked up at them.

"What do you guys want?"

"We want to know about your love life," Jeremy said.

"It's none of your stupid business."

"Whoa, Roger. Don't throw a hissy fit. Did you call her or not?"

"Yes. I called her. Now—"

"Did you ask her out?"

"Why do you care?"

"What'd she say, Roger? Come on."

"She said she's busy this weekend, but maybe—"

"I knew it. I told you a girl like that wouldn't be interested in a dummy like you. What a loser."

The General Manager had stepped behind Jeremy and he had his arms crossed over his chest and was waiting for him to finish. When Jeremy sensed this he turned and caught the GM glowering at him.

"Sorry, boss."

The GM looked over his crew and gave his hair a toss.

"I need you all on your game tonight. One of you morons took two big-top reservations without checking with me first and now we're way overbooked. To make things worse I had two servers call in sick, one of whom I canned, and now I've got a bartender limping around like he lost a cage fight. It's time to step it up, gang. I need your tables turned fast tonight. Get those desserts down right away. And don't let me see those check presenters sitting on the table. Once they've signed their slips I want you to pull 'em. Pull everything. Thank you folks, have a good night, now get the fuck out. You got me? Paul, I'm looking at you on this one. You're solid, but you're slow. Pick it up, buddy. Any questions?"

Roger raised his hand and said, "Who got fired?"

"You'll figure it out. Let's just say if you're gonna have your boyfriend call in sick for you, you oughta make sure you and him have your stories straight. And don't fuck around with meth. It's just disgusting."

A couple of the servers muttered, Allison.

"Let's make some loot tonight, gang. Chef, what have you got for us?"

By seven o'clock that evening the restaurant felt more like a battlefield than a fine dining establishment and for four hours straight Cash had no fewer than five tasks simultaneously demanding attention. Food runners were delivering the wrong plates. The kitchen had lost multiple tickets and even so they were so inundated with orders some of the entrees were taking close to an hour. As Cash was attempting to entertain an especially impatient table he watched Charley heft a massively overloaded tray onto his shoulder and then saw him stumble through the door of the dishpit followed by the sound of glassware cracking like shots from a rifle.

Cash turned back to the table and continued trying to pacify the guests. At the head of the table was a fat and imperious man who finally punctuated Cash's attempt by barking, enough.

"I didn't bring my wife and her friends here to listen to you stammer about for paltry excuses."

His wife put her hand on his arm and said, "Honey, please."

"When I pay top dollar for a meal I have certain expectations and those expectations are not being met, young man. Do you understand that?"

"Of course I do, sir."

"We've been out sailing all day and now we are very hungry. Why on God's earth does it take this long to cook a meal?"

"It's just extremely busy tonight, sir."

"You've already said that. I believe you've already said that twice."

"I'm sure it will be ready any moment. Would you like me to bring you out another basket of bread?"

"I think I'd prefer to speak with your manager. There's obviously nothing you can do about this situation."

"Yessir. He's right there."

Cash pointed at the GM who stood behind the host desk while repeatedly running his hand through his hair. Before him in the lobby were at least thirty guests waiting for their tables like a herd of cattle ready to be led into a paddock. The host hurried up to the GM's side and was given two menus and whisked another couple into the restaurant.

"You see how busy it is," his wife said. "Please don't make a scene. I'm sure our waiter is doing everything he can."

"I'll bet I can get a couple of free desserts for you folks," Cash said. "For being so patient."

"You see, honey. He's very nice."

The man sat back in his chair, looking somewhat wounded by his hunger.

"I'll bring more bread," Cash said.

When the night was finally all over Cash had made more money than any other day in his life and he was sure it wasn't worth it. The synapses in his brain felt fried beyond repair and he was wearing a majority of the restaurant's sauces. He could think of only food and beer and sleep. Charley followed him to a late night taco shack down the street and they exchanged their war stories. Afterwards, Charley went home and Cash rode over to a bar so he could decompress.

He took a stool at the bar counter and ordered an amber ale when the barmaid came around. It was like a tonic for the onslaught he'd taken that night and when he was finished with it he ordered another. In the corner of the bar a band was covering songs he'd heard countless times before. Four guys were playing doubles at the pool table and four more were watching along the rail. A drunk woman went listing into the bathroom like a doomed ship and when she returned Cash watched her insert the same coin again and again into the jukebox until someone told her it was only a nickel. Cash watched a soccer game on the television.

Ten minutes later a man sat two stools from him and he turned and saw it was Jeremy. They nodded at each other. Jeremy ordered a Corona and two shots of whiskey. The barmaid poured them and Jeremy passed one of the shots to Cash.

"Crazy night," Cash said.

"I feel like I just got raped by a donkey. Cheers."

They took the shots, Jeremy observing his empty glass with some rumination.

"I always think I might like it," he said. "But I still can't stand whiskey."

"You ever seen the restaurant as busy as it was tonight?"

"Once or twice maybe. But we weren't running with two no-shows and a cripple. Didn't help the kitchen went down in flames."

"I had some angry people in my section. One of 'em totally stiffed me."

"That's nothing. I had two tables walk out on me."

"You get in trouble for that?"

"Lawrence didn't say anything. And I wouldn't have let him if he'd tried. Wasn't my fault we were overbooked. I'll bet he mucked it up himself. He does that. He uses us as the scapegoats so he doesn't get in trouble from the owner."

"This restaurant has been an eye opener for me," Cash said. "I guess I was expecting a higher caliber of people. Seems like everybody there's got a lot of problems."

"You've been here for what? A month?"

"Like six weeks."

"You don't even know the half of it then."

"Fill me in."

"Okay. Start with Barry. He went to prison for dealing coke. Alexis is addicted to pain pills. Dennis owes like forty large to the IRS. Stu's a good story. He got drunk one night and threw a construction sign through a Hooters window, injured a person or two, and then fled the scene drunk in his car. I think that was his third or fourth DUI. He spent sixty days in jail for that one and can't get a driver's license again for six years."

"And what about you?"

Jeremy stared at him for a moment.

"Fuck it. I'll tell you. Ten years back my cousin set me up with this job running drugs from Jersey to San Diego. Big time money. Like ten grand for taking a five hour flight. I'd done a couple runs no problem and then one day they busted me and another guy with five pounds of reefer and two kilos of cocaine. I was up against ten to thirty years in the slammer. Imagine that? I spent all the money I'd made on a lawyer and after a year in jail he finally got me out on a technicality. The lawyer found out they'd searched me a half hour before my warrant was issued so they had to let me free."

"What was the first thing you did when you got out?"

"Got drunk with my uncle."

"So how did you end up down here?"

"Just wanted to go someplace warm and far away from home. In Jersey I'd been accused of six different aggravated assaults. Only three of 'em came to court, but one more little thing and they were gonna lock me away for a long long time. Fort Myers was a throw a dart at a map kind of thing. I guess I sorta knew one guy."

Jeremy picked at his coaster.

"Hardly anybody in Florida is from here. They're mostly all like me. Running away from something. Even all these old geezers who come here to retire. It's like they're running away from their families. People just get it in their heads that it's paradise down here. That some sunshine and beaches are gonna solve all their problems and then they realize pretty quick that they're just the same mope they were when they left."

He swigged the rest of his glass.

"You want another beer?"

The brothers had borrowed Spencer's SUV and they
were driving north on I-75. Charley with his seat reclined and his
feet propped up on the dashboard.

"What's the name of this place again?" he asked. "Mykala?"

"Myakka."

"You see how fried I am. I can't even remember a dang name."

"I hear you."

"Eleven days in a row. I feel like a slave. Why can't Lawrence
just hire more workers?"

"Season's almost over. At four bucks an hour it's cheaper for
him to pay us overtime than it is to train new staff he's just gonna
have to let go in a few weeks. It's economics."

"Seems like economics is just an excuse to screw the little guys."

"Pretty much."

"I'm glad we're getting out of town. I think if I had to look at
another bus tub full of dirty plates I'd start throwing 'em back at the
guests."

They rolled north.

"Dad called me last night," Charley said.

"Oh, yeah? What'd he say?"

"He just wanted to know how things were going."

"What'd you tell him?"

"Told him we were getting rich and tan."

"What'd he have to say about that?"

"He said those don't mean nothing unless you're getting laid too."

Cash laughed.

"He say anything about a new job?"

"Not too much. Just said he was staying busy."

"I still picture him working those roofs sometimes. Alone. In the rain. Slipping, cussing."

"Wearing that bright yellow climbing harness."

"Yeah, tied off to nothing but some crumbling old chimney."

"Working the edge."

Cash envisioned it.

"That's real work, Charley. Working the last row of shingles while you're looking down at concrete from thirty feet. You wanna go back to that?"

"You know, it's kinda surprising none of us ever fell off one of those roofs."

Cash looked at him.

"Dad did once," he said.

"What? You guys never told me."

"He made me promise not to mention it to you or Mom. Thought you guys would worry too much."

"What happened?"

"It was that big private school job a couple years back. I don't know if you remember. Took us almost a week to finish. I mean, they let that roof go to shit. All around it were these pine trees and man, we must've blown about a thousand pounds of moss and pine needles off that sucker. On the flats there was a layer about an inch thick and we're talking a hell of a lot of square footage. They finally got a leak from it, that's why they called us. Anyways, we get finished with this massive school roof, get it all hosed down and the debris blown into the bushes and then Dad notices this little toolshed thing that's got a roof on it about ten feet high. He says he's gonna blow it off real quick. Ten minutes. A snaperoo, like he says. Problem was the roof wasn't shingled, it was made of this slick plastic stuff and I could see his boots weren't gripping it hardly at all. He got most of it blown off from the ladder but he's so damn crazy about being thorough he decides he's gonna climb onto the ridge so he can reach the last few spots. So he gets up there and he's spraying it down when all of a sudden his boots come out from under him and he starts sliding down the roof like it's a goddamn slip and slide. I'd kind of been expecting it could happen so when he shot off the eave I ran toward him and threw my arms around him as he was coming down like a big bear hug, you know, to soften his fall. And he just landed right on his feet. Couldn't believe how springy he was for an old guy. Meanwhile the pressure washing gun had shot out of his hand and got wrapped around the power lines and it's spraying every which way, and Dad and I, we just started laughing. Patting each other on the shoulders and laughing."

"You miss the work sometimes, don't you?"

"Nah. I just miss him."

At the outskirts of Sarasota they spotted the sign for Myakka River State Park and headed inland. Though it was only April the day was as hot as Longview in August and twice as humid and when they reached Myakka it took only the fifty paces from the car to the ranger station for them to grow sticky and uncomfortable.

In the station the brothers waited in line for the ranger. Ahead of them a woman was asking many questions about birds and after several minutes the ranger gingerly brushed her aside and the brothers stepped up and paid for their campsite and bought a bundle of firewood.

"So where can we go swimming?" Charley asked.

The ranger looked up from the forms.

"Oh, there's no swimming in Myakka."

"What? But it's so hot outside."

"I'm sorry, son, but this is an alligator sanctuary."

"How many alligators are there?"

"About two thousand."

"Have you had any attacks?" Cash asked.

"Not too long ago we had an alligator tip over a canoe and bite a lady pretty bad."

"I heard they're more likely to drown you than anything," Charley said.

The ranger looked at him like he was a nincompoop.

"Fella, you're dead either way."

Beyond the ranger station they soon entered a jungle of palm trees and live oak that overhung the road and it was all so dense and dark and dooming at midday the park seemed inhabited by unseen sinister. At the end of the drive they parked the car and walked out to a small gazebo that stood over the Myakka River. Below the gazebo a thin concrete divider stretched some yards into the tea brown water before terminating in a murky opaqueness. Charley pointed.

"Dare me to walk out on that thing?"

"No."

"Come on. Dare me."

"No."

"Whatever. I'll do it anyway."

He dropped down to the ground and tiptoed out until he was standing but a few inches above the surface of the water.

"Charley, I can literally see an alligator in the water right now."

"Where?"

"To your right."

Charley looked and he saw the studded armor scales of the alligator floating motionless fifty yards away.

"Come on, Cash. Try this. It's spooky."

Cash shook his head but he also dropped down and inched his way out.

"Charley, you can't see more than a couple feet into the water."

"I know. Makes you tingle a bit, doesn't it?"

Right then another alligator surfaced half as near as the last and from that close the brothers could see teeth snaggled all along its snout.

"That's pretty big," Cash said. "Not huge, but big enough."

"Don't be scared."

Cash couldn't help it though and he turned and scanned the water behind him. He looked up at the gazebo and saw a family now watching them with morbid fascination. A gurgle in the water made his head jerk down again but it was only an eddy swirling in a slow gurgling circle. He searched the water to be sure and then he heard Charley make a horrific gasp. Cash flinched and threw his head around. Charley was convulsing and shrieking with monstrous laughter.

"You should have seen you just now."

"Goddamnit, Charley. You get yourself eaten if you want but I'm gone."

Cash clambered back onto the gazebo and read what the bulletin board had to say about fishing regulations. A minute later Charley joined him.

"I thought you loved it down there," Cash said.

"I didn't feel so brave after you left."

"We'd better head to camp. It'll be getting dark here pretty quick."

The brothers were halfway to the car when Cash stopped and turned and looked up into a massive oak tree. Perched throughout its branches were more than a dozen black and hulking vultures. Every one of them with their eyes trained directly on the brothers and now more swooping in noisily to join them.

"This place is super creepy," Charley said.

"Yes it is."

By the time the brothers had found their campsite and put their tent together they could barely see for the dark and Cash set about getting a fire going. With his switchblade he cut the twine around their bundle of wood and then stood three of the pieces against one another in a tripod. The space underneath he filled with kindling and newspaper and it took off in a crackling fire and then died. Using the last of their starting material Cash built it up higher this time and yet the logs still wouldn't take. Next he circled their campsite collecting dead palm fronds which burned good and hot, but they still would not ignite the wood.

"Damn this," Cash said. "I can barely see anymore. Charley, where's the lantern?"

"I didn't bring it?"

"Why not?"

"I couldn't find it."

Cash rummaged through his pack and found his headlamp. He clicked it and clicked again and nothing happened.

"Remember when I took the batteries out of this for the DVD remote?"

"Yeah."

"That's where they're at."

"I'm getting hungry, Cash."

"It's awfully hard to cook steak and potatoes unless you've got a fire. Why don't you help me out here."

Charley began gathering piles of palm fronds which Cash continually fed into the fire and still the logs weren't alighting. As the brothers continued in futility a diesel truck with an astoundingly long trailer backed into the neighboring site and soon two young guys emerged from the cab. Charley dumped another load of palm fronds and Cash fed them one after the other until they'd all fizzled out in a dull smoke.

"It's almost like this wood is fire retardant," Cash said. "I mean, we had no problem in Cayo Costa."

"Cash?"

"What?"

"We suck at camping, don't we?"

"Pretty much. Try asking these guys if they have any fire starter."

"No way. It's embarrassing."

"Do you have a better idea?"

"There's some toilet paper in the bathroom."

"Just go ask these guys, will you?"

Charley went and explained their predicament and the neighbors immediately produced a fire-starter log and passed it to him graciously. Within a minute flames were leaping up out of the fire pit and they set their steak and potatoes to sizzle on the grill. When the potatoes were soft and hot inside and the steaks were cooked through the brothers took their plates to the picnic table and cut in with belated zeal. By this time their neighbors had gotten settled into camp and they sat alongside their fire while one of them strummed his guitar. When the brothers were finished with their meal Cash opened their cooler and removed two beers from the icy slush. He walked over to the boundary between the two sites and held the beers out.

"Thanks for helping us out with the fire, guys. Can we give you a couple beers?"

The guitarist looked up.

"That's okay. We've got plenty. Our last gig paid in beer."

"Alright then. Let me know if you change your mind."

"You guys are welcome to join us if you'd like."

The brothers carried their folding chairs over to the fire and cracked open their beers. Cash asked them their story and the guitarist said they were friends from Massachusetts and that one month ago they'd given up their time clock lives and left home to travel the country playing music. He was young and wild-haired and handsome and he spoke with constant enthusiasm, often interrupting himself for more urgent tones. The other was built somewhat spindly and though he was older he was always watching the guitarist to see where things were going next.

"So what do you play?" Charley asked him.

"I'll show you."

In a moment he returned from the trailer with a full-size stand-up bass which he looked at proudly.

"I traded my old motorcycle straight up for this," he said.

"Let's hear you guys jam," Cash said.

"I'm pretty lousy," said the bassist. "I just started learning when we left."

"You're too modest," the guitarist said. "He's too modest. You guys have any requests or you wanna hear an original?"

"An original," Cash said.

"Let's do Sultry Sue," he said to the bassist. "You ready? Come on, you know it's tuned. Ready? One, two, three."

The guitarist played as energetically as he spoke and he sung with a soulful boyish voice. He knew he was good and it gave him great pleasure and he seemed both incapable and disinterested in concealing it. The bassist, however, was even more of an amateur than the brothers expected and he followed along with incredible simplicity. His play was so slow and incongruous with the guitarist that it was hard to tell if he was even hitting the right notes. The guitarist seemed not to notice or not to mind and when the song was finished he looked back at the bassist and said he'd played well and the bassist smiled sheepishly.

"So how do you guys line up your shows?" Cash asked. "You got a manager hiding in that trailer too?"

The guitarist smiled.

"Nah. No. Nothing like that. We've just been driving around

the country asking bars and clubs if they'll let us play, but it's hard to find a gig that way. Hard, man. Sometimes they let us play, but most of the time they're booked up already so we just wander on to the next place. Try again, you know. Sometimes it works though. We had a good one in Virginia, couple in North Carolina. Georgia was tough though, man. Georgia was tough."

"Problem is even when we get gigs they don't want to pay us," the bassist said. "They might give us a burger and some beer, but that's about it."

"Yeah, but see, we're starting to figure it out now. We've been playing out in the streets lately. We just find some crowded spot like outside a mall or whatever and we play there. Like with our cases open on the ground. And it's been working. Right, Dustin? It's been working."

"Sort of."

"We made almost seventy bucks in Venice yesterday. Enough for beer and gas. And we met some cute girls too. Damn, I meant to call her tonight. Tomorrow. Dustin, remind me to call her."

"So where are you guys trying to get to?" Cash asked.

"That's what's so crazy,' the guitarist said. 'We don't even know. It's just like this big adventure. We can go wherever we want. Maybe tomorrow we'll wake up and want to be in New Orleans. Bam. We just drive there."

"It's not that simple," said the bassist.

"We could though. If we wanted, we could be there tomorrow. God, that'd be dope wouldn't it, Dustin? New Orleans."

"We were there," Charley said.

"I'll bet it was sick wasn't it?"

"Yeah. Pretty sick."

"Nice. That sounds awesome. Did you guys go for Mardi Gras?"

"We were just passing through. We rode our motorcycles here from Washington. The state."

"Holy shit, man. Yes. Dustin, did you hear that? On their motorcycles."

Dustin gave Cash a look that seemed an apology for his friend and the guitarist continued.

"You guys know exactly what I'm talking about then. You know, just getting out in the world and going for it. Living huge. Most people, it's like they don't ever even try anything brave or original in their entire lives. They just work in their office or their factories and it's so fucking depressing. I wasn't built that way. I've got too much energy. I mean, sometimes I feel crazy even. Like my bones wanna jump out and dance, man. And that's good. That's the way we're supposed to be. You guys are great. You guys are adventurers like us."

"I guess I never really thought of us as adventurers," Cash said. "We just came out to Florida to live with our cousin. We always knew where we were going."

"What about Texas?" Charley said. "We didn't know we were going there."

"I'd call that more of a debacle than an adventure."

They all sat in silence for a few moments, sipping their beers and listening to the fire crackle and hiss. The guitarist finally looked somewhat subdued and he took up his instrument and gave it a few strums.

"You know," he said. "I don't think being an adventurer is really all about where you're going. I think maybe it has more to do with why you left in the first place."

They all pondered it into the fire.

"Let's play another song, Dustin. Let's play some Oasis."

"Sure."

They played many songs that night and the four of them stayed up drinking and yakking until it was very late. When the brothers finally stood up for bed Cash told them to carry on playing if they wanted, that he didn't mind a bit. As he began drifting to sleep he could still hear the guitarist singing a tad above a whisper and the bassist plodding along, his rhythm sounding better now. Cash felt lucky to have met them and he hoped very much that there was a place in the world for them to really make it. And then he fell asleep.

It was noon on Mother's Day and Cash was cooking rice and chicken on the stove. Charley sat at the kitchen island playing a game of solitaire.

"What time does Mom start her lunch break usually?" Charley asked.

"Eleven."

"So we should…"

The front door swung open and showed the owner of the house looking down at her feet which she was wiping on the welcome mat. Her wrist bangles and ornate necklace jingling with the motion. She stepped inside and looked up at them with an expression of surprise and then some hostility.

"Who are you?" she said.

"We're Spencer's cousins," Cash said.

"And how long will you be visiting?"

"Well. Actually, we live here."

"Since when have you lived here?"

"Since February, so I guess that makes it about three months now."

She slapped her purse against her leg.

"Where is he?"

Cash moved his food from the burners and shut off the gas.

"He's out running errands. What's the problem?"

"The arrangement was for him to be my caretaker until I could get this house to sell. And he promised me he'd be the only one living here. He never mentioned anything about that to you two?"

"He said you were trying to sell the house but he never said we weren't allowed."

"He lied right to my face then. I've been putting him up in this house rent free and he pays me back by lying right to my face."

Cash leaned forward.

"Wait a second. Did you just say rent free?"

She looked from Cash to Charley and back to Cash.

"He got you too, didn't he? How much were you paying him?"

"A hundred a week."

"Well, it looks like all three of us have been duped. And quite a little racket he had going for himself. Three months times eight, nine hundred. Plus what he was saving on rent the whole time."

"Hold on now. Just hold on," Cash said as he put it all together.

"You see how he was working us?"

"Yeah, I got it. He's a damn good liar."

"Yes, he is."

"So what happens now?"

"I'm sorry guys. I'm sure this comes as a shock but you're going to have to find someplace else to live. I'd like to give you a couple of days but I don't think that'll be possible."

Charley straightened up in his chair.

"But we don't have anywhere to go."

"I pray you at least have some money," she said.

"We've got money," Cash said. "Thanks for your concern, but you don't need to worry about us. And we'll get out of your house as soon as we eat and get packed."

"I could call my property manager friend for you. She might have some apartment vacancies."

"That's alright. We'll figure this out on our own."

She opened her purse and took out a business card.

"The number to my cell is on the back. You give me a call if you change your mind."

"What's gonna happen to Spencer?" Charley asked.

She snapped her purse shut.

"He's about to regret this very much. Speaking of which, if you decide to kick his ass I'd appreciate if you did it out on the lawn."

She began backpedaling toward the door.

"Don't you want to wait for him to come home?" Cash asked.

"I'm gonna speak to my lawyer first. Good luck guys. You've got my card if you need it."

The door clicked shut behind her. Cash dished up two plates of food and placed them on the table.

"So what do we do now?" Charley asked.

"We do like we said we'd do. We eat this food, we pack our stuff and we get out of here."

"And then what? Where do we go?"

"I guess we go find ourselves a hotel room."

"We should take some of his stuff, or bash in his tv or something."

"No. It wasn't exactly like he was stealing from us. Or her even. We would have had to pay rent somewhere. He was just using us."

"You say it like it's not bad."

"Trust me. I think it's pretty rotten."

Cash cut a hunk of chicken, ran it through some hot sauce and brought it to a stop just before his mouth.

"I've got an idea, Charley."

An hour later the brothers had their packs loaded and resting against the wall of the entryway. They were wearing their riding gear and waiting patiently in the kitchen when Spencer returned.

"Yo yo, I'm home," he called.

They watched him shuffle across the hardwood floor and set two grocery bags on the counter.

"What up guys? You going somewhere?"

"Looks like it," Cash said.

"Where you headed?"

"We don't know yet."

"What do you mean?"

"Hey, Spencer. You wanna see a magic trick? Charley can make a hundred dollar bill disappear."

"Alright."

He opened a fresh gallon of milk and took a few gulps straight from the jug. Charley stood up from his chair and pulled a hundred dollar bill from his pocket.

"Watch closely now," Cash said.

Without saying a word Charley held the bill aloft and he fanned his other hand theatrically across the air. Spencer chuckled. Charley then lifted a lighter from the countertop and produced a flame which he held under the edge of the dollar until the fire began climbing and eating its way up.

"I don't get it," Spencer said.

"I'm making it disappear," Charley said.

"But why would you burn your money?"

"It's not his money," Cash said. "It's yours."

"What the fuck, guys."

Spencer leapt forward and snatched the flaming dollar and ran it under the tap. More than half of it had been burned away and he tossed it in the sink with disgust.

"Seriously, guys. What the hell is going on?"

"Well, cuz. The owner came by about an hour ago. She had some interesting things to say."

Spencer looked dumbfounded.

"Come on," he said. "Who you gonna believe? Some crazy lady or your cousin?"

"There's no use blathering. It's already over. We're gone."

"We can get another place, guys. I'll pay half of it. Look…"

Spencer turned and walked into his bedroom. They could hear him digging around in his closet and then the percussion of his fist against the wall. He came out and stood bitterly in the doorway, chewing at the inside of his cheek.

"Where's the rest of my money?"

"It's around."

"You ungrateful pieces of shit," he screeched. "I set this whole thing up for you. I got you jobs. I gave you a house to live in. So what if I got something out of it. You would have paid twice that if you were on your own. You owed me. Now where the fuck is my money? Tell me where it is."

Cash took a sip of water and set the glass back down.

"You used us. You lied to us. You got us booted out on the street. We may be blood but we're not family anymore."

He stood.

"The money's at the bottom of the pool. Let's go, Charley."

Spencer bolted through the kitchen and slid open the door to the patio. The brothers crossed the living room and as they were swinging their packs onto their shoulders they heard Spencer splash into the pool. Outside they strapped on their helmets and knocked their kickstands back. Cash looked over.

"Maybe we shouldn't tell Mom about this today."

"I think that's a good idea."

Early in the afternoon* they left the cool of their room and
stepped out into the sweltering furnace heat that had come to
everyday dwell on the region. With their beach things in hand they
took the stairs down to the ground floor and entered a creaking door
labeled office. Behind the desk a hog-faced woman was watching a
courtroom show on the television with a bag of potato chips in her
lap.

"There's some fresh coffee there if you boys are interested."

"It's too damn hot for coffee," Cash said. "I mean, thank you
though."

The woman pulled a thick wavy chip from her bag and aimed
it at the television.

"She didn't bring the bill of sale with her to court. Where do
they find these people?"

Cash had stepped up to the desk and the woman put the chip
back in the bag and brushed her lap for crumbs and set the bag
aside. She swiveled around to face him.

"Staying on another night, honey?"

"Yes ma'am."

"That makes five nights now. It'll be a better bargain for you
boys if you pay the whole week in advance, you know."

"Yeah, we know."

"So just the one night again?"

"Yes ma'am."

"You know the drill then."

Cash passed her the money, already counted out exactly to the penny.

"How long do you figure you boys will be staying on with us?"

"We don't know."

"You'll save yourself some money if you pay it by the week."

"We'll keep it in mind."

Charley opened the door and a speaker in the back room went ding dong.

"Watch out for them sting rays if you plan to do any swimming," she called.

"We will."

"Couple little girls got stung this morning."

"Thanks for looking out," Cash said. "You have a good day."

"Oh, you too, honey."

She swiveled back to the television and Cash shut the door behind them. They crossed the street. Hardly a car moving anywhere. The lazy quiet of the afternoon reminding them of childhood summers in Longview.

A path between two condominiums brought them to the beach and they slipped out of their sandals and unfurled their towels to lay lumpy on the sand and then padded over and stood ankle deep in the water. Stopped there watching sting rays glide through the ocean shallow, their sepia-toned bodies looking like dusty old book jackets.

"Still wanna swim?" Cash asked.

"We'll be fine."

"You catch one of those stingers in your leg you won't think you're fine."

"They say you just have to shuffle your feet. It's not like they want to sting us."

"I'm a little burned out on trust right now, Charley. Maybe there's a better spot down a ways."

They walked the beach a quarter mile in each direction and all along they could see sting rays flapping their wings in a tight patrol of the shore. Cash walked back and sat on his towel. A moment later Charley joined him, saying, "What's the point of living by the beach if you can't even swim in the ocean?"

The boiling humidity was incredible and they smeared their sweaty forearms against the sweat of their faces and watched the waves. A dozen terns skittering about in the wet sand. A pair of pelicans divebombing one after the other and then again. Beyond that a few small cottony clouds drifted toward the horizon and then went out of sight as though banished by the tyrannical blue of the sky.

Cash wiped his face again uselessly and said, "Lawrence had a chat with me last night. I guess I didn't feel up to telling you about it until just now."

"Are we fired or what?"

"May as well be."

"What'd he say?"

"He said the season is over. Told me that starting with the next schedule the best he can do is give us a few on call shifts. Said that Jillian and some of the others that have seniority are his first priority."

"So we get the scraps."

"If anything."

"Isn't there laws against that? I mean, don't we have to at least do something wrong first?"

"What kind of laws would there be? It's not like he can force people to take vacations. Why would they want to come here anyways? It's like a sauna from dawn to dusk now."

"So we're fucked."

"And not in the good way."

"We're about to be homeless and unemployed."

Cash snorted.

"How is that funny?"

"It's not."

"We're gonna go broke if we keep staying in this hotel."

"We can hold out for a little while."

Charley worried his face into a faraway stare.

"I didn't think it was gonna be like this," he finally said. "This isn't how it was supposed to work out."

"Shows you what supposed to be's are worth."

"It's not fun anymore. We don't even have any friends. I mean, we rode all the way across the country to get here and for what? To wind up living in a shabby old hotel room next to a beach where we can't even go swimming because it's full of sting rays."

"Now don't be losing heart on me, bud. We just hit a rough patch. Well, come to think of it we've hit quite a few of those but what the hell else are we gonna do? Go back home? Clean roofs for the rest of our natural lives?"

"It's better than being a hobo."

"We're not hobos, Charley. We're a couple of badass pilgrims. Brave young brothers who set out from home to reach the promised land."

"And where is the promised land? Cause this isn't it."

"I guess we just haven't found it yet."

Cash opened his pack of cigarettes and flicked his lighter and took a puff.

"You know what I miss?" Charley said.

"What's that?"

"I miss riding with you."

Cash looked at him and Charley went on.

"I guess I miss how that made me feel."

"Tell it."
"Like there was nothing else in the world that mattered."
Cash flicked ash into the sand.
"We could be gone tomorrow."

257

All morning they rode the freeway north. Their engines crooning gruff two-tone ballads as the green country slipped past in the pure race against fear and routine and stagnation and time. They knew not where they were headed, nor why. Only that this was good. Intent and forwardbent to the highway and the wind-dazzled going of it. Inventing songs to hear echo around in their helmets. Silly things sung seriously. Of booze and girls and sudden haphazard joy. Each of them believing secrets only velocity and danger knew to whisper.

An hour past Tampa they exited for gas and food. Their visors and leather jackets blotched and discolored with the carnage of uncountable lovebugs. The nearest town was a few miles from the freeway and en route they passed a farm with a sign along the road advertising fresh produce. Cash pulled over and they waited for a pickup truck to pass and then looped around and parked their bikes in the dirt lot.

"Why are we stopping here?" Charley asked.

"Seemed like the thing to do."

Charley shrugged and they wandered over to the produce stand which was set in the shade of an old oak with wispy beards of moss hanging from the branches. Ringed around the stand were wooden bins of melons, strawberries, oranges, tomatoes, carrots. At least six different peppers. Behind these a Hispanic man was eating a peach and as the brothers approached the man stood up from his stool and tossed the pit over his shoulder and then reached into one of the bins and grabbed another.

"Let's get us a little appetizer," Cash said. "What do you want?"

"Those peaches look tasty."

Charley faced the man.

"Is that peach really good?"

The man wiped his chin.

"Yes. It's much juice."

"Alright. We'll take two peaches then."

"Two or three is same price," the man said. "Take three."

They picked out three peaches from the bin and paid. As they were walking away Cash looked back and the man nodded politely and threw another pit into the yard.

"That doesn't seem like such a bad gig now does it, Charley? Sitting around eating peaches all day long."

"Until you get diarrhea."

"What are you talking about?"

"If you eat too many peaches it gives you diarrhea."

"Are you sure that's true?"

Charley took a slurping bite.

"I think so. Could be something else I'm thinking of maybe."

They strolled through the yard kicking at the grass. An osprey flew overhead and across the road and landed in a nest it had made in the crook of a telephone pole.

"So what's our plan?" Charley said.

"We don't have one."

"Do you want to start heading for home?"

"Not really."

"What are we gonna do then? Wander the country like those guys we met in Myakka?"

"Not unless we learn to play some instruments."

"So what then?"

"I don't know, bud. We'll think of something."

Charley took another bite of his peach and withdrew yelping.

"What happened? You alright?"

Charley swallowed.

"I just had an idea."

"What?"

"Georgia is the next state up from us right?"

"Yeah."

"Well, those guys from Myakka. Didn't they say that hippy hostel was in Georgia? Near Branson. Brussels. Something like that."

"Brunswick."

"Whatever it's called, we should go there. Tonight. We could sleep in a treehouse. A treehouse, Cash. With real life hippies."

"Hold on."

Cash brought out his phone.

"How far is it?" Charley asked.

"About three hours."

"That's nothing. We have to do it."

"Well…"

"I'll skip lunch if I have to."

"I suppose we don't have anything else on our schedule."

Late in the afternoon they crossed into Georgia, riding west on Highway 82 and looking for some advertisement of the hostel. When they saw the wooden hand-painted sign they'd been going too fast to make the turn and so they pulled over to the shoulder and then rolled themselves backwards with the thrust of their feet like they were operating toddlers bikes without pedals. For the next two miles they weaved along the already winding dirt road, sliding through the sluiceway grooves and attempting to dodge potholes an overloaded wheelbarrow couldn't fill. Finally they came to where a half dozen cars were parked in a turnabout and they let down their kickstands and hung their helmets on the handlebars.

At the end of a sandy footpath they came to the center of the hostel grounds where they saw several geodesic domes squatting in a tight cluster. The domes seeming both more modern and more atavistic than a typical house, the shape and shinglework of them resembling armadillos half curled up for sleep. All of the structures so accommodating of the forest they looked as if they'd taken root and grown up that way just the same as the trees had. A rooster came strutting along and they watched it pass and then took four steps up onto the deck marveling at the place like it was some recurring dream of theirs, always forgotten by morning and yet come to fruition anyways.

"I feel really good about this," Charley said as a slim tomboyish brunette came outside and smiled at them.

"Do you live here?" Charley asked.

"I do."

"This place is really cool."

"I'm glad you think so. Are you staying with us tonight?"

"That's why we're here. We'd like to sleep in a treehouse."

"Do you have reservations?"

"Well, no. We thought—"

"It's okay if you don't. Come on."

She led them inside the dome which emanated a soft pumpkin glow. Every square inch becluttered with books and couches and all manner of curios and trinkets and art. She went around and stood behind the desk.

"Is it just the two of you tonight?"

"That's right," Cash said.

"Well, we've got a few beds left in the Palapa. That's the bunkhouse. Unfortunately we're down to our last treehouse so I guess you'll have to flip for it. The cost is twenty-five dollars per night. Cash or travelers checks only. Have you read our website?"

"No."

"That's okay. I just wanted you to know that the price includes a communal dinner which we prepare for our guests every evening. Wouldn't want you to drive all the way to town for Taco Bell or something."

"Sounds good."

"We'll ring the dinner bell when it's ready. You'll be able to hear it fine even if you're back at the lake."

"About what time might that be?"

"I don't believe in time. Time is now."

He nodded.

"Can I just see your IDs real quick for my logbook."

They passed her their licenses and she leaned over and scrawled their information on a yellow notepad as they watched the jiggle of her small naked breasts through the gaping peephole below her neck. They each looked to see if the other was watching and Charley made his eyebrows dance. When she was finished she passed them each a bundle of bedding and brought them outside and explained how to get to their rooms. Charley had removed his cell phone and he was aiming it at one of the domes for a picture when she said, no phones. He looked at her to see if she was in earnest and again she said, no phones, and he put it back in his pocket.

They shambled on down the path she had described and soon stopped and looked up at the treehouse which was not built into a tree at all but instead was a wooden cube of a room standing twelve feet high on stilts and accessed by a twisting external staircase. They went up the stairs and opened the screen door and set their things on the bed. Three of the walls were all windowed to the forest and they looked out at the dense and unreal green of the canopy just above.

"This is the beez neez isn't it, Charley?"

"I want to live here."

"How you wanna decide who gets it?"

"Rock paper scissors."

"Best out of three?"

"For this? Has to be at least five."

"Make it seven then."

"One two shoot?"

"One two shoot."

On the seventh round Charley won with scissors and he made a good show of consolation and then set Cash's things on the floor and made his bed. Afterwards they changed into their swimming trunks and went downstairs and passed the domes where a few guests were now lounging out front in homemade rocking chairs. When they found the boardwalk the girl had mentioned they followed its sloping planks through the forest until they came to a small lake at the back of the property. In the middle of the lake was a floating platform and they swam out and pulled themselves aboard and then listened to the birds chirp as their feet dangled in the water.

From somewhere in the woods they began to hear the reedy cry of a harmonica and soon a man appeared at the far bank. He was barefoot and barechested and then he removed his shorts and was naked. He saw the brothers for the first time and he waved at them and then dove in and flapped and spluttered his way to the platform. It took him a few tries but he heaved himself up and pushed the bangs of his moppy blond hair to the side, standing and dripping and facing them without bashfulness.

"Hey," he said.

They kept their eyes on the platform and said hey back.

"You guys don't mind me being naked do you?"

"Do your thing," Cash said. "But maybe you could aim it another direction."

"Sure, sure."

He rotated a few degrees and then took a seat.

"I'm Dave," he said. "You guys must have just arrived."

"Yeah, we did. How about you?"

"I've been here for about a week now. I like it here."

"Where you from?"

"South Carolina. You guys?"

"Washington State."

"How'd you end up out here?"

"We rode our motorcycles. It's a long story."

"No shit. I rode here too."

"On that scooter?"

"Yep."

"From South Carolina?"

"Yep."

"Damn. And I thought he was crazy for riding a two-fifty. How fast does that little scooter even go? Like fifty?"

"Like thirty. It's not running really well."

"So what, you just took backroads?"

"I took the freeway, man. Just rode the whole thing on the shoulder. Dodging tire shreds and glass bottles and every other thing. About halfway here this cop stopped me and said I was breaking at least three laws and that he wasn't gonna let me keep going unless I had a helmet. Said he was gonna write me up and this and that and then the craziest thing happened. This pickup truck pulls up behind us and the driver shouts, hey what's the matter, so I told him about how I needed to get a helmet, and the guy says, hold on a minute and I'll bring you one. And the guy comes right back and gives me a helmet. And the cop lets me go. So now I'm here for a while."

"They got you working?"

"I do some chores and they let me stay. I guess I'll just drift around for a while."

They heard a splash and turned and saw two girls swimming

toward them. When they reached the platform they climbed the ladder and looked at Dave.

"Hey," he said.

Both girls looked as young as Charley and the bolder of the two, a tan and busty Persian said, "Dude, you're like naked."

"Join me. Life's better this way."

"Maybe later."

The other girl was auburn-haired and petite and she seemed to find many things to smile at. Her shoulders were both overrun with freckles and altogether she looked like a flower in its final stage of a late bloom. Cash would have called the Persian the prettier of the two but he noticed that Charley had eyes only for her friend. When the girls weren't paying attention Cash leaned in and said, "Go easy, bud."

Charley whispered, "I feel like I swallowed a butterfly net. And it was full of 'em."

Dave asked all the questions and they learned the girls were from Orlando where their parents mostly worked for Disney World. They were college roommates and they were about to finish their freshman year and then start summer jobs. The Persian girl said she was going to be a Snow White. Her friend said she would be working with horses in Wyoming. The sun was down below the treeline now and when they heard the dinner bell they all swam back to the lakebank and Dave went and got his shorts and then led them to the dining hall in a building behind the main dome.

The table was set for at least twenty and they entered the room as employees and guests were carrying platters and cakes and huge bowls of food in from the kitchen. The girls took their seats and Cash was trying to discretely usher Charley into the chair next to her but he was already around and sitting and asking her questions about Wyoming. When everything was assembled a man with oriental tattoos down his arm and his hair tied back in a ponytail asked for everyone's attention and the guests drew quiet.

"Thank you all for being here and welcome to our home in the forest," he said. "For those of you who have never stayed with us before we have a little ritual we do every evening. It's very simple. We're all going to hold hands and say something that we're grateful for. So come on, guys. Hold hands."

Cash took his brother's hand and then he reached out as an old woman clasped him tightly. Most of the visitors expressed gratitude for simple things like their dog or sunshine or the restful day they'd had. It went around to the girls and then to Charley who said he was grateful that so far he'd managed to keep his motorcycle on two wheels. It came to Cash. He looked at Charley and back around the circle.

"My brother and I are a long ways from home," he said. "Seven months ago we basically ran away from everything to see if there wasn't something better for us out in the country and I guess we're still figuring that out. We thought we had something good in Florida but it turned out it was a fool's gold. So we're still looking."

The woman squeezed his hand and he looked at her and saw that she'd had her eyes closed and was bobbing her head like there was some inaudible rhythm to the proceedings.

"I'm supposed to say what I'm grateful for," he continued. "My intention was to do this trip by myself, but this guy here next to me, he wouldn't let me. He was too damn stubborn. Our first night on the road, back when we were still in Oregon, he told me I was gonna be glad he came along, and you know what, bud. I am. I'm grateful I didn't have to go it alone."

The woman gave his hand another warm clench and opened her eyes and said, that was just right. She said she was grateful to be surrounded by so many beautiful loving people and at last it went to the guy with the tattoos.

"That was great guys. Thank you."

"What are you grateful for?" someone called.

"I was getting to that," he said. "I was gonna say I'm grateful for our meal tonight. I'm grateful for our strawberries. I'm grateful for our fruit salad with wild mint grown from our garden and…"

As he listed that night's fare he began swinging his arms so that it made two others swing theirs and so on around the circle with increasing tempo until it appeared some flailing schoolyard game with a round of cheering after each new item.

"I'm grateful for mushroom quesadillas. Mashed potatoes and gravy. French onion soup. Chocolate cake. Pineapple upsidedown cake. Let's eat. Dig in. Let's eat."

If he'd been a mere spectator Cash would have likely scoffed at the ceremony but he'd been flailing and cheering like all the rest and by the end he was positively thrilled to dish up. When his plate was loaded the way he liked he took it back to the table, realizing midway through that it was the best meal he'd had in months.

After everyone had eaten Cash helped clear the table and when he was finished he went out to the deck. It was full dark now but still quite warm. Dave and the Persian were rapping on a massive bongo drum. Charley and the other girl sat side by side in rocking chairs drinking wine as he told her about all the places he'd been.

Cash pointed at the railing where two boxes of Franzia and some keg cups stood.

"Who do I have to pay for some libations?"

"Have all you want," the Persian said.

"You girls came prepared."

"Duh. We're in the forest."

Cash helped himself and ten minutes later he helped himself again. After his third glass the red wine had cast its spell. His whole body warm and tingling like a casual euphoria. He patted at his shorts for a cigarette and they weren't there so he stood up and walked the path to the bunkhouse. He came back smoking and saw that everyone was gone except for a man who puffed on a small ceramic pipe.

"Where'd everybody go?" Cash asked.

"The lake, I'd imagine."

Cash nodded and took a step to go.

"What did you think of that meal tonight?" the man asked.

"I thought it was pretty damn great."

The man shook his head.

"It was good," he corrected. "But it could have been great if they had incorporated some of my chia seeds."

"Ah."

"Chia seeds. You know what I'm talking about right?"

"Guess I don't."

"They're a super food. Full of Omega 3, Omega 6. They regulate your pancreas like nothing else, boy. You really don't know. Okay, look. Chia seeds require no freezing, not even refrigeration. They've got a three-year shelf life. But do not take too much of 'em dry. You hear me on that part?"

Cash was looking everywhere but his direction.

"Don't take 'em dry," he said.

"Well, a little bit is okay. I'm saying don't take too much. Aztec warriors used to ingest them dry during their twenty-four hour forced marches. You know the Aztecs right? Before Christ and Mexico. These Aztecs, see, they couldn't carry water cause water weighs eight point six pounds per gallon so instead they'd give 'em one tablespoon of chia seeds and those warriors, they'd march for a day straight. I mean, what does that tell ya?"

"Must be good. Hey, I'm gonna—"

"Damn right they're good. They're a super food. If you're interested I could get you started. You can check out my website. I've got some—"

"Excuse me. I'm gonna head to the lake."

Cash left the man standing there and took the boardwalk again through the forest. So nightblack along the path he had to stop several times to feel with his hands where the edges of the planks lay. He heard laughter and began to see the lesser dark of the lake ahead. When he emerged from the forest he could see the platform clearly and he stopped and smiled and went on removing his clothes. Every last person was as naked as they could be, the platform crowded into a pale huddling of flesh. Cash heard his brother shout his name and a woman catcalled, show me the money. He slipped out of his shorts and swung them around over his head a few times and then threw them to the ground and dove in. At the platform he pulled himself up alongside a girl with nipple rings encircled by dark oversized areolas and he looked around.

"Sure are a lot of nice titties assembled here tonight," he said.

Everyone chuckled, especially the girls. Someone passed him a half empty jug of wine and he took a huge gulp and licked his lips and passed it to someone else. Charley was sitting next to the girl on the opposite end of the platform and Cash caught his eye and gave him a wink. People were all around mingling in small groups and Cash was content listening until the girl with the nipple rings tapped him on the shoulder.

"Hey, man. I really liked what you said tonight at dinner. About how you're still looking for something better. You're a searcher. The world needs more of those."

"Am I a searcher?"

"You must be to ride your bike all the way to Florida like that."

"Maybe."

"Wherever you go next I just hope you get to sleep out under the stars as often as you can."

At that he looked up and saw them all shining in their ancient places. She looked there with him and they gazed like that in silence for some time.

"You know," he said. "We always sleep under the stars. It's just that we forget."

In the morning the brothers loaded their bags and when they were ready they walked the girls to their car. Charley somewhat grave about it. The Persian tossed her things in the trunk and said goodbye and got in behind the steering wheel. Charley helped her friend and he shut the trunk for her. She said she hoped that she would see him again someday and then gave him a hug and squeezed his hand and got in the car. They backed up until they were turned around and drove off waving.

They had talked about staying at the hostel for a few days but in the end they'd decided they ought to start heading back home and so they rode a number of country highways that afternoon in the general direction of Atlanta. Outside of Macon the sky clouded up a dismal gray and when it started to rain they stopped at a small diner and took a table along the window. A young man with half a mustache brought them waters and then coffee and then took their order. Charley stared out the window. Cars going past with wipers on high. Cash stirred his coffee.

"Neither of us has any luck with girls."

Charley looked at him without turning his head, rolled his eyes back to the street.

"At least it's useful to know which types are interested in you."

"She's not a type. Her name is Madeleine."

"I know that. I'm just saying… You're right."

Cash looked around the diner. Busy for a week day. He watched the waitresses moving about and then saw their likenesses in picture form above the expo line, each of them rendered into grinning cartoons by some artist. He looked back at Charley and found his eyes waiting for him.

"I'm going to Wyoming," he said.

"Boy did she snare you."

"She's gonna be in Jackson Hole this summer."

"At a dude ranch somewhere?"

"Yeah, something like that."

"What are you gonna do?"

"I'll find work. She says they're always looking for people at the National Park."

"Yellowstone?"

"No, this one's called the Grand Teats."

Cash chuckled.

"I thought it was a pretty funny name too."

"Charley, it's called the Grand Tetons. Tetons."

"Oh."

Cash took a sip of his coffee.

"So you're gonna follow her to Wyoming?"

"Yeah."

"You put all this together in the last twelve hours."

Charley shrugged.

"Alright," Cash said flatly.

"Don't be mad at me. I'm just doing what…"

"I mean, alright. I'm coming with you."

"Really? Just like that?"

"Just like that."

"Her friend won't be there."

"She wasn't my style anyways."

"You'll really come with me?"

"Yes."

"We're just gonna get on these bikes and ride to Wyoming?"

"Soon as it quits raining."

Charley looked out the window where beads of water were streaked against the glass pane.

"What's gonna happen to us, Cash? Where do you think we'll wind up when this is all over?"

"Bud. It wouldn't be nearly as much fun if we knew that, now would it."

www.ingramcontent.com/pod-product-compliance
Lightning Source LLC
Chambersburg PA
CBHW022016120726
47902CB00012B/278